2019

Please return this book on or before the date shown above. To
renew go to www.essex.gov.uk/libraries, ring 0345 603 7628 or
go to any Essex library.

Essex County Council

ABOUT THE AUTHOR

Anbara Salam is half-Palestinian and half-Scottish, and grew up in London. She has a PhD in Theology and is now living and working in Oxford. She spent six months living on a small South Pacific island, and her experiences there served as the inspiration for her first novel, *Things Bright and Beautiful*.

Things Bright and Beautiful

ANBARA SALAM

PENGUIN BOOKS

PENGUIN BOOKS

UK | USA | Canada | Ireland | Australia
India | New Zealand | South Africa

Penguin Books is part of the Penguin Random House group of companies
whose addresses can be found at global.penguinrandomhouse.com.

First published by Fig Tree 2018
Published in Penguin Books 2019
001

Copyright © Anbara Salam, 2018

The moral right of the author has been asserted

Printed and bound in Great Britain by Clays Ltd, Elcograf S.p.A.

A CIP catalogue record for this book is available from the British Library

ISBN: 978–0–241–98225–9

www.greenpenguin.co.uk

Penguin Random House is committed to a
sustainable future for our business, our readers
and our planet. This book is made from Forest
Stewardship Council® certified paper.

For my grandparents:
Rasha and Walid, Jock and Marion

Beatriz knew it was wrong to hate a missionary, but when it came to Marietta, she couldn't help herself. Marietta liked to hum. Interminable, tuneless humming, like the dirge of a bluebottle. Bea was acutely aware of quite how often Marietta felt the need to serenade the Lord. Marietta sang 'Onward, Christian Soldiers' in the garden. She droned 'All Things Bright and Beautiful' in her bedroom. She whined 'Jesus, Mi Lavem Yu Tumas' under her breath while they ate supper together. Upon interrogation, Max claimed he hadn't noticed, but Bea didn't believe him. The noise filtered through the cracks in the bamboo walls, and crawled right into the ears. Mission House was simply not built for two people, and one hummer.

When Marietta and Max were out witnessing, Bea found the normal sound of the jungle a blessed relief. The tickling of ants stirring in the earth, the rain in the palms. She accomplished the housework with unusual gusto. She scrubbed their clothes in the bucket. She picked large curls of rat droppings out of the rice sack, chopped firewood with her bushknife, and swept their bedrooms for scorpions. And then, invariably, she would catch herself launching into a half-remembered chorus of 'Lead, Kindly Light', and curse the God who had chosen Marietta as His missionary.

Marietta appeared in Bambayot on a Wednesday afternoon. That morning, Max had been further north along the coast, visiting a tiny village in the shadow of a waterfall. He was climbing the hill towards Mission House when he saw her sitting on the stump outside the front door. As Max's shadow fell over her, she looked up and smiled, exposing long yellowed teeth. Marietta was a short, portly woman in her late fifties with a round face and silvery hair. Max realized he was having trouble not looking at a protuberant pink mole on her left cheek.

She shook Max's hand so vigorously her gold cross necklace trembled over her breasts. 'More missionaries in my village,' she said. 'Well, praise the Lord.'

Max smiled, though her immediate and exclusive claim to Bambayot fluttered around in his chest.

Bea was up 'on top' in the hills picking naus fruit, and Max felt clumsy trying to entertain this unexpected guest. In the kitchen, he dropped the pot so hard it bounced, and chuckled pointedly to cover his embarrassment. He heard a stool scrape in the living room, and Marietta materialized behind him. She took hold of the pot and dismissed him with a pat on the arm. Whistling, she strode outside to draw water at the pump. Back in the kitchen, she settled the pot over the fire, blowing on it gently until the embers glowed. Max realized she must have lived in the house – their house – for years.

She muttered to herself, 'Let me see, they were here. Where did I leave them?'

Max cleared his throat. 'The cups are hanging from the hooks on the left wall.'

'So they are, thank you.'

Within minutes, Marietta was back, carrying two tin mugs of black tea. She sat down on the other stool at the table with a groan. After a minute of silent blowing and sipping, Marietta exhaled. 'So, Pastor. You must tell me everything. How long have you been on the island?'

'Around four months, I suppose.'

'Goodness.' Marietta whistled through her teeth. 'As long as that? I did hear about a new whiteman, but I didn't realize it was so long ago.' She looked off into the distance.

After another sip, Max cleared his throat again. 'I hope you won't think this an odd question, but –' he paused, realizing he didn't actually have a question '– but well, we had no idea there was still another missionary on the island. Have you been away for a long time?'

Marietta gave him a flat smile, 'I guess Filip never mentioned me?'

'Filip Aru?'

Marietta nodded.

'No, not at all,' Max said.

'*Quelle surprise*,' she said, raising her eyebrows. 'Yes, I have been away for a while.' She stifled a yawn, and stretched a little, folding her arms behind her head, pointing her breasts towards Max as she did so. 'I left for the East at the end of the last dry season, and that's where I've been,' she said.

'Ah. East,' Max parroted.

'Yes,' she shook her head, as if he had said something insightful. 'East. It's been an adventure, I can tell you. You're familiar with Chief Liki, of course?'

Chief Liki was a renowned sorcerer on the east coast. Most villagers on Advent Island were wary of the East. It was widely regarded as a swampy wilderness, governed by leaf magic, and populated by vampires. Even people who had lived their whole lives in the mountains of Central had never ventured to the East. This was partly due to fear of the vampires, and partly because there were no roads. Instead, a couple of tracks wound along tight precipices that disintegrated into mossy footholds, gouged into cliff faces overhanging deep gorges. The hillsides leading to the East were so steep that during the monsoon season, people in Central called it 'the brown rain'. The slopes became a waterfall of noxious, slippery mud that coated the

3

mountains, and made the route impassable for months. The terrain was mostly slimy cliffs, tabu hilltops, and patches of dense jungle whirring with mosquitoes. To make matters worse, there was no significant land mass between the east of Advent Island and South America, and winds blew straight off the ocean, smashing nightmarish waves on to black rocks. The climate was so dire, villagers huddled together inside one smoky thatched hut for months on end until the rains stopped. Max looked at Marietta again and felt a nudge of admiration for her. It was no mean feat for anyone, let alone an elderly, clearly unfit, lone, white, Christian woman, to travel to the East.

'And you were there for the whole of the rainy season?' he asked.

'Yes. Well, you can't cross the roads until it's very dry.'

'I imagine.' Max sipped his tea.

'And there was my leg.' She patted her left shin.

'Oh?'

'Yes, darned tropical ulcer. Horrible. The whole thing was swelled up. Could hardly move. It was months before anyone could walk up to the North and get antibiotics. Pus everywhere. A whole scoop came out in the end.' She exhaled in a laugh, still rubbing at the shin.

Max couldn't help but look at her pale leg, exposed under a canvas skirt. It was covered in sparse grey hairs, and marked with an inverted round scar, as if a large lipsticked mouth had given it an open kiss.

He made a noise of non-committal sympathy. 'Is it healed now?'

'Oh, yes.' She took another gulp of tea, brushing hair back from her eye.

'And for the whole of this duration, you were staying with Chief Liki?'

Marietta nodded.

'What was it like?' Max asked.

She shook her head slowly. 'I would barely know where to begin. That place is in bad need of the light of Christian leadership, I can tell you. He's a difficult man.'

Max leant forward in his chair. 'And were the people – were they receptive to the Word?' This was the reason why he had come to the New Hebrides, this very reason. To think there were still villages, here on the island, which had never heard the Word. It was the last frontier. His chance to carve out another kingdom for the Lord.

Marietta had not answered. She had pursed her lips, and was breathing heavily through her nose. She cleared her throat. 'Liki is not likely to allow Christian worship, no. But he allowed me to stay there, to preach, with no harm done to me. We met every so often, he wanted to ask me questions about the new religion. But really, he seemed to think he was preaching to me!' She gripped her knee in emphasis. 'You see, he thought I would go back South and spread the word about his wonderful leadership.' She laughed again.

'What kind of leadership is that?' Max pressed his fingers against the tin mug, now it was cool enough to touch properly.

'Well, he's a sort of –' she paused, then caught Max's eye. 'I'm sorry, I've been speaking Pansi for so long, my English is a bit rusty. What's the word – he controls every aspect of life?'

'A dictator?' Max filled in. 'An autocrat?'

Marietta slapped her knee, 'Yes, exactly. That exactly.' She opened her mouth to continue, but the door swung open and Beatriz appeared in the door frame. Her face was flushed, and she was carrying an island basket with the strap braced across her forehead, so the knot stuck up from her hair like a straggly headdress.

Bea half stepped forward, and stopped abruptly. She looked

between Max and this strange white person. Max was perched on the edge of his stool, one elbow leaning on the table, and the woman had paused mid-sentence. Bea felt suddenly like she was intruding. She started to say something but only opened her mouth and then closed it again.

'Bea!' Max stood quickly, his eyes bright. The sitting woman smiled at Bea with enthusiasm.

'Bea, this is Marietta Hardwood – the old missionary,' he said, holding out his left hand.

Bea took hold of Max's hand, unsure why he was greeting her with a formal handshake.

Max read the confusion on Bea's face, as it occurred to both of them he had meant the 'last' missionary, and not 'old'. They looked at Marietta with a synchronized glance of simultaneous panic, like two small birds. Marietta smiled and waved the comment aside, leaning back on her stool. Max hovered, glancing between Bea and the remaining stool. Bea removed the island basket from around her head, and rubbed the indent it had made in her skin, settling uncomfortably into a half-perch on the window sill. Marietta was gazing at Bea with friendly curiosity. Max desperately wanted to return to their conversation, but was conscious a polite time would have to pass while Bea's entrance was acknowledged.

'Well, I must say, this is lovely.' Marietta grinned her yellow grin.

Bea twisted the strap of her island basket in her fingers and smiled back at her uncertainly.

Marietta turned her head to Max. 'Just lovely to see a young couple working together in the service of the Lord.'

Max nodded humbly.

'And where have you been?' Marietta addressed Bea again, in a perceptibly louder voice, the tone of a headmistress questioning a pupil.

Bea's stomach constricted. 'Natsulele,' she said. Max's eyes were pleading, so she added another smile.

'Witnessing?' Marietta asked, enunciating each syllable.

Bea was taken aback. 'No – with a friend. For storyan.'

'Oh, storyan, that's nice.' Marietta leant back on the stool. 'Nothing like a good old storytelling session to lift up the spirits. It's so important to keep up friendships, you know,' she said to Max.

Max nodded sagely. He heard Bea's voice behind him.

'Are you visiting for long?'

Her expression was the picture of innocent hospitality, but Max knew better.

'Well, I'm not sure. Don't worry, though –' Marietta held up her hand, with a smile '– I won't get in your folks' way. Last thing you need is an old biddy like me under your feet.'

Max and Bea tittered politely.

Marietta got to her feet, sighing. 'I must declare, I'm beat. I'm going to lay down for a siesta. Which room are you two using?'

Max and Bea exchanged a glance. Somehow, Max didn't want to admit they each had one room. Maybe it was extravagant; but he snored, and Bea was so messy. Bea bit her lip, wondering if she would have to give up the only space she had to herself. And would Max even want her beside him? She recalled the state of her room – the bed was unmade, the table nubbly with spilt candle wax. By the window she'd left a glass of water which contained a drowned purple moth.

'I'll set up the small bedroom for you,' Bea said, standing up and brushing the dust from the seat of her skirt.

'When I lived here, that used to be my laundry room,' Marietta called after her.

Bea cleared up in a hurry, sweeping everything into the

trunk, laying fresh sheets on the bed, listening to the low bray of Marietta's voice mixed with Max's through the wall.

The next few nights were uncomfortable for both Bea and Max. Bea felt a little shy, approaching Max's bed, her face covered in cold cream, her hair pinned up with rags. It made her feel strangely vulnerable for him to see her in such a state of domestic frumpiness. Max thoughtfully tried to make space for her in the bed, but as soon as he fell asleep, he would sprawl sideways, his thick limbs hanging over her like heavy branches. If he rolled over on to her in the night, she could hardly prise herself out from under his weight. She had to stretch her knees out into the mosquito net, and tangled herself up in it. Max snored, and his hot breath condensed against her neck – as if the nights were not humid enough, she thought crossly, heaving his calf off her thigh with frustration. When, in the early mornings, Bea woke to feel the stiffening of his erection against the small of her back, she found the slight pressure oddly comforting. But she knew it was just a reflex, not an invitation, and Max would only feel humiliated by a body he could not control properly. So she pretended to sleep on, oblivious.

Max, for his part, wasn't enjoying the new arrangements much either. He breathed in the tail ends of the rags in Bea's hair, making him sniff and tickle. Bea pressed her cold toes up against him while he slept, slipping them into the most vulnerable corners of his body. Once asleep, she wriggled continuously, turning over and over, scratching him with her toenails all the while. And her sleep talking in Spanish disconcerted him. Once, she woke him urgently in the night, her fingers gripping his shoulder. But when he asked her what was wrong, she rolled off an incomprehensible Spanish emergency, and fell back down, still asleep. He lay awake for hours after this, a nebulous jealousy tugging at him. No matter how long he was married to Bea, she would always have had a life before him, a life he knew nothing about.

After the sixth night, Bea sat up in the early hours of the morning with a muffled squeak. Tears hung in her eyes, her hair sticking in all directions. 'I can't bear it any longer!' she said.

Max sat up too, his eyes heavy.

'How long is she going to be here?' she demanded.

Max shushed her, but Bea could see he was wondering this, too.

'I don't know,' he admitted, wiping his left eye.

'How can we go on like this?' Bea gestured to the bed with one hand, clutching a hollow pillowcase she had wrestled out from under his head. Max was relieved to hear she was genuinely asking his opinion, and not rhetorically threatening a tantrum.

'I don't know,' he said, trying to stifle a grin.

'What?' Bea mirrored his smile. 'What's so funny?' Putting her hand to her head, she felt curls of escaped hair loosed from the rags. She put a self-conscious palm over her face and he pulled her into him to muffle her giggles.

The next few nights were better as they established a pattern. They would fall asleep with her head inside the crook of his shoulder, and once asleep, turn to face the same direction, Bea's head in the hollow of his neck, so he would not choke on her hair. And though she would not have thought to tell him, Bea began to enjoy sleeping in Max's single bed. She took cautious comfort from their restful intimacy, since sleeping was all Max would want to do.

At first, Max found Marietta a welcome guest. He enjoyed, although he would never have confessed it in so many words, having someone to properly talk to. Marietta and he would sit on twin benches in the vestry and talk by the paltry light of the hurricane lamp, its pink shade abandoned like a shed skin. They shared readings from the Bible, or compared notes from his library of exegetical commentaries. They rarely agreed on anything, and Marietta was prone to long, honky sermonizing, but they were both Lewis aficionados, and sometimes Marietta would read aloud from *The Screwtape Letters*, performing the voices with flair. Sometimes they worked on Marietta's pet project: a lexicography of the sand-drawing language that Chief Liki used in his sorcery school. Eventually, she wished to translate the Bible into their language for use in witnessing.

Marietta was always up at daybreak, and they drank black tea at the table while the last cockroaches sleepily wound down around the table legs. They went out to witness together, visiting villages in Central and along the west coast. Marietta had a veritable second stomach for kava, and cheerfully ignored the strict tabus that prohibited kava drinking for either women or churchmen. 'Witnessing begins at the watering hole,' she would say, nodding her head from side to side as if it were a Bible verse. After perhaps the thirteenth time she delivered this aphorism, Max began to wonder if it actually was a kind of paraphrase, and guiltily flipped through Leviticus one evening after Marietta had commenced her cacophonous snoring.

Bea, meanwhile, tried her hardest to keep her opinions about Marietta to herself. But she interfered with the housework in a way that should have been a blessing, but felt like a curse. Marietta fussily chased Bea away from the kitchen, and recommenced banging pots and pans together with the cheerful buoyancy of the terrible cook. She was out with Max all day long, and in the evenings, after a walkabout, Marietta came back to the house and dropped on to her stool with tumultuous sighs. Bea never understood why, with all that walking around, Marietta never got any less fat. After eating supper, Max and Marietta retreated to the vestry, and Bea followed the departure of their only hurricane lamp with narrowed eyes. She would be left in Mission House alone with their preciously rationed candles.

It became obvious, as the weeks passed, that Marietta was not going anywhere. In the evenings, once the muffled sounds of wheezy breathing could be heard, Bea and Max argued in low voices.

'But she doesn't even contribute –' Bea gestured vaguely with her hand.

'Beatriz!' Max looked shocked.

'Well, it's true.' She fixed him with a look, knowing full well Max was not as holy as all that. For weeks they had been feeding Marietta from their stores. All the money was donated by Max's church, and his savings from when Marybelle's was sold. That's all they had, and when it was gone, there would be nothing.

'We can't ask her to leave,' Max pre-empted, before she could suggest it.

'Why not?' Bea tipped her nose up.

'Bea! This is a Mission House! Moreover, it was her Mission House before we even arrived. We can't ask her to leave her own home, for goodness' sake.' Max glanced nervously towards the room where Marietta slept, pausing every few words to listen for any change in the snoring.

Bea made a whining noise, and curled her head against the top of his thigh. 'But why? Why does she have to be here?'

Max rubbed his fingertips into her scalp and sighed, worried that if he said anything diplomatic she might fly into a temper.

Bea looked up at him. 'I don't want her here. She's so . . .'

and Bea, normally so quick with insults, trailed off, exhaling through her nose. 'She's so big,' she finally murmured.

Max gave her a quick kiss on the forehead, feeling a strain pull through his spine.

But Bea was right, Max thought to himself the following day, while strolling down to the coast, smoking his pipe. Marietta was just so big. Everything about her was big. Big voice, big appetite, big opinions. Her bigness expanded to occupy space he hadn't even known was available in their tiny hut, in their tiny village. And there was a slight change, in Bambayot. A slight, but absolute change. Aru might not have mentioned her, but he certainly seemed to have no problem heeding her counsel. There was not one single incident of dark praying while Marietta was back from the East. No chanting. No screams in the night. Max watched her carefully, as she delivered the sermons on Sunday in his stead. As she spoke, her bare feet wiggled in the dirt on the floor of the church. He must have an awful lot to learn from her, he thought.

And as the days turned into weeks, it became clear Max would have to find a way to keep Bea and Marietta apart. The humming had reached epidemic proportions, and when it rose unbidden from Marietta's bedroom, Bea's eyelids visibly twitched with irritation. Marietta only addressed Bea in the loud, slow voice that Bea suspected she must once have used on her Latina maid. One Sunday, after church, Mabo-Mabon asked Bea if Marietta was her mother, and Bea had shouted, 'No!' so loudly that even Mabo-Mabon had raised her eyebrows in amusement.

Mealtimes were particularly difficult. There were still only two stools in Mission House, and until Willie, the self-declared village carpenter, could be bothered to carve a new one, two stools there would remain. Marietta always sat on the far stool, on the right, Max on the stool at the head of the table, and Bea perched awkwardly on an upturned crate, which left her half a head lower than Marietta and Max, and in direct eye contact with their mouths. Marietta ate hungrily, stopping to clear her throat in an unnecessarily gruesome way every other mouthful. Each time she cleared her throat, Bea paused, her spoon in mid-air, waiting for Marietta to spit out whatever she had dislodged, but she just swallowed, and Bea shuddered inside. And it was always God talk. Bea sat, patiently eating, while Marietta and Max lectured each other about the fulfilment of the Holy Spirit, or the story of Naboth's vineyard. Or else they talked about the island.

'And is it true he has his own currency?'

'Yes –' Marietta coughed and swallowed '– now this is interesting –'

That phrase had a special power to make Bea's spirits drop.

'– he only permits the use of "the Liki", can you believe it?' Marietta raised her eyebrows.

Max and Marietta chortled.

Max shook his head. 'What an egotist.'

Bea watched him with disbelief. Why did he always have to speak so pompously when he talked to Marietta? Max didn't behave normally when he was around her. He was trying to impress her. And she was flattered by his deference to her authority as the island know-it-all.

'Now, "the Liki" is nothing more than young namele leaves punctured with holes. But you can't buy anything with actual currency – only these leaves!' Marietta continued.

'And they say money doesn't grow on trees,' Max quipped.

Marietta snickered again.

'I don't understand,' Bea heard herself saying. 'How is that any different to our money?'

Max and Marietta both stared at her.

'What's that, my dear?' Marietta asked.

'I mean – our money is from paper, also from trees.'

Max and Marietta shared a look, and Marietta stared down at her plate, grinning to herself. Bea saw a flicker of humour dilating Max's nostrils.

'No, my dear, it's just a saying,' he said.

Max and Marietta exchanged another look of suppressed hilarity, and Bea had to restrain herself from smashing her plate on the table and walking out. Stupid little Bea wasn't a missionary. Sitting here, taking smug looks from her husband and this awful, annoying woman. Max read mutiny in Bea's expression and maintained a polite silence for the rest of the meal.

In the early evening, Max and Marietta went to the village nakamal, the men's traditional drinking hut. Women were not supposed to even look too hard at the path to the nakamal, although apparently Marietta was an exception to the rule. Perhaps, Bea thought bitterly, she was so old and fat she didn't count as a woman any more. Bea, in a desperate act of rebellion, spent her evenings reading on Marietta's stool, resting her feet on her own crate. She kept the fire going, and sipped endless cups of watery tea. In the beginning, in the days before Marietta, the night-times had been the worst. The sudden blanket of darkness yanked over before you had a chance to strike a match, the unplaceable movement of insects in the house. Now, the early evenings perversely became her favourite part of the day. The wind breathed heavily into the jungle, boys on the beach strummed aimlessly on a ukulele. Bea would pick up one of Max's books and pretend to herself she was reading it, while pausing every few minutes to gaze out of the window. The village was quiet, the hush of kava settled upon it. Faint smudges of light from fires could be seen as women cooked for their families. There was the soft giggling of girls sent to lay food on the path to the nakamal, the beats of a ching drum as the girls alerted their fathers to the arrival of their taro.

Max spent all his time with Marietta, together in the vestry, or out on walkabouts. Before, Bea went with him on his witnessing missions. Yes, it was boring, but she at least had a chance to leave the village. Now, it was always Max and Marietta, Max and Marietta. They traded the death tolls of Pacific battles, and prayed together for the poor heathen souls in Korea. They snapped Bible verses back and forth and bickered imperiously about theologians with German names. Those private conferences, shared jokes, pious remonstrations – they were all the influence of Marietta. There was something about Marietta, thought Bea, as she scrubbed her clothes furiously in the bucket; there was just something all wrong about her. Something inherently bad about the way she cleared her throat like that. About the way she picked island cabbage from her teeth with her finger. About Marietta's colossal grey brassieres hanging from inside her room – what had been her own room. About the way she pushed the floppy lock of hair back from her face, over and over. Why didn't she just pin it back? Bea brushed and brushed. Bea dropped the brush into the bucket and cried hot tears into the knees of her skirt. She wiped her face with the back of her forearm, picked the brush up again, and sighed. It would be fine. Maybe Marietta would go back East. Maybe she would go back to Australia. Eventually, she would leave and they could be alone again.

Max was starting to regret his own insistence that Marietta stay with them indefinitely. At home, her presence was unavoidable, as if the moment they entered through the door of Mission House, she grew to be three times her size. Marietta's body was like an exclamation mark. She would just appear, and announce herself. Corpulent. That was the only word for her. Her sniffing and wheezing, her heavy breathing as she moved about the house. She bathed only once a week, and the dank, goaty smell coming from her clothes repulsed him. She scratched under her arms at the dinner table, so he could hear a rasping sound from where fingernails met hair. Her very footsteps began to irritate him. She had a flat-footed way of walking, where each tread slapped heavily down on the floor all at once. It woke him up in the morning before the sun had even risen. Max became convinced she was walking like that deliberately, to remind him he was lazily dozing in bed while she was already up and about, ready to start the day in the service of the Lord.

When they walked up the hill to the villages on top, and out of respect for Marietta's impaired leg, Max slowly made his way up the path, he would hear a honk behind him, 'No, not that way – this way is much quicker. Really, Max, haven't you been this way before? I'm amazed.' Marietta knew the villagers by name, and Max was forced to trot along behind her as she talked animatedly in badly accented but fluent Kunu, asking after the health of old people, murmuring appreciatively over people's pigs or new wives, confirming rumours and gossip. Max stood towering over her shoulder and mimed comprehension, sucking at his pipe, desperately trying to pick up any words he could. He could have asked Marietta for lessons, but she assumed he already knew more Kunu than he did, and he was too ashamed to declare his ignorance. Sometimes, he wished she would just go away on a walkabout, and stay away.

In a way, Max got his wish, because almost two months later, he killed her.

PART ONE

Five months earlier

I

Advent Island didn't at all resemble the postcard of tan, smiling honeymooners that Max had shown her. It was not even a landscape, Bea thought to herself – it was just land. She looked out at the ocean. It was flat and lifeless, unmarked by even a slit of foam. The day was so overcast that the sea and sky blended on the horizon in a leaden grey haze. The air was still and thick with water. It was difficult to breathe.

On their honeymoon in New York, Max had taken her to see *South Pacific* as 'preparation' for their trip. She ate two hot dogs during the intermission and smeared mustard on her blouse. Watching George Britton and Martha Wright dance about the stage of the Majestic had hardly been appropriate training for the dank beach and drab sea lying before her.

Tiny translucent hermit crabs stirred along the shoreline, and the sand wavered like an optical illusion. Four metres to her left, the bloated and skinless corpse of a cat was washed on to the beach. Bea closed her eyes. She had lain awake in Port Vila only three weeks before, imagining a beautiful riot of flowers and gilded parrots. But there was only jungle, and air, and sea. And everything was only green, or grey, or black. Except for her and Max. She opened her eyes. At least with no breeze she couldn't smell the cat.

Instead, she could smell the sickly perfume of the rainforest. It reeked of a complex confection of decay. Even on the beach, far from the treeline, she could smell the rotting trail of smashed papayas that littered the coastal path, and the musk from the warm, hairy bodies of the two long-limbed black monkeys wheezing in the coconut palms. And there was the damp mustiness of her clothes. It didn't matter how often she soaked, and pressed, and hung, and scrubbed, and rinsed them. She could detect it on her skin even after she had undressed at night. She stank of the treacly mildew of the jungle.

The sun was beginning to drop towards the horizon. Soon, it would curdle with red, and minutes later, there would be whole, complete blackness. Bea stood up, brushed a hermit crab from the lap of her skirt, and began the walk back to Bambayot.

Bambayot village was set on top of a hill about a ten-minute walk up from the coastline, in a small clearing of rainforest. Behind the village, the land rose almost vertically. The mountains were well tracked with footpaths to and from the farming allotments, but to Bea's untrained eye, at first it had looked as if an unbroken green sheet of jungle simply sprang from the back of the settlement.

The village itself was a jumble of bamboo houses and chicken droppings. There were eight families living permanently in Bambayot, and each family had two huts: a larger one for sleeping in, and a smaller bushkitchen. Chief Bule also had a 'holiday home' he occasionally slept in, further east of the village. The houses were distributed over a slope that rose gently upwards towards the rocky forest in the north.

From the boat on the way over, it had been easy to see how isolated they were. Impenetrable jungle spread out as far as the eye could see over the island, and Max had pointed out the white dot of Bambayot Church in the midst of all that green. As the boat drew closer to the shore, Bea could see a six-pronged waterfall through the jungle to the north, and a glimmer of an old-fashioned western building high up in the hills to the south. Here and there along the shoreline, she could make out the odd clearing among the leaves, where smoke from village fires wound up into the air.

The main features of any island village were usually either a church, or a nakamal, the low-roofed ceremonial hut used for drinking kava. Bambayot was unusual, because it had both. The nakamal was south of the village, at the bottom of the hill, a stone's throw from the huts of Willie Kakae and Edly Tabi, the only two confirmed 'bachelors' of Bambayot. The rest of the villagers lived on top of the hill. Smoky, cramped and muddy, the village was overrun by blond-haired, brown-skinned children with swollen bellies and running noses, poking pores in the dirt with hibiscus switches. According to Max, possessing both brown skin and blond hair was a native quirk of the islands, and not, as Bea had thought, the resultant product of one white and one black parent. The church had been built at the front of the village at the bottom of the slope, where it could easily be accessed by boat. And behind the church, at the top of the hill, was Mission House, the place Bea now thought of as home.

Mission House was made from woven bamboo and pandan leaf, with a natangora palm thatched roof and a generous porch. Their central room was outfitted with one of the two stone floors in the village, with a lean-to kitchen that had been nailed on to the right-hand side of the building. The 'living room', as they generously called it, was bare of furniture, apart from their two stools and a splintery, unsanded wooden table which sat under the window on the left.

At the back, a narrow corridor led off into two bedrooms on either side. Bea's bedroom faced the church. From her window, she could see the top of the huge wooden cross nailed to the top of the building, and an expanse of grey water beyond. In bed at night, if she listened carefully over the shifting and sucking sounds from the jungle, she could hear the ocean against the shore. Max's bedroom also had one window that looked out past the edge of the village and on to a steep forested incline.

On the boat from Caracas in the early days of their marriage, Bea and Max had shared a narrow bunk for the duration of the journey. In that narrow bunk, Max dedicated himself to performing his nuptial duties with solemn administration. But as soon as they arrived in Boston, Max had retreated into his childhood bedroom, allocating Bea his father's old room, still fusty with the faint aroma of a long illness.

It had been some relief, therefore, to find Mission House equipped with two bedrooms. Bea begged Max to take the larger one, since they discovered in there a mysterious trunk containing a squealing nest of rat babies in the tattered shreds of what had previously been women's underpants and a collection of crossword puzzle books. Bea refused to stay again in a bedroom haunted by someone else's belongings.

Their bathroom was set in an outhouse to the left of the main house, behind a rough semicircle of banana trees. The lavatory was only a great hole in the ground, and there was a crude but functional shower, improvised from a small rainwater well, a pump and a rusty-looking pipe suspended at Bea's shoulder height. Max declared the previous missionaries must have gone through a lot of bother to set it up. Bea wished they had bothered to make a door as well, since both facilities, although separated from each other by a pandan screen, were nevertheless completely open to the elements. Max reminded her it could be much worse. The other women from the village splashed themselves along the banks of the river using buckets, or simply sat in the stream, fully clothed, rubbing themselves with slabs of soap. Bea thought back to her bathroom in her father's house. It had been tiled and white, with a proper door, and a lock with a key. There, she had had

Elizabeth Vera to heat water for her on cold, rainy days, and fill up the tub with the heads of camomile flowers.

To make matters worse, the only route to reach Mission House bathroom was to leave the front door and circuit the whole building. During the daytime, Bea found this mortifying. Often, while crossing in front of the house, someone from the village would spontaneously pop up over the hedge, and demand to know where Bea was going. At first, she had pointed vaguely into the shrubbery around the back of the house, colouring in shame. As time went on, Bea began to lie cheerfully, and declare she was going 'walkabout'.

Night-time trips to the bathroom were, however, intolerable. It was barely worth lighting a candle for such a short trip, but unthinkable without proper navigation. After dark, the grass was squelchy underfoot with dew, and concealed an innumerable plenitude of teeming insects. After sunset, the outhouse became a zoological garden of creeping terrors. The floor and the walls became coated in lively, twisting spiders, furred centipedes, and all manner of antlered monstrosities for which Bea did not even have a name. It was only possible to use the lavatory by trustfully baring your behind to this spectacle of crawling nightmares, while simultaneously performing a sort of hopping dance. Allow one's legs to stay on the ground for more than five seconds, and its inhabitants crawled up them and into one's nightclothes. The first few twilight trips were so traumatizing for Bea that she stopped drinking water after supper, and without mentioning it to Max, in cases of dire emergency, she began to use a chamber pot.

Max and Bea had arrived on the island the morning after Chief Bule had presided over a generous feast, the centrepiece of which had been a freshly slaughtered bullock. Rainson Tabi and his eldest son, Edly, had inexpertly split the beast in half with their bushknives, and hung it from a rope attached to the beams of the Chief's bushkitchen. Sepater, Rainson's second son, had grabbed the freshly severed tail of the animal, and wrapped it around his waist in high-spirited mockery of the ceremonial red mat his father was wearing.

All this meant that on the day of Max and Bea's arrival, the earth around Mission House was trailed with dark cow's blood and frothing with ants. Bule met them on the coast as they waded in from the launch, but he was sluggish and grumpy from drinking too much kava. In a moment of last-minute observance of the proper etiquette, Othniel Tari ran back to the village to procure for Max and Bea two wilted salu-salus of browning hibiscus flowers that had been made for Bule the day before, and trampled underfoot during the celebrations.

Max was delighted when he first saw the church. Passion flowers had been tucked into the slats of the windows, and palm fronds cut into fans were tied in arches over the door-way. As Max circled the room, a pink lizard paused motionless on the ceiling, before scuttling noisily through a hole in the wood. On the wall behind the altar there was a crude and rather faded painting of a white man with a beard, and a help-ful label of 'Jesus' added in broad brushstrokes underneath. In front of the altar were arranged two sets of wooden benches so the women could sit on the left of the church, and the men on the right. There were a handful of battered paperback Bibles with 'M. Hardwood' ink-stamped into the flyleaf.

Max sat on one of the benches, unknowingly picking the women's side, and looked up at the pulpit, daydreaming about nothing in particular, but enjoying the warm breeze inflating the back of his shirt. He looked around to see a handful of children ducking below the window sill, and heard a murmur of hushed giggling as they ran away. There was a tentative knock on the door frame, and Max stood up to greet a man with short hair, and a round face with deep-set eyes. This was Mr Filip Aru, who spoke decent English as a result of the Protestant boarding school on Santo.

'I have been running the religious programmes until now,' Aru said shyly, nodding his head, rolling a paperback Bible in his hands so the white seams of the book strained. 'It's very good to have a Pastor here to help us in the ways of the new religion.'

Max smiled. 'That's splendid. Have you received any training?'

Aru smiled, a dimple appearing at the left corner of his mouth. 'No, no training. I only have the grace of the Holy Spirit.'

'That's splendid,' said Max again. 'Tell me, has it been long since your last missionary left?'

'The last missionary?' Aru echoed in English.

'Yes, a woman, I believe. I'm afraid I can't remember, perhaps from New Zealand?'

Aru raised his eyebrows in affirmation, but didn't reply.

Max nodded silently for a moment before changing the subject. 'Maybe you can help me, then. We should talk about the religious programme you have run so far.'

Aru smiled broadly, showing two rows of small, white teeth.

Max began work in his small kingdom the week after they had arrived on the island. After consultation with Aru, he agreed to run services in the church every Wednesday and Sunday morning, during which he could expect not only villagers but converts from the surrounding area, who would rise early to walk to Bambayot.

On his third morning on the island, Max had woken to the sound of hymns. He was used to the New Hebridean form of singing, a chorus of childlike, high voices whose discord ultimately produced something queer and beautiful. He lay in his cot, dreamily transported back to his days of service during the war. And then, all in one tumultuous lurch of childhood terror, such as when one recalls they are already late for school, Max realized the music was coming from the church. He sat bolt upright in his cot in a flurry of panic, realizing he must be, in fact, absent from one of his own services. He dressed as quickly as he could, and dashed down to the church two strides at a time. This was not how he had planned his introduction to his new congregation.

When he arrived at the church, he was relieved to see there was only Aru and a group of seven young women inside. Three he vaguely recognized, but the others were strangers to him.

Aru shuffled over. 'These are the church singers.' He gestured to the women.

Max nodded hastily, looking around for the arrival of the rest of the churchgoers who were no doubt already on their way. Aru walked backwards, still facing Max. He picked up his ukulele from one of the benches, and continued to accompany them. Max stood behind the lectern, flipping through his Bible and praying for inspiration for an introductory sermon.

A girl of about thirteen in a blue island dress watched him and tittered, nudging the girl next to her. He realized he must look quite unkempt, and smoothed his hair down, wondering if the creases on his face from his pillow were still obvious. Aru continued to sing along with his small crowd of girls. Max stood at the lectern, flicking through the Bible and feverishly composing a speech in his head. The singing continued for another twenty minutes. As the sun rose higher in the sky, and the day began to warm, it became increasingly obvious to Max that no one was coming for a service. Instead, Max had interrupted a practice session.

Aru's church singers gathered at the break of day and the close of night to practise. After awkwardly hanging about at the first several sessions, Max realized he wasn't needed, nor even particularly welcomed to the singing practices. Aru was clearly in charge of the musical arrangement for the services. He was a talented musician, who not only coordinated the chorus of girls, but accompanied them on a ukulele. Their singing was beautiful and unpredictable. It was a combination of old church favourites set to a sort of island rhythm, and substitutions made in Bislama or in what was simply known as 'Language' – the umbrella term for any of the hundreds of local dialects.

When he wasn't preparing his services, Max was occupied with the everyday small tasks of missionary work. He administered yaws injections and distributed mosquito nets. He doled out spoonfuls of Milk of Magnesia, dispensed Bufferin pills, rubbed antiseptic cream on cuts, and occasionally handed out Atabrine tablets to malarial children. He attempted to acquaint himself with each member of the village, and offered his services to Othniel Tari for the religious education of the small band of children he intermittently and reluctantly tutored. Max held a Bible reading group on Monday evenings, inviting all the villagers to participate. These were sporadically attended by Othniel and his wife, Jinnes, and their five-year-old daughter, Lorianne. Aru dutifully came to every meeting, as did Abel and Gracie Poulet and their daughter, Judy. Occasionally, Patro Tarileo and his daughter, Leiwas, joined in. But never his wife, Mabo-Mabon, who was decidedly unconverted.

Max often worked alongside Chief Bule, who had been converted to Christianity some ten years previously. Standing at around five foot, he reminded Max of a garden gnome. Bule appeared to own only one shirt, a strawberry-coloured affair with a pussy-bow collar that had clearly once been a lady's. It was spotlessly clean, but tattered about the hem and the sleeves, so that all edges of the blouse hung in shreds. Max supposed Bule found the colour to be cheerful, and never thought to mention it was clearly an item of women's clothing. Bule was of an indeterminate age. He might have been fifty-five or seventy-five. His beard and hair were peppered with grey hairs, and he wore a constant toothless smile of mischievous good cheer. Bule was lean, his muscles taut and powerful. He had the aura of a man with a potential reserve of explosive energy, like a cat about to pounce. Bule sometimes took Max on walkabouts to other villages in the area, and Max could barely keep up with the man, despite matching his stride by almost double.

Bule introduced him at all the nakamals in the surrounding villages on the south coast. He pointed out the garden allotments on top and showed him the paths to the North. Max quickly learnt that 'path' was more of a euphemism for hours of trudging upstream through ice-cold rivers. He dreaded those short cuts. Deep, hungry ravines appeared out of nowhere, requiring a steady heart to clutch on to mucusy vines and leap between slippery boulders. Vast, gummy spider's webs hung across the whole width of the river. Sinewy things crept over his feet. Every now and again, Bule would point to something in the bush – a completely indistinguishable branch, or a tiny white flower – and draw his bushknife across his heart, miming death. It was thoroughly unnerving.

Once, Bule took Max along a 'path' to the East that he would be able to use when the rainy season was over. After the usual vertiginous spiral up the hills, the track broke on to wide meadows dotted with the odd brown cow. Max caught his breath. The grass was thigh-high, with soft green weeds that closed in upon themselves when touched. He could look behind them, and see the coiled-up buds tracing their wake. Bule pointed out a nakamal in the distance, which, he claimed, served the best turtle on the island.

It wasn't long before the 'path' plunged back over the edge of the land. Max stepped into the crunchy shell of a hornets' nest and froze in terror as a stream of stripes poured out, trailing barbs as long as pencils. Bule rolled his eyes at Max, and began winding down and up and down again, round the hill, underneath the old colonial house. Max had to scramble on his hands and knees, heavy rocks turning in the mud underneath his wrists and ankles. He slipped several times, and almost slid back down the slope, grabbing desperately on to liana to steady himself, while Bule nimbly sprang up ahead of him, pausing to watch him in amusement.

As they passed the ridge under the shadow of the old house, Max allowed his neck the odd rest to look up at it. It was two storeys high, with one window on the top floor, looking out towards the ocean. The ground floor was covered in vines that had busted through the window frames. Two ionic columns flanked a heavy doorway, coated in moss. It was quite uncanny. Max asked if they could go up to take a look, but Bule merely shook his head, made the bushknife 'death' sign, and offered 'tabu' by means of an explanation.

Knox Turu later claimed the old colonial house was built by a French prince, who had intended to create for himself the first two-storey construction on the island so he could be closer to the gods. Unknowingly, he had chosen a tabu hilltop, and had died horribly from leaf magic. If anyone ever went in there now they would also die horribly from the tabu. When Max shared this story with Willie at the nakamal, he laughed and slapped his thigh.

'No, no. It was a copra farmer. He lost his money before it was finished. It's not a good place for a house. Too wet for the wood. So he gave up and went to some other island.' Willie waved his cigarette vaguely in the direction of the shoreline. He hunched over to take a draw of smoke, and turned back to Max, suddenly serious. 'It is tabu, though. You must not go there.'

While Max spent time on walkabouts with Bule, or in church with Aru, Bea found it tricky to get to know the other people in the village. Each day, she strolled through Bambayot, hoping to strike up a conversation with one of the other women. But the women weren't in the village in the middle of the day; they were farming in the gardens 'on top'. There were often men congregating by a fallen tree near the nakamal at the south of the village, chewing tobacco or sharpening their bushknives. But Bea was far too nervous to approach them. She was not used to talking to tall, half-naked black men wielding machetes. She wasn't even sure if it was 'allowed', since there were so many tabus around what women were and weren't supposed to do.

She wasn't supposed to go walking around by herself. She wasn't to show any skin above her elbows or knees. Even while bathing, she had to swim fully clothed, in her island dress, or in a pair of Max's long shorts. She wasn't allowed to go out in a dugout canoe. It was tabu for women to fish. She shouldn't make too much eye contact with men, in case she seemed indecent. She wasn't to wear her hair loose. She mustn't dry her clothes outside, especially any underclothes. She wasn't to point directly at anything, because it was unlucky. It was also unlucky for women to walk on the path to the nakamal. She wasn't supposed to run anywhere. And on Sundays, it was considered ill-mannered to do anything that might constitute work – no mending clothes on the front porch. It was like being a pilgrim. It made Bea feel a little wild.

All she wished to do was leap from her house on a Sunday morning, wearing only her underclothes with her hair shockingly loose, and run straight down the coast into a dugout and start fishing.

For the first couple of weeks, Bea's main companion was an ugly little stray dog that had decided to follow her around. 'New Dog' was a scrawny piebald Jack Russell mutt with an overexcitable temperament. On the afternoon of their arrival, it had accosted her from the grass around Mission House, bursting out of the underbrush, yelping, whinnying and trying to leap up on to Bea's clothes. Othniel had dropped the half of Max's book trunk he was carrying up from the coast, and rushed over to her rescue. He kicked the animal in the snout, yelling, 'Kranki dog!'

The dog whined and slunk off behind the house, looking over its shoulder with its tail between its legs. Its flank was crawling with hopping fleas, its nipples were distended and swollen. Apparently, the beast craved attention, and any new arrival from another village would cause a mania of hysterical joy as the dog cavorted and frolicked, licking and sniffing. There had been so many attempts to catch the animal that it was considered basically demonic. Othniel explained he had tried to snare it in a net. Bea asked what he would do when he caught it, and he had smiled, miming eating.

'Kakae,' he said. Bea wasn't sure if he was teasing her or not.

Bea found that whenever she left her house, it was only a matter of minutes until the dog followed her, flattening its ginger ears against its head, trotting territorially around the porch while Bea scrubbed clothes in the bucket.

It even, to Bea's mortification, followed her into church. After trying to casually hustle the animal out of the building with her Bible, she had to relinquish herself to its company. It would shimmy underneath her pew, contenting itself with breathing heavily up into the folds of her skirt, attracting flies with its repellent stink. Occasionally it crawled out during the sermon to stretch itself, yawning casually before investigating the other members of the church, who were only too happy to release old-fashioned Christian vengeance on the beast by beating it with their hymn books and smacking it towards the doors, but with no luck. It let out strangled howls of annoyance and squirmed back under Bea's pew. But as her only friend on the island, Bea didn't feel she was in a position to be picky.

2

It was their third Saturday on Advent Island. The sun had begun to rise, and the sky was stippled with yellow clouds. With one hand on the door frame of Mission House, Max pushed himself towards the church, towards the sound of the screaming that had woken him. It was the screaming of a young woman. It echoed between the huts and the mountains beyond the end of the village. Over the wailing, he heard muffled voices, maybe prayers. It sounded like someone was in pain, and a group had gathered to offer consolation.

As he approached the church, a brilliant splash of crimson streaked up through the sky. He was now certain the noise was coming from the church itself. Through the slats in the windows, Max could see people had congregated inside. He paused by the door frame. A woman was lying prostrate on the floor. Maybe someone had had an accident? What could he do? He had so few medical supplies, and so little training.

He realized, with a sinking feeling, that the woman lying there was Leiwas, Mabo-Mabon's eldest daughter. He was fond of Leiwas. She was so young. She was a sober and sweet teenage girl who had brought Bea a gift of a beautiful hollowed-out, lavender-coloured lizard's egg. She was supposed to be married next month to an older man from the North. She and Mabo-Mabon had spent the last two weeks collecting and drying pandan rushes on the roof of her house for her wedding mat.

The murmuring had grown clearer as he descended the hill, and he could hear the five or so people gathered around the young girl were chanting prayers. He caught the odd exclamation of, 'Oh, Jesus!' Something was clearly terribly wrong. He paused by the door of the church, suddenly unsure. There were only young girls inside. And Aru. Together they had formed a circle around Leiwas, who was lying on the floor, her wails rising and subsiding.

Aru and the girls were shifting from side to side and flapping their hands, as if shaking hot water from their fingers. Leiwas let out another agonized wail. The mutters of, 'I cast you out in the name of *Jesus*,' came more clearly now. Leiwas' eyes had rolled back in her head, and she was sobbing uncontrollably.

Aru approached the fallen girl with a Bible in his outstretched hands, and crouched beside her. He grabbed her firmly by the shoulder and placed the Bible on her forehead. Leiwas' screams grew louder still. Max stood outside the church watching, unable to move.

Aru and his 'church singers' were performing an exorcism.

Max slunk back to Mission House, an odd prickling on the back of his neck. Surely, as the resident missionary, he should have been consulted. What was he to do? Entering the church like that, in the middle of all the commotion, would only have served to undermine his position. It would only have made it more obvious he hadn't been invited. Instead, Max reasoned, he could ask Aru about it in private.

Max sought him out later in the afternoon, and asked him to join him in the vestry. He sat down on the small bench in front of the table, while Aru lingered by the door.

Max cleared his throat, 'Forgive me, Mr Aru, but I couldn't help overhearing the, uh, the disturbance from the church early this morning.'

'Pastor –' Aru dropped his head, then looked up at him again. 'Pastor, this is dark praying. It was necessary.'

A thrill passed through Max's stomach. 'Dark praying?'

'Yes, Pastor. For the health of the young women in this village.' Aru was nodding gently, as if in agreement with himself.

'What –' Max began, looking off at the corner of the door of the vestry '– what makes it "dark" as such?'

Aru looked at him. 'We pray to protect against the power of darkness.'

Max sat back and crossed his legs at his ankles. 'Do you believe the power of darkness was in Leiwas?' he asked.

'Yes,' Aru said quietly. 'It is all around us in the hills. The power of the Devil, and his servant Ukunu. We have to protect the innocent in Jesus from these dangers.'

Max re-crossed his legs. Aru had something of a literal interpretation of sin, but this was not so unforgivable. 'Mr Aru,' Max began, smiling, so he might not seem as if he were rebuking the man. 'Do you feel that Leiwas is still in danger?'

'No.' Aru shook his head. 'For now, she is safe.'

This answer did not much reassure Max. 'May I ask?' He maintained his smile. 'I would like to know more about this risk. When you –' he corrected himself hopefully '– if you feel, again, that Leiwas – or any other innocents – are in danger, perhaps you and I can talk more about it? Before you pray over them?'

Aru broke into his small white smile. 'Of course, Pastor.'

After Aru had left, Max sat alone in the vestry. Aru was a gentle, kind man. It was undoubtedly part of the effort he had made while there was no missionary in the village. It was his way of trying to help a young woman under his care. Leiwas was sixteen or so. Perhaps it was a misunderstood fear of menstruation or another kind of female ailment. Perhaps pre-wedding jitters; Leiwas was afraid she might be found wanting in some way by her new husband. Max rubbed his fingers over the bristles of his moustache. He smiled to himself, sighing. This was where he could truly make a difference.

In 1942 Max had accompanied the American troops to a base in Luganville, Espiritu Santo, a rabbit-shaped island in the New Hebrides, so large that the first explorer overenthusiastically declared it to be Australia. On Santo, Max was truly happy. He spent most of his time living with the soldiers, offering them advice and cigarettes, delivering services in the church on Sundays, and spending every other waking moment in the villages around Luganville working with the Australian missionaries to spread his faith. For Max, his faith was like his nationality; an immovable part of himself. The stories from the villages on Santo disturbed and sickened him. The men and women of the New Hebrides he met were truly ashamed of their cannibalism, the ferocity of the Big Nambas. All Max had to do was help the natives he met to understand how to turn their backs on their heathenish practices, and accept the Word of God.

On Santo, no one had ever questioned his right to be there. Not all the boys came to see him with their problems, but they listened to him, though he was pretty near the same age as most of them. He ran services on Sundays, offered smokes and sympathy to anyone who wanted either, and travelled around the island in an open-backed truck for the rest of the time, visiting men building roads and airstrips. He learnt Bislama, and got a chance to meet the locals there. Even among the white men, he was something of a novelty – being six foot six, with red hair. He was invited into churches, to circumcisions, to pig-killing ceremonies. The top brass were keen on churchmen being there too, so he never had any problems. 'Important for the morale of the boys,' they said. It wasn't just the Japs they were trying to flush out of the South Pacific – it was their lawlessness, their godlessness and, Max understood as time went on, their fearlessness.

Luganville might have been the biggest city on the island of Espiritu Santo, but everyone called the city and the island by the same name: Santo. Before the war, Luganville hadn't been much more than a squalid assembly of shacks looking out on to a rough, white-topped sea. But in '42 when the Americans arrived, Santo was plugged full of money it had never even dreamed of. The Seabees built roads all over the island – great, flat roads. The Americans were young, brash and bored. They established three new hospitals, built Quonset huts that looked surreal nestling between the palm houses of the villagers. They rigged up unreliable electric lights, and ran outdoor cinemas from their generators.

Santo had a feel to it. A feel that Max only later came to understand was excitement. Santo in the forties was close enough to the fighting on Guadalcanal to feel perpendicular to the action. It had enough tall-necked coconut palms and men with three-stringed guitars to be exotic. And the wealth the boys brought in, it made Max feel good. They built a new pool bar on the waterfront, shared smokes with the locals on the benches in Unity Park. They bought brown braids of tobacco from the market and sold on extra oil and rice. Kids on the street waved as they went by. It was the best three years of his life.

At the end of the war, the same festive atmosphere continued even as they set about destroying the place. Orders came to trash everything – forklifts, oil, jeeps, cases of untouched tinned peaches. And so the whole lot went into the sea. Men with comically white ghost-shirts painted on their skin spent weeks driving trucks to Million Dollar Point, smashing years' worth of equipment and supplies down into the waves. Lines of islanders watched on, whooping in amusement at the sudden madness that had overcome the GIs, or making frantic dives for cases of Coca-Cola, or barrels of oil as soon as they hit the water. It was a shameful waste as far as Max was concerned, but it was still kind of fun. Like stomping on your sandcastle after a day at the beach.

Max was surprised to find himself disappointed the war was over. A lot of the men felt the same way. The lucky ones went home to a hero's welcome – having spent three years drinking gin and tonic as guests of the British and French Administration. The unlucky ones had been on the outer islands trying to set up insane labour projects, or in New Guinea with the Australians. They turned up on Santo every four months, pock-marked with insect bites and riddled with worms. Their hair grown to their ears, half-baked with malaria, they nervously took in the flickering electric lights, smoked endless cigarettes, and frustrated the hell out of everyone else by draining all the day's hot water in twenty-minute showers. Max listened to their stories – sleeping in the bush, surrounded by tattooed islanders, worshipping ancestors, cooking with hot stones, wandering around naked with red mats or straw nambas strapped to their groins. The men's stories were laced with contempt for their peers, their three-year holiday on Champagne Beach, dipping in the Matevulu Blue Hole and frolicking with dolphins. While all the time they sweated themselves half to death in some smoke-hole in the jungle.

But Max was impressed. These places were among the last serious challenges for a Christian. These people, living in wild, untamed jungle. Eating each other, killing their children, turning to witches and sorcerers for advice and spiritual guidance. The missionaries who had dared to make it that far hadn't met with a happy fate. There were stories of white people arriving on outer islands and being immediately speared on their boats. In some cases, the missionaries had early successes, gaining converts, witnessing to scores of people. Later, when those people caught European diseases from the missionaries and died, the villagers traced the cause of their death to their new religion, blamed the missionaries, then killed and ate them. It was exhilarating. Max had no desire to end up in the cooking pot of some bone-nosed island savage, but the idea that the Word was still unheard in these places – not denied, nor ignored, but unheard! That there were Christians who could bring the Good News to untouched communities – there could be no higher purpose.

Max stood up and crossed to the doorway. He could hear the whine of Aru's instrument being tuned. 'Mr Aru,' he called.

Aru emerged from behind Othniel and Jinnes' house, ukulele in hand. But now Max had summoned him, he wasn't sure what more there was to say. After a moment's pause, he gave him a thumbs up.

Aru smiled and waved.

The tension in Max's chest relaxed. It was never going to be easy, weaning the natives off the corrupted parts of their faith. But such were the perils of the missionary life. And such were its pleasures.

3

'What do you think he'll be like?' Garolf slugged from his kava shell and walked to the back corner of the nakamal, where he spat on the dirt floor.

'Thin. Little round spectacles. Poor bastard probably spent the whole journey up stopping at each village handing out trousers,' said Jonson.

Garolf laughed, wiping his mouth with the back of his hand. 'Worse than Hardwood?'

'At least this one's a man.' Jonson passed him the bowl of papaya, and Garolf took the last slice.

The dinner ching boomed three times at the north of the village, and a chorus of whistles relayed the end of the day to those still at work in the coconut palms. Handknives clattered against stone, the pump squeaked as workers rinsed their hands and feet. As they filed slowly into the meal hall, a noisy brew of chattering voices echoed between the trees; coughs and giggles, a baby crying.

Garolf stuck his head out of the nakamal door and whistled until a young Vietnamese man wearing jeans and a black T-shirt appeared in the doorway. Garolf pushed the empty bowl into the man's hands, and he ran off towards the smoking bushkitchen. Garolf sat on the bench and sighed, crossing his hands behind his head. 'Does this one have a launch?'

'Not according to the LMS.'

Garolf tutted. 'Why do they even need more missionaries in Bambayot anyway? They're all kranki down there.'

Jonson fingered his empty kava shell. 'Heaven knows.'

I. A. M. Jonson was a Christian, but island spirituality confounded him. Superstitions about flesh-eating dwarves, gibbering about demons and devils, about flying sorcerers and magic leaves. And now all coated in a respectable churchgoing varnish. In his first four years on Advent Island, Jonson had endured the reign of two resident missionaries: first Reginald DeWitt, then Marietta Hardwood. He'd humoured the seven crusading missionaries who had travelled the island spreading the Word during his tenure. Three Americans, three Australians, and a Spanish Jesuit who'd caught crookworm and been housed in Jonson's spare room for two weeks while village girls massaged his feet with coconut oil and picked out the parasites with a pair of tweezers. Jonson imagined Pastor Hanlon would be yet another of those stooped, sunken-looking men with a feathery patch of hair, drab and subtly faded like an old watercolour. Those men with too-large Adam's apples and unnaturally clean, oversized bony hands with knobbly, chafed knuckles.

'And he's American?'

'So I've heard.'

'An American to save the day. Step in at the last minute? Help you out, huh?' Garolf nudged Jonson, hard, in the ribs, and Jonson gripped the bench to catch himself from toppling over.

'Very droll.'

'At least it's another whiteman for you.' Garolf pulled a squashed, black cigarette from the front pocket of his shirt and lit it with a match. 'A friend,' he added, drawing a strand of tobacco from his lower lip.

'A friend. How generous.'

The nakamal ching struck. Jonson walked to the doorway of the hut and collected a refreshed bowl of papaya slices from the path. He watched as a middle-aged Vietnamese woman climbed the hill to the meal hall, chewing on what was presumably an errant slice of papaya. Jonson wrinkled his nose at the bowl, laying it on the bench and wiping his fingers with his handkerchief.

'How is the health issue progressing?'

Garolf cleared his throat. 'Fine.' He reached for another slice of papaya.

Jonson raised his eyebrow. 'Any more, uh, expirations?'

Garolf sighed. 'One last week. That's good. Dying less quickly now.'

The plantation hosted 133 workers, and also a constant rotation of fevers, coughs and influenza. Garolf hadn't said the word out loud, but an outbreak of measles had claimed the life of six camp babies since the beginning of the year. Their tiny bodies were fresh bumps in the earth on the far side of the stream. Garolf had initially ordered the victims burned, but his camp manager, Ephraim Bule, had advised him the workers didn't like that one bit. So instead he ordered white chopsticks from Port Vila, and offered small sacks of rice to the mourning parents.

'Don't tell the Pastor.'

Jonson frowned. 'Whyever would I do that?'

From outside came the heralding cry of, 'Whiteman!'

Jonson looked down the nakamal path at the silhouette of a tall man ascending the hill against the pink glow of the sunset.

'Dr Jonson, I presume,' Max said, with a smile, as he approached.

Jonson blinked up at Max's great bulk. His broad nose was sunburnt and freckled, and his ginger hair was coarse and damp at the temples. He held a pipe between his teeth. Jonson shook his hand. And though his hands were clean, they were not in the least bony.

'How do you do?' Jonson cleared his throat. 'It's not Doctor, it's only Mister.'

'Oh,' said Max. 'Of course.'

'You must be Pastor Hanlon.'

'Please call me Max.'

'I. A. M. Jonson.'

Jonson was middle-aged, small-boned and short, with the grubby kind of a tan a pale man can only achieve in the tropics. His hair and moustache were the white-fat colour of Stork, and his eyes a diluted blue. The left side of Jonson's face didn't cooperate well with his right side, and when he spoke it was from one corner of his mouth.

'This is Mr Garolf Sugarcraven.' Jonson gestured to Garolf.

Garolf stood to shake Max's hand and, even slouched, his head scratched the thatch. His skin was dark brown, and his face was wide with high cheekbones. His black hair was slicked down in waves with coconut oil.

'Ah, Mr Sugarcraven himself! I've heard great things about your plantations,' Max said, although all he had heard was that his plantations processed copra.

Garolf smiled, prompting two deep dimples either side of his mouth. 'Thank you. Tomorrow I'll take you on a tour.'

'Would you care to join us?' Jonson searched on the shelf under the bench and pulled out a clean shell.

'Thank you, but I never got the hang of kava.' Max ran his thumb along the strap of his island basket. 'That numbness – I always feel a bit like I'm about to get a filling.'

Jonson smirked.

'Food, then?' Garolf asked.

Max glanced at his watch. 'I don't want to put you out – I know it's early. Are you gentlemen eating?'

Garolf fixed him with an incredulous look. 'You really don't drink kava, do you? No. We're not hungry.' He crossed to the

43

nakamal door and whistled. A bare-chested teenage boy sharpening his bushknife with a leather strap answered with a whistle and ran down to the door.

'Kakae,' Garolf said.

The boy nodded and ran to the meal hall.

'How long did it take you to walk?' Garolf said.

'About ten days,' Max said.

Garolf struck another match and revived his cigarette. 'Did you take the coastal path?'

Max's eyelids fluttered. 'Is there – is there another route?'

'No,' Jonson said.

'So,' Garolf rested his elbows on his knees. 'Do you still have that kranki priest down there in Bambayot? What's his name – Aru?'

Max was startled. 'He's not exactly a priest.'

'He owns the store, though?' Garolf said.

Max nodded, although 'store' was a generous interpretation. Aru's shop was comprised of three shelves in a sheet-metal shack. His main trade was in slabs of pink soap and wide-toothed, white plastic combs.

'You know –' Garolf squeezed the end of his cigarette and inhaled the last of the butt '– his wife's a vampire.'

Max laughed, but Garolf was staring at him evenly.

Jonson shook his head. 'Leave the poor man alone, he can't help it if his priests have vampire ex-wives flying around the forest.'

Max looked uncertainly between them, unsure who was teasing whom.

The ching on the path struck, and Garolf gestured Max towards the doorway. From the path, Max retrieved a warm banana-leaf parcel filled with slices of taro. He sat on the bench next to Jonson, and silently offered thanks to God before breaking the taro into chunks with his fingers.

44

'So. Where was your old missionary, um, place?' Garolf said.

'My last station?' Max caught a crumble of taro at the edge of his moustache. 'I guess one could say I was last on mission in Venezuela. Though I was also in Santo during the war.'

Garolf raised his eyebrows at Jonson. 'The war, huh? Me and Jonson would love to hear storyan about the war. Brave Yankee Doodle Dandy helping us out on Santo.'

Jonson rolled his eyes.

Max smiled politely, swallowing a chalky mouthful. 'Did either of you gentlemen have much contact with the former missionary?'

Garolf scoffed. 'Hardwood.'

Max blinked at him before remembering the name stamped into the Bambayot Bibles. 'Did you know her, Mr Sugarcraven?'

Garolf licked his lips. 'No.'

Garolf had invited Marietta to take a tour of his plantations, with the vague idea he might set up Protestant churches on-site, though not out of any religious motivation. Rather, Garolf had been impressed by the sour-faced converts in drab smocks who staffed the Protestant boarding school on Santo. He reasoned anything that could encourage such structured and gloomy dedication to productivity would be a benefit to his industry. But Marietta never came. He wrote to her on four separate occasions, but didn't even receive a reply. The only time he had met her was a chance encounter during a visit to Chief Liki's sorcery school.

Liki's proficiency in leaf magic was renowned throughout the island, and Garolf had heard rumours of a special leafy brew that bestowed upon its consumer superhuman powers of concentration. It enabled men to stay awake for days at a time, jittery with energy. Liki used this concoction in potent spell-casting to stave off winter cyclones, but Garolf had other uses in mind. Liki had never warmed to Garolf, pronouncing him the archetypal island boy corrupted by the lure of louche 'modernity'. Garolf knew it was unlikely Liki would part with the recipe for this potion, but he had nevertheless trudged through days' worth of slimy jungle to reach Liki's miserable outpost near Black Shark Rock.

There, Garolf had been instructed to leave his shorts and T-shirt outside the compound, to cleanse himself in the salty marsh near the rock, and tie a nambas over his groin. He stood in the mud outside Liki's hut for an hour, waiting to be received, and being bitten by midges. At last, Liki emerged from his hut, accompanied by an elderly whitewoman, dressed in Western clothing, and hobbling on one leg with a stick as a cane.

Liki waved imperiously in the air at Garolf, instructing him to kneel before him in the grass. Garolf begrudgingly obeyed. He watched with disbelief as Marietta Hardwood, for that was the only person it could be, kissed Liki on both cheeks, smacked him playfully on his bare behind, and limped off towards the nakamal. Garolf spent another twenty minutes grovelling before Liki at the front of the hut with his request. After Liki delivered a long soliloquy on the importance of maintaining island tradition – kastom – in the age of machines, Garolf's appeal was promptly rejected.

Garolf did not write to Marietta Hardwood again.

'And are the natives at Bambayot treating you well?' asked Jonson.

'Fantastic, thank you. I've had phenomenal support.' Max gathered the taro crumbs in the centre of the banana leaf, and tipped them into his mouth. Not knowing what to do with the leaf, he folded it and placed it inside his island basket. He pulled out the Johnson's Baby Powder tin he was using for tobacco, and packed his pipe. Garolf shuffled forward on the bench as he threw the end of his cigarette into the earth, and the wood creaked all the way to the far wall. Max wondered if he would be sleeping in the nakamal, and looked around for a mosquito net. On the walk up North, he'd imagined the Sugarcraven plantation as a gleaming mansion, white as a wedding cake, with servants dressed in pressed linens. But on the stretch from Mangarisu, he'd passed through miles of monotonous coconut palms attended by scruffy Vietnamese workers wearing caps improvised from woven pandan and cardboard breakfast-cracker packets, so he'd begun to have his doubts.

'And Mr Jonson, you're based in –?'

'Bwatapoa,' Jonson said. 'West of here, on the coast.'

Max nodded.

'I'm the British District Administrator for the province.'

'Right.'

'I've been stationed here for five years.'

'Super.'

Jonson shot a despairing look at Garolf, who wriggled his eyebrows and grinned.

'And did you have much contact with Mrs Hardwood?' Max asked.

'I never had the pleasure,' Jonson said.

Jonson had made the journey to the yam festival in the South at Rangi, for the express purpose of making the acquaintance of the only other white person on the island. It had been a miserable journey on the *Duchesse*, as an unexpected storm had swept in, and the ocean had been rough, the boat unsteady. He'd been terribly seasick for the first time in his life, and gratefully hobbled ashore at Rangi almost delirious with the desire to brush his teeth. To celebrate the festival, there had been many days of dancing and intricate rituals that appeared to involve the liberal daubing of each other with red earth. The night after Jonson's arrival, the locals had prepared a feast, with a slaughtered bullock, flying foxes, and even a couple of cats. He was surprised at the lack of yams on offer, and only later learnt it was the festival to celebrate the fertilization of the yams, not their harvest. All the women and children were shuffled into one hut to eat their feast, while the men sat together in the nakamal. The chiefs were seated at a huge log outside the nakamal, near to a large bonfire.

Jonson, meanwhile, was led curtly away from the entrance to the nakamal, to a separate log on the other side of the bonfire, where a stool had been set to act as a table. On the stool had been placed the only piece of cutlery in the village; one solitary spoon. As an honoured guest, Jonson had been offered the luxury of the use of the spoon, and an esteemed position directly in the smoke where there were fewest mosquitoes. Eyes streaming, Jonson dolefully spooned up his supper of bullock and rice, trying his best to ignore the laughter and whooping from the nearby huts. Serge, one of the chiefs, strolled over to offer him the choicest cuts of cat from a platter of banana leaves. This delicacy was proffered along with a detailed explanation of how the creature met its demise; a hollow bamboo stake inflated up its paw featured in one of the stories. Jonson's seasickness thus returned with vengeance, and he spent the rest of the meal emptying the contents of his stomach behind an avocado tree.

After the festivities had wound down, and after he had relieved himself of the worst of the queasiness, it became apparent that after being jovially hosted in the ladies' hut, Hardwood had disappeared without even stepping out to introduce herself. After a long and confused discussion about how Jonson was not related to this other non-islander, the two men sent out to retrieve 'the whiteman's mother' reported that Hardwood had last been seen daubed with earth, dancing at a festival in Central. Jonson spent the night sleeping on a bench in the nakamal in the company of stupefied kava drinkers in various stages of sedation. In the middle of the night, one of the men roused the rest of the hut by leaping on to the bench, screaming about a huge snake at the top of his lungs. The 'snake alarm' was duly sounded, machetes were grasped, torches were lit, someone proficient in leaf magic ran outside to pick the special foliage that would supposedly hypnotize the snake. They searched the hut for signs of the beast for ten minutes before the screamer was further interrogated. At which point it became apparent the chap had been sleepwalking. Jonson never felt the urge to court Marietta Hardwood's company again.

'Thanks for the meal,' Max said. 'Lovely taro.'

Garolf smiled, a gold tooth glinting.

Jonson cleared his throat. 'Do you follow cricket, Pastor?'

'Afraid not,' said Max.

Jonson and Max exchanged closed-mouth smiles. The first cockroaches crawled from their nests and scuttled across the floor.

The next morning, Max was woken by a booming ching at the north of the village. The sun had not yet risen, and dark shapes still crept across the floor of the nakamal. Max hopped in the doorway until the plantation workers were all gathered in the meal hall, then relieved himself behind a banyan tree. Shortly after 5 a.m., Jonson attempted a muffled knock on the thatch of the nakamal. As the sun rose, a young Vietnamese boy served them two bowls of rice pudding made with powdered milk and sweetened with mashed banana. After they had scraped their bowls, Jonson ordered two cups of black tea. They sipped from their cups in silence, as Max glanced over to the doorway, wondering when his promised tour would materialize. The nakamal was dank and gloomy, and Max's shoulders were tight from the hard bench.

'Can you tell me a bit about Sugarcraven. Is that his real name?'

Jonson wiped a dribble of tea from his chin. 'Garolf's father adopted the name. His father – Lomani – was blackbirded to Australia. You know what blackbirding is, don't you?'

'I do,' said Max, tersely.

'Barbaric practice. Just dreadful.' Jonson shook his head. 'Basically kidnapping. They say thousands of island men were taken to work on those plantations.'

'Mmm.' Max thought it best to keep his opinions about the British role in repopulating Australia to himself.

'Apparently, the name was given to him by his overseers on the plantation. Craven and Kendall. The sugar company – you know.'

'Yes, I know.'

'I mean, he wasn't really blackbirded. He stole a canoe and went out himself. Voluntarily.'

'He volunteered for slavery?' said Max.

'Well,' Jonson shook his head, 'it wasn't *quite* slavery. Even blackbirded men were paid wages, after all. In fact, his father used most of his wages on the Tongan whore in the local "Sugarhouse". Hence where I suspect he actually got his name.' Twin pink dots appeared at the top of Jonson's cheeks. 'That was how he was, uh, conceived. Grew up care of an albino nursemaid from the Solomon Islands, hanging around the outskirts of the plantation with all the other swollen-bellied bastard children of the kanaks.'

'Gosh, that's awful,' Max said, staring into his teacup.

'Well, eventually his nursemaid was fired – went blind. So Lomani brought Garolf back to the New Hebrides to get him circumcised. Lomani was wealthy, by native standards, he'd stashed away some traditional currency – pig tusks, brace-lets and mats, confiscated from his Melanesian underlings. Actually, we take exactly those sorts of items at the kastom bank now.' Jonson paused, tactically, poised with trivia about the success of his bank.

Max picked a scrap of tea leaf from his tongue. 'So he came back home?'

'Not exactly. Lomani couldn't go back to his own village. As I said, he stole a dugout to leave. And without the permission of his chief, well, it's a big tabu.'

'I can imagine. So he's from Advent Island?'

'Yes,' Jonson said. 'Although, as I said, Tongan mother.'

'Ah yes, of course, sorry.'

'So, they caught a cargo ship to New Caledonia, then from there another freighter to the New Hebrides. And ended up here in Sara. Have you heard of Masoe-manu?'

Max twitched, but before he could answer, Jonson shook his head. 'Sorry, no of course you haven't. He was the old chief here. Agreed to tutor Sugarcraven in kastom.'

'So he's a chief?'

Jonson nodded. 'In a sense –' he rubbed his fingers together to indicate money '– or rather, should I say –' he curled his fingers to demonstrate tusks, and spluttered, flushed with pride at his own witticism.

Max nodded.

'And Lomani, he knew what he was doing. All this flat land –' Jonson waved his hand at the village. Although Max had not seen any of the flat land, he nodded. 'Within two years, he'd started the copra business.'

Max sat back. 'And his father still lives here?'

'Oh, no. Deceased. And the plantations went to Garolf.'

Max whistled. 'Some story.'

Jonson swallowed the last gulp of tea. He'd barely strung so many words together in two years, and his throat was burning. 'Yes,' he said. 'He's got quite a story.'

*

51

Garolf took Max on a tour of the plantation just before midday. He walked him through the anonymous palm forest and handed him coconuts, inviting him to gauge their age by the amount of liquid sloshing inside. He pointed out the workers' wooden dormitories, and the two wash houses with pump-showers. He showed him halved nuts drying in the sun, and the fabulously expensive piece of machinery that squeezed the coconut fat into drums sent off on cargo ships to New Zealand every six months. He pointed out the company store where workers could buy tins of Spam, slices of Chinese soap and Australian cookies from their wages. Meals were cabbage, bananas, and taro farmed on an allotment behind the plantation.

'Kids are all in the gardens,' Garolf said, pointing behind the plantation to the far north of the village.

'You employ them?' Max asked, trying to keep the conspicuous judgement out of his voice.

Garolf laughed. 'No. But they come anyway.' He turned around and grinned at Max. 'I leave the Tonks to *that* part of life.'

At the west of the village, behind the meal hall, Garolf pointed out a small thatched palm hut in the shade, under a rock boulder, where Max could hear a child wailing.

'That's our hospital.'

'You have a doctor on staff?'

'A nurse. There she is – that's Trinh.' Garolf pointed to a short Vietnamese woman with grey hair peeling a banana in the shade of the nurse-house doorway. 'She was in Santo selling cookies and waiting for the French to put on more boats. But,' he shrugged, 'you know what the French are like. The Japs were being rounded up for the "work camp" on Gaua Island and everyone was getting shaky. Got to snap her up! My own nurse!'

*

The dingy nurse house at the back of Sara plantation was the closest the workers came to healthcare, since there wasn't a doctor on the island. Do Thi Trinh's equipment box lived on the top shelf, outfitted with a rusty lock. She carried the key around her neck on a thin chain as prevention against theft. Although the sum total of her treasure chest was: three rolls of bandages, a box of safety pins, a thermometer, six vials of iodine drops, a bottle of phenobarbital tablets and twelve packets of Australian vitamin pills. All the workers had received cholera injections upon their arrival in Vila, and WHO workers had come to the plantation to administer yaws injections. But aside from that stab on the arm – and their mosquito nets – medical supplies were paltry, and supplemented by home-brewed lime-leaf tea and lozenges made from wild garlic. Between the chopping and the husking and pressing and baking, the plantation was full of people with scalded wrists, nubs for toes, stumps for fingers, creeping sores and swollen bellies.

And now the measles.

It was Nurse Trinh who had buried the six camp babies on the far side of the stream. And it was Trinh who had advised a young married couple, Lien and Thieu, to take their new baby and run away from the plantation.

Since the first camp baby fell ill, Lien had become obsessed with the measles. She chattered about it at every opportunity, reeling off home-made remedies, and delivering long, gruesome anecdotes about plague until her bunkmates begged her to stop talking. Thieu tried to divert her attention, requesting a recital of her filthy French limericks, or tempting her with gossip about Ephraim Bule, the plantation manager. But Lien remained fixated on pestilence. She rose in the night to check on Minh as he slept on his little wooden shelf, watching him as he dozed in limpid baby sleep, convincing herself all the while that he was dead. It was his impossible stillness. She could only bear it for a few moments before poking him with a fingernail. She hadn't managed more than half an hour of rest at a time for weeks. Thieu's bunkmate, Nguyen, reassured him it was normal for new mothers. He patted Thieu on the hand, and told him Lien would get over it.

'He sleeps now,' he said, 'but you wait. When he's screaming through the night, she'll never look back. By the time the next one is born, she'll laugh at the idea of waking a baby.'

But Thieu hadn't heard her laugh since Minh was born.

Lien wore her tiredness badly. Her attention wavered at work, her fingers slipped as she cut the coconut flesh from the cups, and she sliced herself across the forearm twice in a single day. Then she developed a rash. It appeared only days after Tran's two-month-old baby had taken ill. Tran and her baby were moved from the dormitory into the nurse house, but Lien lay awake at night, her heart racing, listening to the infant squalling in the shack. The rash began to spread over the outside of Lien's thigh, and she insisted that Thieu 'inspect her' for signs of the disease. Behind the guava trees at the south of the plantation, she stripped off her T-shirt and jeans, and stood naked in front of him, turning so he could check for any red spots.

Thieu watched the expression on his wife's face as she spun round, gesturing to the splotches on her thighs. He pointed to the purple scabs over his knuckles, and tried to reassure her it was merely a patch of copra itch or ringworm. But over the next week, she started picking at the rash. She scraped off the top layer of skin so that the scales glowed through, scarlet. She picked until it became infected and blistered with pus.

When Tran's little girl died, Lien didn't sleep for three days. She cried silently into her taro, and began to pick at a mosquito bite on the soft flesh of Minh's belly.

Gently, Thieu suggested she pray to St Aloysius.

Trinh suggested they run away. That they take their baby and go to Port Vila. And that Marietta, the whitewoman at Bambayot, would help them.

'But isn't it just a rumour?' Thieu jiggled Minh up and down in his arms. 'I never heard of this whitewoman.'

'Of course it's not a rumour. Everyone knows it's not a rumour,' Lien insisted. 'Her name is Marietta – she's an old whitewoman, a missionary. And don't you remember Nguyen Thi Huong? And Pham Van Phu? She helped them both get to Vila, to work at the hotels.'

Vila's two honeymoon hotels were the gold standard in Lien's hierarchy of luxury. The invocation of them now brought Thieu brief reassurance. 'You want to go back to being a housegirl?'

'That's not the point,' she said, licking her lips. She tapped Minh on the nose. 'I don't care where we are, just as long as it's safe for Minh-Binh.'

This was a new nickname, and Thieu hated it with the same suspicious dread he projected on to the manic energy which had produced it. 'What if it's a scam? This white-woman takes money from Sugarcraven to trap us?' Thieu imagined the three of them huddled in a cage, like birds ready for market.

'Trinh says it will work, that's how we know it's not a scam. And then we'll be on our way to Vila. To a proper city. And it's so much cleaner there. The water is cleaner.'

Thieu frowned. 'How could the water be cleaner than a mountain stream?'

Lien dismissed him with a wave. 'It's a proper city,' she said. 'With a proper hospital. And special equipment, from Australia. And medicines and pills. All we have is that –' She gestured derisively in the direction of the nurse house.

'We can't put our lives in the hands of a stranger,' Thieu said, hearing the tremor in his own voice.

'Don't be dramatic.' Lien scratched at the top of her hip. 'She's not a stranger. Not exactly. Trinh says it will be fine. So I know it will be fine. And she'll cover for me. She'll say I'm ill in the nurse house with Minh-Binh. We can't just wait around here until we all catch it. And Sugarcraven won't even know I'm gone.'

But Sugarcraven would know Thieu was gone, that part was clear. Nurse Trinh was not going to cover for him. If he was caught, he'd be stuck hauling coconuts for an extra year at half pay. Thieu watched Lien limping back to the plantation on her swollen hip, dread curdling in his stomach. He wasn't sure which scared him more – Lien's delirium of scratching and picking, or the fact she was right. What punishment could be worse than risking their son's life?

Over the next month, they created a plan. And to Thieu's relief, even the prospect of their escape was enough to re-assure Lien, who grew almost giddy with the promise of leaving the plantation. Thieu would go first. He'd creep out at night and set up camp in the tabu part of the jungle where no one went. After his disappearance, Lien would pretend she had been abandoned. She'd cry and wail and curse him for being so weak and feckless. After a fortnight, she would feign the beginnings of illness, complain about headaches and swollen white spots in her mouth. She would wait until he left the signal of a shell in the knot of a guava tree by the stream, and that night, she would creep out to meet him in the wash house. Trinh would say Lien and Minh were quarantined in her bunkhouse. In the meantime, they would follow the coast down to Marietta at Bambayot, and she would help them board the *Duchesse* to Port Vila.

*

And so, the second night of the whiteman's visit, Lien watched from beside the meal hall as the fire in the nakamal was stoked. She heard Sugarcraven's whistles and followed the plates of papaya being delivered to the nakamal. It was a dark night, and Sugarcraven was already on his third round of kava. Lien took a great breath of relief. It was time to start their escape. Soon, Minh would be safe. They would all be safe. She imagined tucking Minh under crisp white sheets, the rattling sound of a fan overhead, a gleaming hotel kitchen.

In the meal hall that evening she flicked Thieu on the back of his arm. When he turned she blinked at him, twice, and mouthed, *'Je t'aime.'* Slowly, Thieu nodded, and as soon as she had turned her head, he crossed himself.

After dinner, when the curfew ching was beaten, Thieu followed the lines filing into his dormitory. He lay in his bed and listened to the sounds of yawning and scratching and coughing. After a couple of hours, the chirrupy snoring of Nguyen in the hammock above joined the chorus of soft body noises filling the room. Thieu walked out of the dormitory and into the wash house, collected his pack, and crept out into the jungle.

The moon was covered in gauzy dark cloud, but he knew where he was going – a path wound through the palms on the other side of the plantation. It was still Sugarcraven land, so the coconuts were off limits. But the plants were well trampled, and the track led down to a thin stream bordered by guava trees. Thieu squinted up at the trees in the darkness, but they had been picked bare. He left the trail before the stream, and climbed the hill towards the fallen banyan tree, where he had hidden the escape kit. Over the last month, he and Lien had collected two hammocks, a blanket, a threadbare mosquito net, the head of a small hammer, a rusty bushknife, a box of matches and five candles. He steadied himself on the slimy creepers covering the banyan trunk, and groped his way to the base of the tree. Thieu kicked the earth until he hit a soft lump under the soil, then knelt and dug in the dirt with his hands. He pulled the sack free, brushing wet clods of earth from the fabric. He stood for a moment. What if he just buried the bag back in the hole? What if he just threw it into the forest, and returned to his bed? He could tell Lien that the bag was gone – that someone had stolen it. But he thought of how the escape plan alone had soothed her strange energy, calmed the scratching, the prophecies of pestilence. How would she cope if he asked her to stay? So he pulled the strap of the sack over his head, and looked around at the gloom of the jungle. A warm breeze rustled through the leaves, and insects chattered in the undergrowth.

Thieu walked higher into the hills, placing each foot carefully to muffle the noise. An hour into the bush, he set up a rudimentary camp in the shelter of a mossy boulder. He cut three giant palm leaves, and crawled inside the shallow cave, arranging the branches over its mouth. Inside, there was barely enough space for him to sit with his arms around his knees. He peered up at the dripping walls – what if it was the home of some jaguar? He sniffed the dank air for any signs of musk or droppings. But it smelt only of cold vegetables. Thieu squirmed as the damp moss seeped through the seat of his trousers. He thought about singing to keep any wild beasts away, but then perhaps someone might hear him?

Instead, Thieu sat in his cave in the jungle, cursing Trinh and her whitewoman under his breath until the sun rose.

4

While in Port Vila, Max had insisted on loading a huge wooden crate full of imperishable goods. At the time, Bea had resented the extra inconvenience of shopping and packing. Under Max's instruction, she procured tins of Spam and corned hash, packets of SAO crackers, and dehydrated soup mix. Their most substantial investment was a 25kg bag of rice, which Max carried on to the boat with them. But once they had arrived on Advent Island, Bea was grateful for these emergency supplies. The corned hash was the closest thing they had to meat, and the sack of rice provided their main source of food. Unfortunately, it also provided a happy home for a family of rats who cavorted in it after nightfall, but as long as Bea picked out the droppings, it still served them well.

The villagers ate only what they could grow for themselves in their garden allotments, which was mainly taro or cassava. Bea had heard rumours of the days when Aru's store sold peanuts and fresh loaves of bread, but now it contained a disappointing assortment of cargo-ship oddities. Mabo-Mabon claimed that Aru had even sold individual doses of brandy from a bottle. But that was before his wife became a vampire, and he became a Christian. When Bea informed Max of this, he dismissed her with a wave of the hand.

'Idle rumours. You really shouldn't contribute to gossip.' But after a moment, he had run his finger under his moustache, and looked at her from the side of his eye. 'Willie told me his wife died from malaria.'

'Oh, no.' Bea licked her lips. 'See, they couldn't conceive.

And Aru went to a leaf doctor, and *he* said she was cursed with a feeding demon from the jungle –' she rubbed her stomach '– living inside her. She lost three babies, one after the other. Mabo-Mabon said she would hear her crying all night –'

'Bea –'

'– but then one day she vanished. Apparently, the demon took her over, and she turned into a sort of vampire.' She paused. 'Although, it sounded more like a mosquito type of monster. Mabo-Mabon said they suck the juices out of dead corpses. And they live near Hot Wata –'

'Beatriz, really –'

'– because they like the sulphur smell of the hot spring.'

Max rubbed between his eyes.

'And they sleep standing up inside banyan trees,' Bea added as quickly as she could. The image of Aru's monstrous ex-wife had stayed with her. She saw it again now, with hectic clarity – a woman with a long proboscis curled from her lips, sleeping upright in the folds of a banyan trunk, her wicked face turned away from the light. She swallowed. 'Anyway, that's why his store has no food in it. And why he's so religious.'

'Beatriz!' Max raised his eyebrows. 'That's enough.'

But Bea wasn't listening. 'Do you think, if you asked Aru, he would find a spade to sell us?' She looked down at the callous in the centre of her palm. 'It's terribly awkward to dig the garden with a knife. I can't quite get used to it.'

Bea was not a natural farmer. She had been raised in a shabby, but still grand, mint-green house on the outskirts of Caracas. After the early death of her mother, Beatriz grew up as the spoiled pet of her father, Luis, and her brother, José Rafael, who was older by nine years. At school, she was a favourite of the nuns, who took special pity on her on account of her motherlessness. Bea had long learnt that mentions of her dead mother seemed to get her whatever she wanted. It made adults tip their heads, and then pat hers softly. In truth, she didn't remember enough of her mother to feel any sadness about it, but it added a sort of pathetic drama to her life that she almost enjoyed.

Bea grew up sheltered and indulged, with her own nurse-maid who lived with them long after her babyhood. She had a large room at the top of the house overlooking a row of red hortensias, and a thick-limbed orange tree. She was the proud matriarch of a large family of curly-haired rag dolls in hand-sewn dresses, and the devoted amateur veterinarian to a procession of sickly kittens. Although slow to read and to count, she chattered incessantly, gulping large breaths between sentences like a swimmer. The twittering and gulping continu-ed even during mass, and often landed her in trouble with the nuns. She didn't mind, since the punishment was being sen-tenced to an hour sitting alone in the confessional. There, she would swing her feet over the edge of the seat, place her ros-ary over her head, and pretend she was a magnificent queen holding court over her kingdom.

Her family had grown some vegetables in Venezuela – at least, the gardener had. But she'd had no interest whatsoever in grubbing around in the dirt. Even the closest her father had ever come to farming had been his managerial role on the pineapple plantation. When Max first brought up the topic of their Advent Island vegetable garden, she had imagined her-self in a wide-brimmed hat and long canvas skirt, languidly pruning the stems of some birds of paradise.

Once they arrived in Bambayot, Max had pointed into the jungle creeping up around the corners of Mission House, and declared it an excellent place for their garden. Chief Bule thought this hilarious, since everyone's gardens were on top, carved out of jungle on the flat plains above the first mountain. But Max was insistent – it would be much more economical, he explained, to grow crops around the house, rather than walking for hours each day.

After Max declared victory over the placement of their garden, Bea expected they might work together to oversee the clearing of the land, and the planting of the crops. Max had merely smiled. He told her that, traditionally, farming was women's work. It would make him seem unmanly to the other men in the village if they were to see him growing crops. Besides, it would help her to make friends, he offered generously.

But with their garden now right in the middle of the village, Bea became a reliable source of local entertainment. Eleven-year-old Moses Turu liked to loiter in the corner of the porch, watching her in silence. He was a quiet little boy, with eyes that looked in different directions while the pink tip of his tongue lolled out of his mouth. His mute spectatorship unnerved Bea no end.

Moreover, it seemed to Bea that when anyone in the village felt like stepping out of their hut, they made sure to walk up by Mission House to gape at her ineffectual farming efforts. It was the least elegant way she could have imagined acquainting herself with her new neighbours. As she squatted in the dirt on her haunches, wiping sweat from her face with her forearm, she was the victim of, as she felt it, constant catcalling from passers-by who would holler inane and persistent questions.

'What are you doing?'

'Where were you?'

'What's that?'

'Can I have that?'

She had no idea how to respond to these comments. She had no idea what she was doing. After two weeks of misery and mosquito bites, pulling oily succulents from the earth and piling them up before her, Mabo-Mabon turned up at the hedge border of Mission House. She led in tow her teenage daughter, Leiwas, her ten-year-old son, Clinneth, and little Joylee. Trailing behind Mabo-Mabon's own troupe of children were Abel and Gracie Poulet's children, Judy and Ralph. Mabo-Mabon let herself into the garden and grabbed Bea wordlessly by the hand. Sitting Bea before a pile of twigs, she demonstrated that Bea should cut them into strips, sorting the springy vines from the woody brush.

While Bea and Mabo-Mabon crouched on the floor by the porch, sorting piles of kindling, the small band of children immediately set to work hacking down all the vegetation around Mission House. With furious strokes, not a single mutter or grimace of complaint, the whole area was bare within the hour. Bea watched them open-mouthed. She felt so ashamed of her own ineptitude. All the villagers must have been talking about her, gossiping and laughing about the stupid whitewoman who couldn't even do the work of a child. Even six-year-old Joylee, who was dressed only in a man's old T-shirt, was handling her machete with an astounding power and speed that was beyond Bea's wildest capabilities.

Once the area had been cleared, however, Bea assessed her new garden with a glimmer of imagination. Over the following weeks, she slowly taught herself how to bind fences, to rake the soil with her bushknife, and to transplant seedlings from the bush. She spent hours each day pacing the allotment, patrolling for slugs and pulling weeds with vindictive triumph.

Max watched Bea's increasing obsession with their garden with indulgent bemusement. She spent all day hatless in the sun, and was constantly streaked with grime. She was beginning to

look like a native – she carried her machete with her everywhere, reflexively rolling its handle in her calloused palm in
the manner of a villager. He understood her preoccupation.
While their crops grew, they were resigned to plain, boiled
white rice for every meal. Sometimes Bea forgot to comb
through the rice properly, and a softened and mushy rat dropping would turn up in the supper, like a prize in a cracker box.

The monotony of the rice was supplemented by a sad parade
of depressing island vegetables. Occasionally there were
chalky blocks of taro donated by Mabo-Mabon – or, worse,
island cabbage. This stubborn and abundant weed dripped a
clear, viscous mucus that disintegrated into a slimy, dark green
jelly, not entirely unlike loose wallpaper paste. As if eating it
were not enough of a punishment, Bea liked to deliver it to
Max along with detailed lectures about its proclivity to take
over her garden beds.

But Max didn't have much energy to help with Bea's cru-
sade against foliage. Despite their conversation, Aru had not
ceased his 'dark praying'. Twice, in the last three weeks, Max
had been woken by screaming from the church. The first time,
Max had marched down to the church in disbelief. Aru had
explicitly agreed to consult him if such an occasion were to
occur again. Leiwas was again prostrate on the floor, surrounded by the same five girls. They were chanting, slapping
their fists on the wood of the building to expel the evil. Leiwas
was again sobbing and wailing. Max strode straight in through
the door. He sat on one of the benches at the front of the room.
But Aru and the girls carried on with barely a glance in his
direction. He had hoped sitting quietly in the corner might
dampen the hysteria. But it made absolutely no difference.

The second time, the exorcism had taken place at night. Max
woke in the middle of the night to hear the strangled scream of
a young woman straining on and on. The chanting was louder,

accompanied by whoops and shouting. Outside the church, he saw the flicker of candlelight. There were maybe ten people in the building this time. The church singers were there, but also Edly Tabi. Leiwas was no longer the centre of attention, she was part of the circle. Max entered the hall cautiously. In the darkened room, he saw the eyes of the performers turn, all at once, to look at him. There was a slight pause. The hair on the back of Max's neck rose, and he felt a distinct sensation come over him. It was not threat exactly. It was something closer to territorialism. He was intruding.

Prostrate in the centre of the room was Sousan. She lay on the ground with her legs apart, softly groaning, twitching in agitation. The church singers turned back to the girl, and recommenced their praying. It was utterly haphazard. Some were clapping their hands, others shaking and crying, repeating exhortations to 'cast out' the demon. Some were manically gesturing, as if they were sweeping with an invisible broom.

Max resumed his position on the bench at the front of the church. He wasn't sure what he could do, except wait it out. Maybe he could approach Aru again after they had finished. Or walk the poor girl home, and see if he might talk some sense into her. After only a few more minutes of waiting and watching, Judy Poulet – the eleven-year-old daughter of Abel and Gracie – turned to him. Her eyes were wide. She looked as if she were having a tantrum. She faced him, muttering, chanting, and raised her hands. Walking towards Max, she placed her outstretched hands on Max's shoulder and crowed out, 'In the name of Jesus, I cast you out!'

Max sat rigid. He was being exorcized. By an eleven-year-old girl. If he made any motion whatsoever, any noise, it was bound to be interpreted as his collusion in the charade. He might look as if he were, in fact, in need of blessing. Or worse, he might look as if he were hostile to the blessing.

Max maintained eye contact with Judy, his heart racing. She pressed the palm of her hand into his forehead, and continued to squawk, her eyes still wide, her whole body rigid with concentration. Max suppressed an acute, hysterical urge to start laughing. He watched her face as she continued, her palm rough against his skin. Then she was gone, back towards the circle of worshippers.

Max's eyes prickled. This was absurdity! Eleven-year-old girls exorcizing the Pastor! Why was she even in the church after dark – she should have been in bed hours ago. Did Abel and Gracie know where she was? Did they approve? What was Aru even doing here, at night, with all these young women? And Edly Tabi – he must have been twenty years old. Was he there for a chance to spend time with all these girls? Sousan was still lying on the floor with her legs akimbo, her island dress pulled up over her knees. As if reading his mind, Leiwas carefully picked up Sousan's leg and brought her knees back together, tugging the dress down over Sousan's thighs. Max looked away in disgust.

While Max was spending more time at church, Bea recruited a foraging accomplice in Lorianne, Jinnes and Othniel's five-year-old. Lorianne was a small, plain-looking child, with far-apart eyes and a sprinkling of black moles on the right side of her face. She knew only a few words of English, but hospitably guided Bea through the 'shallow' jungle around the village. She showed Bea where nangalat – the Devil's nettle – grew, and where to find the fish-poison tree, the glue tree, and the tree that produced bright red flowers at Christmastime. She knew spots for collecting six types of bananas across a spectrum of starch and sweetness. She pointed out bush nuts, tiny, chalky apples and hog plums. Bea asked her to repeat the names of fruits, over and over, and laboriously repeated them back while Lorianne snickered. Sometimes Lorianne didn't know the names, and shrugged, offering 'kakae' as a response, patting her belly.

Once Bea realized the forest concealed a larder of sorts, she became considerably more interested in the jungle. Without a refrigerator, Bea couldn't collect too much in any one harvest, since ripe quickly became putrid. It was a matter of careful selection and daily scavenging. Guavas were out, because they were so lousy with maggots that she had become accustomed to the sour tang of half-eaten grub. Pineapples brewed to such advanced fermentation in the sun that they gave off paint-thinner fumes when sliced. If Bea miscalculated the time between forest and plate by even a matter of hours, the disintegrating matter solicited carpets of ants into the house.

Bea begged one of Max's blank notebooks from him, and created a volume of sketchy maps for foraging. She pressed leaves in between the pages, and wrote cramped, gibberish notes to herself about what they were. Where Lorianne's knowledge failed, Bea classified in her own made-up taxonomy – listing such delicacies as 'mushy bean' and 'lumpy gourd'. She resorted to increasingly imaginative ways of supplementing their evening meals, adding flower petals and slices of ginger root to their customary piles of white rice. One night, she served supper to Max while he sat at his stool. After they had joined hands and Max led them in grace, Bea picked up her fork.

'What's this?' Max asked, pulling out a small, lacy green leaf from his mound of rice.

Bea glanced at it and looked back at her plate quickly, muttering, 'Hedge,' with her mouth full.

Max rested on his elbow, twisting the leaf by its stalk in between his thumb and middle finger. 'Hedge?'

Bea nodded, raising her eyebrows. She continued eating,

pressing her finger into a fallen grain of rice on the tabletop and slipping it under her tongue.

'Why –' began Max, as Bea sighed, suspecting an impending lecture. 'Why do they call it "hedge"?'

Bea looked at him, silently chewing. She cleared her throat and said in a slow voice, 'Because, my dear, it's our hedge.'

Max stared at her blankly for a moment, then burst into a loud peal of laughter. 'It's a hedge! We're eating a hedge!'

'Yes,' Bea said hesitantly, smiling, although she didn't understand what was so funny. She was hungry, and it was a tasty salad. 'I like it.' She shrugged, trying in that shrug to express that he could keep his opinions to himself.

He gaped at her in amazement. This woman, he thought. She has humbled herself to the point of eating from a hedge without complaining. When they first married, she had disdained lettuce as cattle food. But here she was, coolly enjoying a pitiful plate of tiny, damp little leaves.

Bea, distracted by his silence, looked up at the warm expression on his face, his mouth open, his pupils dilated with a gentle awe.

'What?' she asked.

'You are a marvel,' he said at last, his voice serious, but with a smile.

Bea turned back to the hedge to cover her blush.

5

Inspecting her face in her compact mirror, Bea picked at a scab on her cheek, drawing a scale of skin and a speck of blood. She licked her finger and rubbed at the lump. She had never been beautiful, even as a girl. The misshapen line of her nose she had grown accustomed to, grown almost to like. But now she had to contend with dark scars from bug bites studded across her cheeks and neck. She rubbed a penny of cold cream into the new sore and sighed. Once, the scarring might have mattered to her. But the life of a missionary's wife didn't leave much room for vanity. And Max claimed not to care at all for her appearance, only if she had opened her heart to welcome Jesus.

But holy salvation was not the first time Bea had opened her heart. She first fell in love just after her fifteenth birthday. Luis noticed that Bea had succumbed to long spells of sulky withdrawal. She spent hours sitting in her bedroom, glumly flicking the pages of American movie magazines. She lost weight, and wore a single frown-line cut into the centre of her forehead. She hunched her shoulders. She stopped combing her hair. She lay in bed for hours late into the morning, and yet still had purple marks under her eyes from tiredness. Luis and José Rafael conferred, with some worry. Misinterpreting her misery as boredom, Luis encouraged her to take pianoforte lessons. Maybe she could have her hair fixed, or take a boat trip with a school friend. At these suggestions, Bea did little more than bite her lip, and hug her father with unnecessary force. He was relieved to have solved her malaise so efficiently, but Bea was merely overwhelmed with pity. He had misunderstood so sweetly, and his offers of a child's luxuries made her feel somehow protective of him.

But the cause of Bea's misery was not boredom, although equally mundane. She had met Jorge while buying ice cream during the Holy Thursday festival. He was ten months older than her, with thick, coarse brown hair and black eyebrows that arched to graze each other in the middle of his forehead. He was not especially handsome, but his skin was a copper brown and his lazy, heavy-lidded eyes a queer green in direct sunlight. When selling her a strawberry cone, he had been distracted by the suggestive gap between her middle teeth, and dropped a single pink drip on the corner of her gingham blouse. He spent his days between dozing in Cementerio del Este, catching fish for a meagre income, and trying to seduce every pretty girl who paused to return his smiles. And so, in 1945, Beatriz's life became undone.

Bea wanted him instantly, and with such ferocity, she suddenly understood the meaning of the word 'covet' she had heard so much in church. And in the simple equation of a spoiled child, she set her mind to owning him. Was this the same person who had sat at her lessons with her hands folded, talking to the nuns, only weeks before? They met after her lessons, and in the hours she invented in the company of imaginary school friends. Sitting on the rocks overlooking the river, they spent hours in delicious boredom while he set catfish traps, smoked, boasted of the money he'd won at cards, how much he drank, the pretty girls he had met. And Bea listened patiently, waiting for the moment when he would grow bored of bragging, and they could climb lower to a shallow cave obscured by a mossy rock. There, she would let him unbutton her pinafore with blunt fisherman's hands, his face flushed with concentration. Lying prettily in confession about stealing a pin from her grandmother, failing to say grace, Bea discovered in herself a talent for sin she had not even considered. She was only surprised to realize how naturally it came to her.

Bea had heard all about love. It meant God's sacrifice of His only son. It meant a white dress, flowers in your hair on your wedding day. It was the gentle way José Rafael touched the arm of his wife, Isabella, on a Sunday morning outside church, when he thought no one was looking. Bea begged Elizabeth Vera to retell her stories about kings and serpents as she darned her underclothes in the evenings. With creeping distress, Bea realized perhaps she wasn't the beloved bride in her nurse's stories. Perhaps she was the foundling, abandoned in the forest to mate with the beasts. Perhaps her affair with Jorge was something ugly and unnatural. But when she watched Jorge pick threads of tobacco from his clothes, and look up at her suddenly – a flash of green – there was a disorientating seasick movement in her stomach. That feeling, Bea thought, it had to be love.

As months went by, the fumbling behind the rocks by the river turned instead to something else in the furniture storeroom in the basement of her house, and the grassy parades of Cementerio del Este. At night, Bea waited fully clothed in her bed, with the sheet clenched between her teeth. Every now and again, she woke with an acute shock at the noise of a passing cart, the crow of a cockerel, terrified she had missed his signal. Though when Jorge whistled for her, it couldn't be mistaken. Filled with nauseous joy, she shuffled down the sappy arms of the orange tree to meet him. At the bottom, he would grab her wrist with three fingers and they would stumble through the empty streets, her hair pulled up under one of his caps. He would push his hands under her shirt to feel the cold skin on her back. She ran her hands through the coarse hair on his head. They said nothing, there was nothing to say.

And as time went on, Jorge's gleefulness turned to drunkenness, his drunkenness turned to temper, his temper to fists. He started to hide outside the walls of her school, to watch her walking home. He accused her of fucking other men, the son of her father's friend he had seen driving to the house. He claimed not to care, since he was often with other women – better women than her. He described them to her with a connoisseur's dictionary, and in such elaborate detail, that Bea's initial needles of jealousy evolved into a strange form of solidarity with his entourage. She thought about them often, about Maria with the thick curly hair, Marian the waitress at Hotel Avila. She daydreamed about how they might pass each other one day on the street, and turn to recognize each other. Marian with the tiny waist would approach her, and put her hand on Beatriz's. A benediction.

His chief propagandist, Bea became skilled at interpreting his drunken gripping and pinching, the ugly words he used for her, his energetic caresses and his philandering as misdirected demonstrations of his love. Of course he loved her. Or else, how could he hate her so much? During the day, she reasoned with herself. He was right, of course. She was a whore – wasn't she whoring herself with him? She was too ugly, too thin, too boring. How could she be so offended when he told her the truth for her own good? It was no wonder he didn't want to spend any time talking to her any more. As long as he wanted her, she would wait for him. Perhaps, if she was good, tried not to talk too much, if she was patient, he would overlook her ugliness and how boring she was. Persistence, patience, she told herself, was the key to his love.

They never met in the daylight any more. Once, in September, heart thumping, Bea came alone to Jorge's room through his open window. She just wanted to see him in the sunshine. In a mad moment, she almost wanted to check he was real. But he wasn't there. The room looked so different in the daytime. She could smell chicken fat frying on his neighbour's stove, and the floor was sticky with spilt beer. Bea listlessly shuffled through his shelves looking for love tokens from his other girlfriends. A letter, a brassiere, a lock of Maria's curly hair – anything. She pulled out from underneath his mattress a tattered photograph of her that had gone missing from her own house. Picking it up with shaking hands, Bea sat on the unsteady springs of the mattress and sobbed. She replaced it carefully, understanding Jorge well enough to know that if he suspected she had witnessed this token of vulnerability, their affair would be broken off for ever.

Occasionally, Jorge would vanish, for weeks or even months at a time. During these interludes, Beatriz lay indoors, waiting with stoic patience for a stone at her window, a whistle from the hortensias. Terrified it might be the final time he left her, she was almost delirious with panic. She vomited up her food in heavy ropes. Her gums hurt. And when, inevitably, she chanced upon a sight of him in Plaza La Boyera, half smiling, with a rolled cigarette in his mouth, she wondered if it were possible to also vomit up her heart. And when, inevitably, he returned, the declarations of love, the drinking, philandering and endless, joyful bitter-sweet hours on the springs of his dirty mattress would begin all over again.

Every time he took her hand in the dark, she was dizzy, thinking it could be the last time she might have a chance to touch his fingers. That she should make this time 'count' more than the other times. To remember it better, to be better. To be so good, so perfect, it would change something. Each re-union felt like a new scalding – his drunken mouth kisses, hot rain burning on her hot face. And each time they met to grip each other in the streets – the dark night-time shape of their love – she prayed he would see something new in her. See something new he could love.

And from time to time, he would beg himself a different person. Holding his hand over his chest, 'It's different now, let's run away – we'll get married,' he would say, biting her neck, leaving blue trails on her skin. He dazzled her with abstract compliments. 'I am an electron next to you,' he declared drunkenly to the sky, his arms wide, smashing his bottle of beer on to the rocks. Afterwards, she would crawl home, bruised and hollow. She would whisper to herself, 'Never, never, again,' in her room, holding her shoulders. She felt herself drowning, self-absorbed in the suffering of loving.

Four years went by. Neither Bea nor Jorge really assumed their affair would ever end, until it did, abruptly, in 1949, when Bea was twenty. It was another dark night, and she had left her house with nothing. And after the terrible things that happened, she never went back home. And she never saw Jorge again.

But even after that, even in her new life with Max, even in the New Hebrides, she couldn't control the dreams. They sprouted in her everyday life like gorgeous, flame-coloured weeds. She felt the imprints of Jorge's stubby fingers on her waist, the weight of his thigh muscles, and the coarse stubble on his jaw scratching against the underside of her neck. The gravity of her lust made her heart beat asymmetrically. In her dreams, she could not see his face, but she did not need to see it. Because it belonged to him, and she would love his face with its thick brows and flushed concentration if she was blind, and deaf, and dumb.

Always the same, herself dreamt a teenager again, her profile straight, her skin smooth and soft. And him, strong and careful in his lust, calloused hands and hot open mouth. And filled with an overwhelming stab of love in her heart, she would wake with tears running sideways, salting the hollows of her ears. She would wake, and lie there wretched with longing, his name beating in her chest like a child's drum.

But Bea's profile was no longer straight, and her skin no longer clear. On Advent Island, her body had become a constellation of insect meals. Her feet and ankles were swollen with ant bites; embossed pink circles, sunk here and there with festering craters of white pus. Her shins were peppered with puce-coloured bumps from New Dog's fleas. The insides of her thighs were a destination for only the most enterprising and adventurous of mosquitoes that made furtive, dusk-light expeditions up her skirt. Her back and shoulders were ornamented with crimson pinpricks from bed mites.

Bea was itching all the time. Itchiness, she felt, must surely be the fastest route to madness. Her skin crept constantly from bites, until she fancied she could sense the waves of poison rippling through the skin. The lining of her brassiere, the hems of her sleeves and the laces on her sandals were junctions of agony. Any accidental graze triggered the pimples into hot yearning, and she often woke in the night to find she had been scratching her limbs against the coarse thread of the mosquito net in her sleep. On those nights, Bea lay in the dark, dabbing at the needles of blood oozing from her newly open sores. It filled her with claustrophobic panic, to find herself flailing against her pitiful cheesecloth prison.

Before Advent Island, Bea never would have believed that the countryside could be so cramped. She was strangled on all sides by either petty rural scrutiny or insectile mayhem. It was all right for Max; he had the luxury of walking about whenever he felt like it, going wherever he pleased. No one questioned his right to be out for a stroll in the middle of the day, or pestered him with mindless observations as he tried to claim a moment for himself. But even if it weren't tabu to walk around alone, there was nowhere for her to go. There was only jungle.

The jungle. Its constant whirring noises, its fetid organic complexity, its restlessness. So many thousands of trees and bushes and leaves, each populated by slithering, crawling insects, all with tiny hearts pumping and pumping. Sometimes, during the hottest part of the day, Bea lay still in her bed, conscious of the constant movement of the jungle and a humid, ominous stillness of the air.

The jungle was not quite as Max recalled it. He thought perhaps it had been a different *sort* of jungle on Santo; or perhaps there had just been less of it. On Advent Island, the jungle refused to stay outdoors, it lurked at the corners of the village and wormed its way into civilization. Pale weevils cavorted in the powdered milk, black orchids blossomed in the shower, heavy-breathing rats urinated over his sandals while he slept. It perpetuated itself with explosive fertility. Furry dark fungus bloomed over his vestry desk where none had been at breakfast time. Rotten green oranges dropped into the grass outside the church in an arrhythmia of dull thuds. Voluptuous soursop, sweating at their seams, fell softly into quiet explosions of mush outside his bedroom window, producing a seething mass of glistening, onion-white maggots revelling in its putrefaction.

He began to have dreams that he was standing in line at a kiosk in Kendall Square, holding a jar of peanut butter in his hands. A jar that had been wrapped in plastic by a machine. Uncorrupted food, produced in a clean factory, where men and women wore thick safety goggles and starched white laboratory coats. Millions of jars of peanut butter, identical copies of each other, lined up in gleaming rows. Duplication instead of procreation. Not crawling and moving, not sex and suckling, living and dripping and crusting and bursting and hatching.

And Max knew they had come during rainy season, but somehow he hadn't been expecting so much water. It was all right for Bea, who had the luxury of never having to venture far from home. She could always duck back into Mission House and dry off. But the rain was awful on a walkabout. It was short-tempered and unpredictable. First, he would hear a quiet hush, like an old friend calling you aside for a juicy piece of gossip. Looking up into the cracked hills of jungle, a thick, pulpy grey cloud would be dumping gallons of water over the treetops. The cloud would gather pace, engulfing more and more green, speckling, advancing like a great dust storm. And the hushing and rushing of the rain grew louder as it grew closer, until it wasn't even rain, but only water, great sheets of water cascading from the sky.

Holy Week arrived as a series of rainstorms rolled across from the East. Wind hissed through the palm leaves in the hills around the village, building up into a symphony of low rustling. It filtered through all the windows of Mission House until it was like being slowly poached at the centre of a great saucepan. The paths around the village turned into a thick orange sludge. Max gave up washing it off and instead went to bed at night with a crust of mud painted on his shins. In anticipation of Easter weekend, the church singers' rehearsals reached unforetold proportions. Singing practice began at five in the morning, followed by more singing at church at noon, another session with the service at six, then more singing practice after sunset, stretching long into the hours of complete darkness. The singing competed with a horrible chorus of frightened monkeys, whirring birds, and New Dog, who had been stirred into a whimpering frenzy by all the activity. At night, the church singing devolved into low chanting in F minor. Max and Bea lay in their separate beds listening to the dirge from the bottom of the hill. And then the screaming. High-pitched, sinewy, girl's screaming that unfurled in their dreams.

In honour of Holy Week, Aru had invited a group of 'devil chasers' from the South-East. Max stood on the porch of Mission House and received this news with a creeping sense of dread. He had been fixing the bracket on their kettle-balance when Aru knocked on the door, and felt caught off-guard, smeared in ash and grease.

'It is kastom,' Aru explained solemnly, 'to cleanse the village for Easter.'

'But are they *chasing* the devils, or . . .' Max watched Aru's face carefully.

'They expel demons.'

'Aha,' Max said, nodding, 'but – how exactly?' He imagined a ragtag band of witch doctors dressed in red mats with feathers in their hair, knocking at each door in turn, like carol singers.

'They will purify the village. With holy water, and prayers.'

'This happens every year?'

'Oh, yes!' Aru smiled. 'We are lucky to receive them for the holy festival! They tour the South for a month. Many villagers travel here to receive their blessing.'

Sure enough, a stream of bedraggled pilgrims arrived in Bambayot to welcome the devil chasers. They slept on the benches in Chief Bule's hut and in Willie's nakamal, as rain poured through holes in the thatch. Some camped in the shallow bush around the village, constructing lean-to shelters with palm leaves. Max watched as a sodden teenage girl dragging a twisted club foot behind her shivered under a flimsy umbrella made from pandan leaves.

Max pointed the girl out to Bea later that afternoon as they huddled under a sheet of plastic tarpaulin. 'Should we ask her to stay in Mission House?' he shouted over the rain.

Bea's eyebrows twitched. 'Where would she sleep?'

'In the living room?' Max wasn't about to suggest that Bea give up her bedroom. He hoped he could lead her into her own generosity.

Bea blinked. 'Maxis, we can't,' she hollered, as fists of water thumped on the top of the plastic. They both winced, and Max motioned back to Mission House with his head. They walked up the hill in step with each other. 'Imagine inviting her in and turning other people away,' Bea said into his ear, bouncing on her tiptoes.

As they crossed the threshold, she wiped a drip of water from the tip of her nose. 'And it's not like you think,' she continued, 'people aren't crippled here. It's normal to have something wrong with your body. She'd think you were mad if you tried to help her. Mabo-Mabon laughed when I tried to explain about beggars. She said they must be very stupid not to build themselves a house in the woods.'

'I don't know that proves anything,' Max interjected. 'There's what's "normal" and then there's Christian duty.'

'Yes, well, there's Christian duty –' Bea peeled off her sweater '– and then there's people who *want* to camp out. I'm sure she knows how much it rains at this time of year.'

In the end, Max gave up the vestry to a family of pilgrims from Mangarisu. He brought a pile of books into Mission House and scribbled notes for his sermon as Bea darned clothes on the other side of the table, or added to her encyclopaedia of nonsense vegetables. Drenched well-wishers knocked on the door to greet the Pastor, or receive yaws injections. A huddle of giggling children took turns to tap nervously on the lintel and run away. In between these interruptions, Bea and Max played rounds of their favourite 'island games'. These included Guess the Temperature, after which they would consult Max's thermometer. Or Bea's invention: Guess the Time. Sometimes Max hummed a song, and Bea would try to identify the tune. But they didn't know an awful lot of songs in common, apart from hymns. And Aru was providing enough hymns as it was.

On Good Friday, the rain drew aside for a brief interlude of dark, hot prescience before the next downpour. Bea assumed her usual place at the back of the church for Max's service. The benches were narrow and splintery, with legs of apparently random lengths that tipped to and fro according to the weight of their occupiers. Bea had chosen the back pew for her own, mostly because she could lean against the wall, and thus mitigate some of the discomfort. The church was crowded, and latecomers were standing along the walls of the building, with dejected faces peeping through the window from outside. The girl with the club foot was nowhere to be seen, but the congregation was still a relative showcase of injuries and afflictions – missing teeth, elephantine legs, and unseeing eyes quivering like poached eggs.

New Dog had followed Bea in, as usual, but on this occasion, she was followed by a series of strange mutts. They ran in and out through the doors during the service, skittering through legs and attempting to mount New Dog under Bea's bench. New Dog warbled in long, loopy howls, and Max paused his preaching to shoot Bea a look of extreme contempt. Bea pulled an apologetic face at him. With the devil chasers now delivering the Sunday morning service, Max had been working furiously on his sermon from Romans 8 as his only opportunity to witness in his own church. He'd enlisted a young boy called Nelson to translate into Bunti so the Northerners could understand. Bea wasn't convinced the kid wasn't just making it up, but there were lots of nodding heads, so at least he wasn't saying anything scandalous. Yet another dog slunk in through the doors and sniffed in the direction of New Dog, before Abel Poulet kicked it decisively in the snout. At one point in the service, Othniel Tari pushed through the crowd, left the church, and returned with a strip of dried palm he had knotted into a lasso. He tried to wrestle it over New Dog's head, but she merely whinnied and wriggled, diving further under Bea's bench. Othniel gave Bea a look of utter exhaustion and reproach, but Bea shrugged. It wasn't her dog – she had never made any claims to authority over its behaviour.

That evening, Bea came across what could only be described as an attempt at canine assault in Mission House garden. New Dog was barking, her teeth bared, at a pair of strange dogs, one a glossy black animal that looked like a Labrador, and the other, a lean, long-faced dog, the colour of a gingersnap. They were taking it in turns to fight with one another while the other perched up, climbing on top of New Dog from behind.

Bea found herself holding a long branch cut from an avocado tree, shaking it at the animals. 'Get out of here! Get away, get away, go!'

They flattened their ears against their heads and ran off towards a burning heap of compost at the other side of the village. Bea dropped the stick, all the anger flooding away from her body. New Dog was watching after her retreating suitors, her teeth still bared. Bea turned her back on New Dog and walked slowly into the house. The dog came up to the front door, peering inside the house. Bea carefully closed the door and went to lie on her bed, fat saltless tears running into the collar of her shirt.

The devil chasers arrived on Saturday, while Bea and Max were eating lunch. They were a group of elderly women from

Wansan, a remote village in the South-East, led by a woman in her mid-fifties, dressed in a heavy navy-blue skirt and a stiffly buttoned linen blouse. She wore heavy spectacles, and had short hair that was compensated by a fairly luxurious beard growing on the underside of her chin. She introduced herself as Marisa Bulebatan, and inferred that Max should try to stay out of their way while they were touring the island, doing the Lord's work. Max smiled politely, while she waved to the hills around the village.

'We will beat back the powers of darkness. The evil spirit of Ukunu has a strong power here,' she said.

Bea noticed Max was biting his lip so sharply it had blanched white.

When they returned to their lunch, Max sat in silent prayer for several moments before sighing and picking up his fork. He motioned for Bea to start eating.

He tugged a string of runner bean from his fork. 'This Marisa lady, she seems –' he trailed off.

'Crazy?' Bea filled in.

Max spluttered out a shard of rice, smiling despite himself. 'Well, yes. A bit.' He lowered his voice, ducking his head closer to the table. 'You've got to wonder about all this – "devil chasing". I mean, it's practically a pastime here. I've met a few of these types at home.'

'Crazy people?'

He laughed. 'People who think they need to rid everyone of Satan. I'm not saying possession can't happen, but it's really very extraordinary. Casting out spirits requires a lot of training and a steady hand. Going around telling the whole island that Bambayot is inflicted with demons . . .' he trailed off again.

'You think it makes it seem as if you're not doing a good job.'

'Well, exactly. If we were swimming in demons here, you

would think I'd have noticed by now and taken care of it myself. And Aru – with his band of Puritan children. "Devil chasers" are the last thing we need!'

Bea raised her eyebrows in reply. It was the first time Max had said anything to her about the nightly screams from the church. She felt relieved he was finally talking about it, rather than pretending nothing weird was happening.

'You would think the resident missionary should have some say in these things. Or else what's the point in us being here?' he muttered, concentrating on the beans again.

On Sunday, the devil chasers opened their service with a festive musical piece. Two of the old ladies had synchronized a dance routine with strands of string, which they fluttered in the air to the beats of a tambourine. Bea found it oddly funny, and was pleased to see Max's moustache was twitching as well. Once the singing had finished, Marisa invited several young girls from the village, dressed in their best, brightly coloured island dresses, to join the devil chasers at the front of the church. The girls clustered to the left of the altar, smiling and giggling, covering their faces in shy delight. Marisa approached the front of the group, and addressed the church at length in Bislama.

Bea didn't understand any of it, although she caught the word 'relax'. People in the front pews began to stir. Bea looked towards Max, who gave her the briefest stiff smile. The woman sitting next to Bea nudged her with an elbow, and whispered in Bislama, 'They are going to pray over us to release the evil spirit. Don't close your eyes.' Bea had an urge to hug this woman. Two of the old ladies moved to each side of the church to shut the doors. Bea clutched her hands behind her back and thought to herself, 'I am about to be exorcized.' A cold flash of horror ran down her spine.

The group of girls on the left of the altar began to shake their hands, and Marisa approached them, laying her palm on their foreheads, calling on Jesus. The girls in turn fell backwards on to the floor, where they lay fitting and twitching, as if electrified. Those who were not being prayed over had started shrieking and grunting. Bea smothered a fierce urge to run for the door, and glancing desperately back at Max, she saw he was staring at her with wide eyes.

She sat up straighter on the bench, wondering why it was, exactly, she was not to close her eyes. Marisa and the women at the front began to sway backwards and forwards. Suddenly, Marisa stepped over the seemingly unconscious girls, and let out an ear-piercing scream, holding her arms above her head, and calling out, 'Oh, Jesus!' The others clustered behind her.

In single file, the devil chasers began walking along the central aisle of the church and down the sides of the pews, holding their hands out, screaming and wailing, some clicking their fingers, some pulling at their hair. They approached Bea slowly, holding their arms above the congregation. Some of the churchgoers were swaying from side to side, a song breaking out in the middle pews and spreading to the rest of the congregation. Some stood dumbly, looking ahead, as if undergoing a necessary but unpleasant medical treatment. Some of the younger children clutched their parents. Bea looked to Max, who was standing stock-still at the front of the church, his eyes bloodshot.

Max watched as the girls at the front of the church primly closed the legs of those fitting on the floor, and turned his head away in disgust. These children, these women, exorcizing his flock, his wife! Bea had lost all the colour in her lips, and she was wringing her little wooden fan between her hands.

He was, for the first time, grateful New Dog had followed her into church that day. It was sitting in front of her, resolutely gnawing at the fleas on its flank and farting. The devil chasers seemed hesitant to step over the dog, and when they approached the animal, they turned around and started walking back up the aisle, pausing to beat on the walls of the church, or grip a member of the congregation.

After a further hour of wailing, and fitting and crying, and one final tambourine dance, Marisa concluded the service with a prayer of thanks. As soon as her devil chasers began to file out of the doorway, Max pushed through the churchgoers to reach Bea. New Dog sat up at his approach and circled his legs by means of a welcome. Max gave it a cursory kick on the backside.

'Are you all right?' he asked Bea. Her hands felt clammy in his. Bea nodded.

'Will you stay in Mission House this afternoon? I think –' Max looked over his shoulder at the row of well-wishers queuing up outside the door '– it might be best. Let's just keep you at home, nice and snug, OK?'

Bea gave him a wan smile. 'Happily,' she said.

Max strode past Marisa, who was receiving limp handshakes from the congregation. He went to find Aru. But he was not in his hut, nor on the log by Willie's nakamal. He came across Aru's nephew halfway up a guava tree by the coast, and he pointed Max towards the store. Max marched the hour's walk north, indignation tickling in his chest.

As he climbed the hill to Aru's store, he spotted a glint of white teeth inside the building.

'May I have a word with you?' Max called into the metal shack.

'Of course, Pastor,' Aru's voice came from within.

The store was hot, and so dark that white stars furrowed his vision. The soap on the shelves was baking in the heat, and the cabin was heady with astringent perfume.

'I think we should talk about the devil chasers,' Max said, sitting on the painted red stool in the corner. He took care not to touch the scorching steel with his shoulder.

'Have they completed their service?'

'Yes, they have. And I don't intend to ask them to stay.'

Aru was silent.

'Look –' Max said, swallowing. His mouth was dry. 'I appreciate your help. I really do. I'm blessed to have your support.'

Aru looked at his sandals.

'But you must leave me to take care of any sort of devil, or demon, or what have you. Anything like that. Anything to do with Ukunu. This shall be my responsibility from now on.'

Aru said nothing. So Max continued. 'If I need help, I will consult you. But there must be no more devil chasing, or night-time prayers. At all.'

Aru looked up at him sharply. 'But I can continue to purify?'

'Purify how?' Max steeled himself.

Aru thought for a moment. 'With holy water. To cast away any evil.'

Max sighed. 'Sure. Go ahead. Water away. But please, no more prayers.'

'Of course, Pastor.'

That night, Max couldn't sleep. He escaped from his mosquito net and opened the front door, grateful for the salty breeze, and the heavy night – warm and dark as ink. A distant moon cast a smudgy white halo in the sky. Max crouched by the front door, leaning his back on the frame. He took a deep breath. It was easy to take the natural beauty of the island for granted. He allowed himself the luxury of daydreaming about how he could instruct Willie to build a writing desk, when he heard the unmistakable crunch of bare feet on the coral surrounding the house. He held his breath unconsciously, his heart giving a tiny jump. He looked round the left side of the house, and the crunching stopped abruptly. It was probably one of those infernal dogs that had been hanging around the bushes, thought Max, squinting into the darkness.

'Hello?' he called. He heard a scuffing sound, and could make out two bare feet in the moonlight, sticking out from under the shadow of an orange tree. 'Hello?' he said again, standing upright. The feet shuffled forward, and revealed themselves as belonging to the round face of Filip Aru.

Max started back. 'Oh, good evening. Is everything OK?'

'Yes, Pastor.' Aru smiled, nodding.

Max saw he was carrying a plastic bottle filled with water. 'Out for a walk?' he asked, stretching his hands behind his back in a studiously casual manner that he hoped looked natural.

Aru only raised his eyebrows.

'Don't you have a flashlight?' Max motioned to Aru's hands.

'No,' Aru spoke softly, 'the moon is bright.'

'Yes, I suppose it is.' Max looked back around the village. He noted the telltale flickers of candlelight inside three of the houses. It was obviously not as late as he had thought. Aru stood there, gazing at him mutely.

'Were you praying?' Max suggested, which was a reasonably safe guess.

'Yes. And also purifying in the name of the Lord.'

Max looked again at the water bottle in his hand. 'Oh.' He motioned to the house, 'Well, goodnight then.'

Aru gave Max a friendly wave.

Max waited for a few seconds for Aru to leave, but he did not move, so he was forced to go inside his own front door and close it. Without knowing exactly what he was waiting for,

Max paused by the door, putting his face in line with a crack in the bamboo pattern. Aru was still standing by the house. He gave a barely audible sigh, took the bottle in one hand, and placing a thumb over the opening, shuffled backwards, sprinkling holy water over the hearth of their home.

6

Jonson smacked another tree trunk with his bushknife, and the blade glanced off with a bright clink. The tremor travelled through his arm and into his elbow bone. He wiped his face with his handkerchief. A weak breeze was blowing from Tangariku, and smoke from the village bushkitchens lingered in the humidity. 'How much longer?' he called to Garolf, who was leaning against a boulder, rolling a cigarette.

'A little while,' Garolf said.

'This'll be the end of me.' Jonson massaged the tendon in the pad below his thumb. It had been a long time since he'd last wielded his machete, and the muscles in his forearms were trembling. Relief from physical labour was one of the few benefits from his appointment on Advent Island. He employed housegirls from the village to attend to every need he couldn't acquire from them through coercion. The girls washed his clothes in the stream, and yet others came to sweep his house each morning while he slept. They decorated his house with hibiscus flowers, killed every spider, shined his shoes with pressed palm oil, and sharpened his razor with their bushknives. They prepared his food according to his specifications, baking loaves of dense bread from ground cassava flour. They laid his table with poulet fish, and cooled glass jugs of lemonade for him in the stream that ran from the mountains.

'It'll be sunset soon,' Jonson said.

Garolf stretched his back and lit his cigarette. He put two fingers to his lips, and whistled so loudly that a startled parrot flung itself from the palms. Garolf raised his cigarette, as if it were a pistol, and pretended to shoot it down.

'I don't know why you brought me here. It's like a farce,' Jonson said.

Garolf shook his head. 'Why so many complaints? Just a little while longer. It has to at least seem as if we care.'

'And we don't?'

'You're the District Administrator. Do you care?'

Jonson wrinkled his nose. His sole role on the island was sending the occasional routine report back to his CO on the progress of an airstrip project further north, near Panita. It had been half-heartedly started by some Yanks in the early forties, but had since ground to a halt as a muddy, bald patch of jungle, as if someone had melted a pat of wax and lifted a strip of the vegetation away. Runaways were certainly outside his purview, unless they were dangerous. Or intended to rob his kastom bank of ankle beads and painted feathers. 'No, not officially.' He mopped the back of his neck with his handkerchief. 'But I'm not paying his wages.'

Garolf shrugged. 'For now, all that matters is we seem to be looking for him.'

Jonson gestured to the palms. 'And what if, while we're pretending to look, he's actually here? Sitting in a tree – laughing at us?'

Garolf tutted. 'They all make the same mistake. Into the bush. Do you know how many runaways I've had in the last five years?'

Jonson shook his head.

'Thirteen,' said Garolf.

'And they all just died in the hills?'

Garolf laughed. 'No – nothing like that. A week in the bush, two weeks. They get hungry. They get careless, then they get caught.'

Jonson brushed a spindly beetle from his knee. 'Is he a good worker, this one?'

'He is, yes, according to Ephraim. I pulled his papers.' Garolf began to walk through the trees towards the hills, and Jonson fell in step beside him. 'Thieu Nguyen. Came over to work for that French plantation on Epi, in 1930. Papers signed by his mother. Big rubber stamp on the page says "Coolies". No signature, just thumbprints.'

Jonson kicked a young green coconut, and it toppled unsteadily into a crusty cowpat. 'Hell of a long time to stay out here. He's not one of the Tonks the French refused to take back?'

'I don't think so. Papers say he met a woman here. Married.'

'His wife is here? At Sara?'

Garolf nodded. 'Kid, too.'

Jonson shook his head. 'And he still ran? What a bastard. Maybe he got himself a second wife, a local woman.'

Garolf shook his head. 'You know how funny island boys are about Sinwa – they won't even work on the same parts of the plantation as my Tonks. No way an island woman would marry one.'

'I was joking,' Jonson said, smacking Garolf lightly on the arm with his bushknife, 'on account of his employer's fondness for second wives.'

Garolf grimaced. 'Great comedy. I'll share it with Mame, and we'll see if she still cooks you simboro after that.'

'And his wife?'

'Whose?'

'The Tonk – his wife – did he run off because of her?'

Garolf drew from his cigarette. 'Doubt it. Papers said she was a housegirl with a British family. Then a French one. Three or four languages, good handwriting. No way.'

'She must be peeved.'

'I suppose.' Garolf sighed, blowing a curl of smoke. He rubbed his face, suddenly glum. 'I don't want to lose workers. I don't want men to die in the bush. I don't understand why they leave – where do they even think they can go? Join Liki and train in kastom?'

'Maybe they just want to get out.'

'They never stay out,' Garolf muttered.

Neither he nor his father had ever instigated any precautions against runaways. His northern plantation at Sara was bordered on three sides by tabu hilltops and unpredictable streams. And Dadavoki in the South was hutched in by a shelf of mountain, and one narrow pathway to the landing strip. And after all, anyone reckless enough to abscond would easily be spotted on an island populated by 300 black islanders. Once caught, they'd have an extra year added to their contract, and be transferred to the other plantation. There was no conceivable benefit to running away – unless workers wanted to chance the sharky waters and swim to Ambrym. And in the plantations, they were offered decent pay, housing, even medical care. Garolf's workers were not slaves. After their five-year contract was ended, he would pay their fare for a cargo ship to take them wherever they wanted to go. Provided that where they wanted to go was Port Vila.

Thieu's sickness rolled over him suddenly. The day after he left the plantation, he had hiked deeper into the forest, up in the tabu hills. He walked until there were no flattened plants, and the trees were heavy with red berries and fallen nuts where no one dared to collect them. Clouds of webs bloomed between the boughs, and families of monkeys tittered in the canopy. That day, his limbs had been heavy, his head cramped, as if filled with warm porridge. Thieu had put it down to spending a night in the foul cave.

But as he lay in his hammock that evening to sleep, time spun away from him. He lost himself to innumerable days vomiting yellow, his body seeping vile liquid between his legs and out of the corners of his mouth. He dreamed thick hallucinations, as grand as ballrooms. The sun pulsed above his camp. Ants crawled over him, picking off shreds of softened skin. At night, roaring howler monkeys circled round his camp. Slices of starlight through the canopy drew columns of whirring moths. In his half-sleep, Thieu thought he could hear the soft song of their music. He was sure Lien was there with him. He struggled to reach her. She smelt like talcum powder. Thin tears dribbled down his cheeks. She was waiting for him. He had failed her. Maybe Minh had already caught measles, maybe he was already dead.

As he wavered in and out of sickness, he tried to gauge how much time had passed. Spongy hair was growing on his face, and his T-shirt hung off him, crusted with yellow excrement and sparkling with crystals of salt. Silky white maggots wriggled in the folds of the mosquito net. He wrapped it around him like a shroud. He could not walk. He could not even pull off the leeches on his shoulder blades. He sucked on fibrous scraps of sugar cane. He drank water from banana leaves. He slept, dense, dreamless sleep. Sometimes, he was conscious he was awake. He watched black birds with bright crimson heads beating blurry wings as they nosed inside banana suckers. He heard brown pigs, small as kittens, shunting through the fallen leaves.

When he grew strong enough, he propped himself on to his elbows and forced himself to eat as much sugar-cane pulp as he could stomach. He needed to get back to Lien. It took him two days until he could stand upright, and even then, his vision slanted and rang with dizzy sparkles. He scrambled through the sodden leaves on the forest floor, and collected soft, rotting green fruit studded with custard-coloured grubs. He gobbled handfuls of them, the worms popping in his mouth with a metallic taste. Monkeys cackled and chittered in the highest leaves, sometimes thumping down into the lower branches and peering at him. Once, six of them surrounded him while he was emptying his bowels and pelted him with nuts. He crawled towards the nuts with his trousers around his knees and ate them ravenously; grateful the monkeys had already cracked open the husks.

Thieu made a slingshot out of his belt, and spent the better part of a day launching rocks into the tree where the monkeys seemed to live. His shoulder ached from the effort and he had to stop every fifteen minutes to stretch out cramp in his hand. But shortly before nightfall, he caught one of the monkeys right in the eye socket, and it plummeted to the ground with a pitiful squeal. He ran to its quivering figure and bashed in its skull with the handle of his bushknife in a seizure of mad triumph. He built a fire, and pulled off its hair and tufty little moustache. Its naked carcass looked like a small child. He did not know how to prepare it to eat, but sliced open its belly and pulled out the slimy guts. He split it open over the burning wood, filled its flesh with smoke, then pulled off strands of flesh and ate them in ropes. That night, Thieu dreamed he was crouched over a hot fire, feasting on the corpse of a baby.

After two days of eating from the monkey, he gathered some strength. He painstakingly cleared the earth of the sugar-cane pulp, and checked for termites. He spent an afternoon constructing a rain shelter from pandan leaves, and arranging branches as brackets where the mosquito net could be hung. When it was ready, he collected their supplies and buried them in shallow earth under his hammock. It was time to collect Lien.

★

For two weeks after Thieu's escape, Lien made the appropriate pantomime of despair. She cursed him, and she wailed. She deliberately left her hair uncombed. The other women closed ranks around her, forbidding any whispers of Thieu's scandalous desertion. They entreated her to sleep late, and offered to cover her shifts. It was enough to make Lien feel almost guilty. Small presents were left on her hammock – pink hibiscus flowers, or wilting bars of Australian chocolate. She lay awake, clutching Minh to her chest and rocking him, reassuring herself her fraud would be justified, eventually. And then she began planting the seeds of her disease. She complained of headaches, and chewed the inside of her mouth until it swelled up. Twice a day, she walked to the guava trees outside the plantation, and poked inside the knot in the wood for their shell signal. Nothing. She realized, in a moment of shivery clarity during breakfast, that the shell could have fallen on to the ground and been overlooked. Lien jiggled with nerves, and ran back to the guava trees as soon as the meal was over, peering desperately into the mud for the broken shrapnel of the shell. Two more weeks passed. Nothing. There were only two possibilities, she realized; either he was dead, or he had truly abandoned her.

She began to mourn Thieu in earnest. She lost her appetite. She imagined on a delirious, unquiet loop all the terrible things that could have happened to him – fallen into the river, killed by a fallen tree. Trinh offered to look after Minh, but Lien wouldn't let him out of her sight. She refused to move into the nurse house, afraid of the infection that might be lurking in the linens. Trinh slipped her a handful of sedatives and warned her not to nurse Minh as long as she was taking them. But Lien ignored the pills. After dark, she sobbed herself into snatches of deep, oblivious sleep. Often, as she cried into her pillow, Tran would reach out and grip her naked foot through the mosquito net in solidarity. The gifts of peanuts and home-made soap continued.

One night, Lien was roused from warm dreams to the sound of a bird calling outside the window above her head. Reflexively, she ran her fingers over the puffy scabs of her rash, listening as the bird flew by the bunkhouse, showering the slats with grit. She climbed out of her hammock and crossed to shoo the bird away from Minh's shelf. And as she stood there, a pink shell flew through the window and skittered at her feet. She picked it up and turned it over in her hands, heart hammering. Was she dreaming? Another shell knocked her on the elbow. She peered into the darkness. Was it really him?

Lien gathered Minh and walked barefoot to the wash house, her insides squirming. In the dim light of the wash house, she stepped carefully over the puddles on the floor, and kicked away a couple of curious cockroaches. 'Shush, Minh-Binh,' she whispered, jiggling him up and down, although he wasn't fussing.

There was a scuffling noise from the shower room, and she turned the corner with acid bubbling in her stomach. A figure was standing on the far side of the room under the window. His face was splattered in thin facial hair and brown mud. He was wearing a mosquito net over his shoulders like a cape, and holding a rusty bushknife in one hand. Blackened toenails curled over the sides of his feet. A stripe of cockroaches were climbing up into the net and over his left shoulder.

Lien took a step back, and swallowed her scream. It was her husband.

7

As the months passed, Bea became able to notice the great variation that the Creator of nature can achieve using only green. The way one's eyes become adjusted to the dark, Bea's eyes became adjusted to green – she could distinguish the liana's wealthy emerald from the old-pickle colour of the orange tree. The lozenge-shaped spiders were striped with lime, while the tiny beetles that appeared each dusk glowed like resinous, oily grapes. Amidst the gauzy jade weeds in her vegetable garden, she sought out edible clover that unfurled as neatly as a newly minted dollar bill.

But as the rainy season limped to an end, the relentless mire of green began to fracture. Candy-pink hibiscus flowers appeared in the hedges, crinkled at the edges like crêpe paper. Crimson-headed honeyeaters buzzed at the tips of banana suckers. Gigantic butterflies swarmed in and out of the palms, streaked with electric-blue zigzags. Occasionally, in the fringes of the coconut palms south of the village, there was the bright flash of parrots, a conflagration of colours so impossibly lurid they looked like novelty recreations of themselves, made from marzipan. And slowly, the incessant months of rain beat themselves out against the mountains. And slowly, frail seams of coloured life were stitched into the jungle, and on to the sky. And just like that, Bea woke one morning in June and realized Advent Island was beautiful.

Max was astonished at Bea's newfound appreciation for the island. He wondered if her change in spirits was because her garden was now producing edible food. Although it was strange food – no doubt about it. Their evening meals of 'hedge' had been replaced by long, fibrous 'snake beans', starchy chouchoute squash, zucchini flowers and bitter purple-sprouting alfalfa. But Bea was spending less time in the garden, and more time walking about on her own. She never seemed to go anywhere, just strolled up and down the northern path. Max couldn't fathom what joy she derived from it. When he asked her, she claimed she was enjoying the view. Walking alone like that, with her basket tied across her forehead and that demonic dog in tow, people were bound to talk. But he daren't say a word, lest he upset the balance of her unlikely cheerfulness. And besides which, she had finally made a friend.

Bea met Santra two weeks after Easter. Bea had been picking island cabbage from a scrubby patch of land behind the village when she noticed a young woman approaching from over the hill. Bea sighed. Almost every week, a local passer-by would draw close to examine her skin, then stand, gawping at her, drawing small circles in the dirt with their bushknife.

Bea had been forced to realize that her daydreams about friends on the island had been utterly misguided. Only Mabo-Mabon ever spoke to her. In the months before they arrived, Bea had conjured for herself a small group of women who would gather in her house after church to drink lemonade, and sew and gossip, and pray. They would be fascinated by her hair, and squabble over whose turn it was to brush it. She would become an auntie to their sweet babies. She would teach them some Spanish songs, and they would ask endless questions about life in America, breaking into appreciative gasps when she showed them photographs she had brought with them. Instead, children clustered outside Mission House window to watch her while she scrubbed the stone floor on her hands and knees. Giggling, they used dirty fingers to tap on the windows as if she were a tropical fish in an aquarium, before running away.

But Santra was not prone to giggling, or to running away.

'Do you like island cabbage?' Santra asked, swinging an elbow up on to a wooden post. Her skin was dark brown, her cheeks round, and she wore two tight braids in her dark-blonde hair. On her forehead there was an amateur blue tattoo of an 'x', similar to a Christian cross, underlined by two lines, as if for emphasis.

'Yes.' Bea smiled, not even realizing it was a lie. She looked around the cabbage bush, desperately trying to find inspiration for something to say, anything that might lure her into a conversation.

'I like island cabbage,' Santra offered.

They smiled lamely at each other.

'Where are you from?' Bea asked finally.

'On top.' Santra gestured vaguely to the mountains. In silence, she looked over Bea's dress, her basket, her muddied feet. Finally, Santra joined her, and they picked cabbage side by side for the next hour.

Santra was rather taciturn, except when telling stories. And when it came to island scandals, Bea was a captive audience. Bea probed her for details of the marriages, deaths and affairs going on in the other villages, stopping her every few words to work out who was who. Santra told her about whiteman Jonson and his 'bush marriages' with the Bwatapoa girls in their taro gardens. She told her about when Patrice Kwani beat his wife with a tin of Spam at Aru's store, and how Ephraim Bule used 'leaf magic' to cure his impotence. She told Bea of the robbery up North at Jonson's kastom bank, where the assailant had transformed himself into a macaw, and flown out of the window to escape capture. She told Bea about Chief

Willy's wish-granting great eel that lived in Homo Bay on the east coast, while Bea giggled helplessly.

Santra claimed to be in her late teens, although she regularly changed her mind about her age. She farmed her own garden up top, supplemented by foraging in the jungle. Endlessly horrified by Bea's enthusiastic incompetence, Santra tolerated Bea's clumsy attempts to help with the solemn patronage of an older sister. Santra lived in a tiny squalid village in the hills in Central, with her husband Charles. Bea occasionally walked up top with her, and sat outside Santra's grimy, smoky hut, while Santra braided pandan baskets to sell at the market, and Bea merely sunned her tropical sores, whistling. She allowed Bea to join her on some of her hunting trips. She plaited a loose-weave cage, and they trekked for hours upstream to a small waterfall further in the North. They lifted mossy rocks to make a deep, still dam in the stream and dipped the cage in to catch crayfish. It was Santra who had persuaded her that naus fruit were delicious; Bea had been ignorantly eating the unripe green fruit, without realizing it was supposed to be orange, and soft like a peach. It was also Santra who first convinced her to enjoy laplap.

Laplap was a slimy island jelly which came in three varieties: the whey-yellow manioc kind, soft purple taro laplap, and chewy banana laplap – simboro – made from unripe fruit. Once a month or so, in Santra's village, the women would dig small, deep pits, and lay hot stones from the fire at the bottom, layering the stones with banana leaves. Then the grated manioc, or taro, in a great mush, would be spread over the leaves and topped with coconut cream. It would be covered and left to cook for hours, steam gently rising from cracks in the leaves. When the pit was uncovered, the laplap, in all its glistening, gelatinous glory, would be lifted out, and sometimes, for special occasions, adorned with thin slivers of Spam. Once Bea's palate had acclimatized to island cuisine, she looked forward to eating laplap, even savouring its repulsive wobbly tastelessness, especially as when Santra cooked it, she fried tiny baby squid in palm oil to adorn the top with a crispy garnish.

Santra was a meticulous and generous cook, and often turned up to Mission House with extra fruit or a head of cabbage to supplement Bea's suppers. On the day of Pentecost, she came to Bambayot especially to hear Max's sermon in church, and Bea was thoroughly touched. Despite the cross tattooed on her forehead, she was certain that Santra was not at all religious. Her husband, Charles, liked to declare to anyone who would listen that he could turn into a flying fox at night. When they came to Bambayot for Pentecost, Charles jostled Max about the ribs with his elbow, and claimed he could prove his powers of transfiguration.

'Last night I flew down here and I was one of the bats outside your window.'

Max eyed him wordlessly.

'Yes! I watched you and I can prove it.'

Max opened his arms in a silent invitation, smiling at one side of his mouth.

'You came home and lit a candle. I saw you reading, then you went to bed. And you snore like a huge pig!' He whooped with laughter.

Bea couldn't help but giggle at Max's expression.

'Well, he's not wrong!' she added, as Max shook his head and sighed.

Santra didn't appear to be too concerned with the regular transformation of her husband into a bat, since she had brought one to cook for Bea, carefully wrapped in leaves in her island basket. Bea accepted the gift uncertainly, tucking the body on the shelf in Mission House kitchen while they attended service. They entered to Aru's church singers performing 'Amazing

Grace', and Charles crossed to the men's side, while Santra took a seat on the back bench next to Bea. After the girls had finished their song, Aru left his ukulele at the front of the church and hurried down the middle aisle, carrying a Bible. Averting his eyes, he handed it to Bea.

'Uh, thank you,' she said, not sure what she was supposed to do with two Bibles.

'For your friend,' he said.

Dutifully, Bea handed it to Santra, who accepted it expressionlessly.

As soon as Aru turned to the front of the church, Santra handed the Bible back to Bea and instead pulled her pandan fan from her island basket. Bea slipped the second Bible behind her back, and rested against it so it was out of sight. It occurred to her for the first time that Santra probably couldn't read.

After Max preached from Acts 2, the service concluded with Aru's church singers performing 'What A Friend We Have In Jesus'. Max stayed behind to shake hands with the church-goers, Charles went to Noia Saruru in search of Willie, and Bea took Santra back to Mission House. Trying to find a way to thank Santra for coming to Max's sermon, Bea offered her one of their extraordinarily precious cans of tinned tomatoes, but she misunderstood the gift, and asked Bea to open it for her. After half an hour of stirring away, Santra presented her with what looked like a small, bloody baby, with broken bones sticking out of its mutilated body.

Bea squeaked, and half rose from her stool before she had time to stop herself. Santra muffled a wheeze of laughter. Bea looked at the plate more closely. Now she could see more clearly that it was, indeed, a huge bat that had been simmered in tinned tomato sauce. Its leathery wings were still attached to it, crookedly hanging from the side of the plate, smeared in red. The head was twisted to the right, swollen from the heat of the pan, its mouth open. Santra had thoughtfully cut the front of the bat open for her, and she could see the purplish meat surrounding the bones inside the animal.

Santra returned with a fork, and placed it on the table beside the bat with such finality that Bea realized she would have no choice but to sit down, and with a smile on her face, eat the animal. She felt shaky as she combed a scrap of pale lilac meat from around an unidentifiable bone. She lifted it to her mouth, and took hold of the sliver of flesh with her teeth, trying not to let her tongue make contact with it. But once it was inside her mouth, she could taste it against her gums. It was like chewy, undercooked lamb. Bea sat upright in surprise, still suspiciously probing the meat with her tongue.

When Max came back to Mission House twenty minutes later, she was unselfconsciously pulling ropes of cartilage from around the bone and eating them with relish, leaving delicate hairline streaks of red tomato sauce and bat juice across the side of her cheek. Max glanced between Bea's face and her dish. Bea suddenly remembered the plate resembled the crime scene of a brutal baby massacre, and put her fork down by the sad remnants of the swollen bat, barely recognizable now she had pulled out and devoured its insides. Both Max and Bea reviewed the plate in silence, and in the few seconds that passed while he stood and she sat and the bat lay dead between them, Max looked at Bea with a mingled sense of pride in her unfussiness, and the odd feeling he didn't recognize her any more.

8

Before Max and Bea left for their great adventure, his church in Boston had thrown them a farewell tea party. It was a bitterly cold day, the sky a distant pale shade of blue. The church hall was unheated, and the jugs of fruit cocktail sitting by the window had filmed over with a discreet layer of frost. Max was in his element, his cheeks flushed with excitement, his laugh louder than ever. He swept between gaggles of church ladies, reciting their soon-to-be address carefully, over and over.

Bea was a little overwhelmed by the attention. The small community of women had become something like her friends. They had championed her as their own Dolores del Rio – beautiful and exotic – although Bea knew she was neither. They had taught her the Pledge of Allegiance, taken her to quilting circles, patiently corrected her English, and slipped her recipes for pot roast and American cookies. Bea's throat felt thick. She did not really, now she was officially being bidden farewell, want to leave. Irene, an English widow whose daughter had emigrated to America after the war, pushed into Bea's hands a blue hardback book. Bea read the title out loud, *101 Things for the Housewife to Do*.

Irene smiled at her, with a tooth-shaped gap on the left side of her mouth that made her look lopsided. 'My daughter swears by it,' she whispered conspiratorially. 'Now don't forget, God will only make a home so happy. The rest is up to us.' She nodded, and gave Bea a tight, lavender-scented hug.

Bea smiled speechlessly and patted the book with appreciation until Irene had disappeared to find Max. *101 Things for the*

Housewife to Do and the Bible were the only two books Bea had brought with her to the island. She had never been a keen reader. Growing up, she had a shelf of storybooks and fairy tales in English, which her mother had bought before she was even born, hoping for a little girl. These lived on the left-hand side of her bed, and Bea never opened them except to draw a finger over the illustrations of the dancing princesses on page eleven, lingering over their impossibly fair hair and tiny feet. Now, *101 Things* was one of her only possessions. She had gone into the hospital in Venezuela owning nothing. And after some time had passed, she had begun to remember her child-hood room with longing. She thought of the sewing basket stuffed with coloured ribbons and glass beads, and her mother's tiger's eye bracelet. She thought of the wide-toothed comb with mother-of-pearl handle, and her old First Communion dress, which had been kept packed up in a hatbox. Bea used to guiltily unwrap the dress from its tissue paper, seduced by the rustle of the train. Pressing it under her fingers, she would try to imagine what she would look like as a bride in a long white dress and veil.

Now her possessions were few and practical. Max, to his credit, had made gestures towards Bea's love of beautiful objects, understanding it was as much a form of nostalgia as of vanity. For their first Christmas, he had nervously presented her with a white, teardrop-shaped opal pendant. Bea was at once touched and embarrassed. She wore the necklace for the rest of the day, and ever after kept it wrapped in tissue paper in a wooden box that once held a boot polishing brush. Max assumed she was making a brave gesture of rejecting worldly things. Of course, Bea could never have explained to him that opals were desperately bad luck, and its trembling milky radiance recalled a drop of semen hovering glutinously in the hollow of her throat.

The book and the necklace were both among the scant items of Bea's belongings that made it to the New Hebrides. And despite herself, Bea found flicking through the pages of 101 *Things* to be a curious form of self-punishment. Every now and again, Bea opened the book and allowed herself a few minutes of delicious torture. The photograph of the smug housewife, with her carefully set hair, neat day dress and calf-skin pumps. The white carpet across which she effortlessly pushed her vacuum cleaner, holding on to the handle with one carefree hand. Bea enviously touched a finger to the picture of that vacuum cleaner. She didn't even have a proper broom. She looked over at the broom with contempt. It was a bundle of small twigs, held together by vine. When swept over the floor, it didn't so much sweep up dust as liberally disperse the tiny butter-coloured spiders living in its dry climate.

One particularly painful spread exhibited two photographs of a washing machine and drying machine. A washing machine! Bea's heart hurt. She did all their laundry with a wooden slab and a bucket. Sometimes she carried their washing to the stream, and stood with Santra in the foamy water. Santra laughed her high-pitched hissing laugh as she expertly slapped her island dress on the rocks, twisting it in her arms again and again, the arc of her muscles contracting. Bea could barely lift the wet clothes above her head.

It was their fourth month on the island before Bea could finally put 101 *Things* to its proper use. It was about five in the afternoon, the women of the village had stoked their fires ready for the dark evening, and the men were beginning to grind the kava in the nakamal for the first shells. Bea was sitting at the table in Mission House absently running her fingers over a patch of hardened white crust on a tropical sore over her left elbow. Sharp whistles began to sound from the hills, the children gathering on the high ledge that overlooked the sea. The whistles grew louder, until Bea was certain something was happening. She carried her bushknife to the edge of the village, to where women had left their fires, trailing babies and machetes, joining the chorus of whistles.

Down by the shore a large fire had been lit, and a circle of boys were stomping round the flames, whooping and jostling each other in an imitation of kastom dancing. Yellow lights were twinkling low over the water. Tufty red hair rose up from the coast as Max climbed the hill with giant strides, his face alight with joy.

'It's a cargo ship,' he called, holding out his hand for her.

He looked so like a schoolboy standing there – his hair disarrayed and his face sunburnt – that Bea sprang forward to take his hand, forgetting the tabus they would be breaking. Together they hurried to the shore; the months of treading the hill had provided good practice at rolling with moving gravel underfoot, and navigating slippery patches of orange mud.

'The lights were visible about an hour ago.' Max was speaking so quickly Bea could hardly understand him. 'It's the boat that runs from Santo and it will most certainly be stopping here tonight. The boys have lit a fire, I wish I had a stronger flashlight or we could have used it as a signal. That's why they're whistling. It was supposed to have come last month but for some reason it didn't – I don't know why – oh, look –!' He broke off suddenly with a gasp as they rounded the mango trees arching the coast. 'Can you see?'

He stood behind her, the soft hair of his beard against her cheek, and pointed out towards the flickering light where a dull shape was outlined against the deepening pink of the ocean.

'Max!' Bea grasped his outstretched pointing hand, crying out louder than she had meant to. She clung on to his arm and lowered her voice to a strangled whisper. 'Do you think –?' She could hardly bear to risk completing the sentence.

'Our trunks?' Max finished for her, and she felt the smile on his face as the apple of his cheek pressed into hers. 'It's possible, it's entirely possible.'

It took an hour for the ship to finally draw to a stop in the shallows by the village. The Bambayot men brought their kava shells to the shore, and knocked them back under the mango trees before wading into the water to carry boxes of supplies, of kava roots and matches on to the shore. Bea crouched on her haunches as close to the fire as she could risk without setting her island dress alight, slapping at mosquitoes and nudging New Dog out of the way. Max was striding up and down the beach with Edly Tabi, rolling barrels of fuel and making inane small talk about the size of the ship or the quality of the kava roots.

The boat stood in the shallow water for ten minutes before Bea spotted a single pale face jostling through the crowded deck. She squinted harder. Was it a whiteman?

Jonson had boarded the ship at Mangarisu. He strode lopsidedly up to the shore, drying his hands on his pockets. Max stood on the beach and greeted him with an unnecessarily vigorous handshake. 'Mr Jonson, this is a welcome surprise.' Jonson's fingers were smooth as pebbles under his own.

Jonson retrieved his hand. 'I made the trip this far to secure your belongings – you never can rely on the honesty of the locals, I'm afraid. They are prone to forget some objects, indeed, have a destination.'

'Our trunks?'

Jonson nodded, supplemented by a squeak of surprise as Max gripped him around the shoulder.

'Oh, thank goodness. God bless you, Mr Jonson!'

'Yes, quite welcome,' Jonson muttered.

Max and Jonson retrieved the battered trunks from the ship and relayed them on to the beach, where Ralph Poulet declared himself custodian of the boxes and leapt from one to the other with so much enthusiasm that Max didn't have the heart to stop him. Jonson produced a list from his pocket, copied from the ship's manifest from Vila, and they discovered one of Bea's trunks was unaccounted for, eventually located under a dozing, grumpy young woman destined for Ambrym.

As they waded through the shallows to help unload the village's supplies – barrels of oil, boxes of questionable tinned fish, Chinese soap and soggy breakfast crackers – Max felt emboldened by the victory of his possessions. 'Mr Jonson, may I ask you a personal question?'

Jonson tensed, sensing the topic on the horizon. 'Go ahead,' he said, tersely.

'Are you at all related to the esteemed Mr Jonson, the pilot?'

'Yes,' Jonson said.

'Distant cousin?'

'Not so distant,' Jonson said, bending to rinse his hands in the surf.

Jonson was the younger brother to a decorated RFC fighter from the Great War, who had run away to enlist before he was even old enough. Occasionally on the London tube, Jonson would catch sight of that awful government poster of Bernard staring out into a patriotic middle distance, a tasselled blue scarf flapping around his neck, holding his helmet in his hands as if it were a prize-winning cabbage: 'B. A. M. for Britain' printed across the bottom.

I. A. M. Jonson had made a brief flirtation with the army himself, only to have spent two years in 1939 sweating in a miserable hole in Egypt. There, he felt suffocated by flies and hot sand, uninspired by his humourless neighbours and their inevitable diet of onions. He'd been given an honourable dismissal after losing his nerve and shooting a man through the kneecaps, after he was overcharged for a black-market bottle of whisky. His commanding officer, not unsympathetic himself to the locals' booze-swindling, had decided the sand-fever had gone to Jonson's head, and perhaps he'd be better off on government service in a steadier climate. Somewhere with lots of rain where a chap could eat fish. And so, Jonson was transferred to the Colonial Administrative Service, and was sent off to the New Hebrides.

When the last of the items had been piled on the beach, Max and Jonson stretched their backs and waved to the passengers on the ship as the boat slowly pulled away from the shore. At that moment, Jonson was rushed from behind by New Dog. Snorting and twisting, it leapt up at Jonson's back, sniffing him wildly, its tail flapping, pressing mucky paws behind his kneecaps so he momentarily lost his balance.

'Oh, for goodness' sake!' Max offered Jonson his left arm to brace him, while delivering a swift kick at New Dog's snout with his right leg. 'Go! Shoo – get away from here! Kranki dog!' He gave it another shove on the side of its face with his leg, and the beast slunk off towards Mission House, its ears flattened to its head.

'I'm so sorry.' Max brushed the back of Jonson's shoulders, though they weren't at all dirty. 'It's totally harmless but quite wild about visitors.'

'It's quite all right.' Jonson adjusted his cuffs. 'Well,' he coughed, 'let's have a look at your digs then, shall we? Make sure the natives are treating you right.' He placed one small, square white hand behind Max's shoulder blades and gestured him back towards the village.

'My wife will be delighted to meet you,' Max said. 'She'll be so grateful for your help with our items, we've been waiting for months.'

Jonson had heard the new missionary had brought his wife with him, and had been expecting a chubby, dour-faced woman wearing a high-necked white shirt, clutching a Bible. This vaguely Victorian image, plus the caustic smell of carbolic soap from the inside of the few Christian houses in Cairo, formed Jonson's entire lexicon of reference for missionaries' wives.

He was startled, therefore, to spot outside the thatched house a young, brown-skinned woman with a thick plait over one shoulder. She was sitting astride a green stool, her skirt carelessly tucked between her legs as she shelled peas into a basket under her knees. In the dim light, her bent head, long hair and slim shins sent an odd wrench through him. But when she raised her head, he realized she was not beautiful after all. Her nose was too large for her face, and bumped in the middle, as if it had been broken at some point. Her eyes were spaced far apart from each other, and were a bit goggled-looking. Her mouth was wide, and her teeth were white, with a clear gap through the centre. As she stood and smiled, she wiped her face on her shirtsleeve in a singularly unladylike gesture.

'Good evening, gentlemen,' she said, in a hoarse, not-quite-American accent.

'Beatriz, this is the famous Mr Jonson, who has been so kind as to come all the way to welcome us,' Max said. He placed one proprietary hand on her waist, and motioned for her to shake Jonson's hand.

Bea took his hand in her own damp one, and smiled disinterestedly. Jonson found himself stuck for words, being unused to socializing with women.

'Ah, good evening. It's I. A. M.'

'Sorry?' Bea looked at Max, her eyes widening in panic, as if it were a greeting in the local tongue she did not yet know.

'I. A. M. Jonson,' he said, clearing his throat.

'Oh.' Bea looked as if she were fighting a small smile. 'Oh. You're Jonson. I see.' She glanced down into her basket of shelled peas, barely concealing a smirk.

'Poor Mr Jonson has already met your canine,' said Max, an edge of reproach in his voice.

Bea grimaced. 'I'm so sorry.' She looked at Max. 'I did try and tie her – soon as I saw a whiteman – um, Mr Jonson, but –' She gestured vaguely.

'Just keep it away from here, will you, huh?'

Bea nodded.

Max gave her an anticipatory smile, 'So, Mr Jonson has helped to bring our boxes ashore,' he said.

'Oh!' She clapped her hands. 'Bless you, Mr Jonson!' She dropped her chin on to her chest and made a soft gurgling sound in her throat that Jonson feared would be crying, or praying, or both.

'Yes, very welcome, madam,' he said, stepping back away from the porch, lest she try and embrace him. 'Shall we – uh?' Jonson tipped his head towards the bottom of the hill.

'Yes, please!' cried Beatriz.

Max chuckled. 'OK, after you.'

As they walked back down to the bottom of the hill, Abel Poulet chased his son away from the boxes, and with a brief nod, seized a trunk and carelessly hoisted it on to his shoulder and began walking it up to Mission House. Max and Jonson exchanged a glance. They each took one handle of a chipped oak chest that had been Max's grandfather's, and slowly inched it up the slope.

'Have you been married long?' said Jonson, between breaths.

'Almost two years,' said Max.

'And –' Jonson nearly restrained his curiosity, but his chest still bristled with pique from the close encounter with Bernard's accomplishments. He cleared his throat. 'And how did you meet your wife, if I may ask?'

'In Venezuela,' Max said.

'And was Mrs Hanlon also working on mission?'

'Not at that time –' Max licked his lips '– but I've been blessed to guide her as she learns from our opportunity here on Advent Island.'

It had taken Max two weeks to travel from Boston to Venezuela, but almost instantly, he felt the tepid misery of the last few years lifting off him like sheets of vapour from a gasoline bucket. It was hot, it was humid, and the food was awful. It was like being back in the Pacific. Max first stayed with a small chapter in a wooden house a couple of hours away from Caracas. It was overseen by Gustav Horetz, a large German in his late forties, with short blond hair that stood up on his head like the bristles on a toothbrush.

There were eleven people who lived permanently in the house, and they slept four to a room in bunk beds. Although Gustav and his wife, Penelope, were extremely welcoming, they were also bonkers. Gustav was prone to long lectures in the middle of mealtimes, during which he would stand up, tipping over his bowl of rice and beans to orate at length about how the prophecies of Ezekiel were coming true right before their eyes. He declared South America to be the New Jerusalem, and his small, strange band of companions to be akin to the Puritan founders of America, come to civilize the natives. Max decided it might be wise to spend rather less time in that house, and more time visiting the other minuscule chapters of Protestants near the capital.

It wasn't easy making his way around on his own, but it was

certainly preferable to the cramped quarters of the wooden cabin. Max had tried to learn some Spanish on the long trip south, but languages had never been his forte. He had to make do with a set of phrases dutifully copied into a notebook that expressed his intentions in a woefully old-fashioned and formal Spanish that made people on the street break out into gleeful hilarity whenever he opened his mouth.

While visiting a small Mission Hospital outside of Caracas, Max met a young woman. Her nose had been broken, and her face was still swollen and split in places like an overripe plum. She had been deposited outside the hospital three weeks previously, and had spent most of her time inside her narrow cell, refusing to talk, and staring blankly at the walls. Nurse Abilo, a middle-aged woman with a cauliflower-shaped birthmark on her neck, told him the girl had been in an accident with an automobile, and was now developmentally damaged. She would probably be sent to the asylum when she recovered. But while buying oranges from José Martido, the caretaker, Max was told the girl had been beaten by 'some bastard' somewhere in the city, and left on the doorway of the hospital.

José crossed himself apologetically. 'Sorry, Father, for using such language.'

Her name was Beatriz. Max sat with her sometimes on his visits to the clinic. She barely turned her head to look at him when he first came to sit with her. He couldn't do much more than read out Bible passages to her in English from a wicker chair in the corner of the room, while she pointedly ignored him. He tried to engage her in conversation, making inane small talk in his shaky Spanish. But after four visits, she had astonished him by addressing him in English. Her face was still healing, and had joined back together asymmetrically. Looking at it straight on was a bit peculiar, it seemed to wander in a squiggly line.

'Your Spanish,' she had said, in a low voice. 'It's too formal. You sound like a ridiculous old man.'

Max found himself speechless with equal parts of amusement and embarrassment. He was delighted to discover she understood English, even if she wasn't prepared to speak more than a few terse words at a time, unless she were rebuking him. No one at the hospital knew anything of her background. But Max was surprised to learn she even knew some words of German, thanks to the mottled heritage of an émigré housemaid. And Max was even more surprised to feel relieved when he realized she must have been well educated. A wealthy man's daughter. A girl who had probably owned ponies, and ridiculous little hats with feathers in them. God knows what blows life had dealt her to bring her to this place. Although he would never have admitted it, a part of his relief was also due to a new reassurance that no matter what had happened to her, she was too refined to have been a prostitute.

Three weeks into his trip, Max stepped into the small, dusty garden at the back of the hospital to light his pipe. He sat on the splintery bench and scratched at the back of his sunburnt neck. He turned his head to a soft brushing noise, to see Bea ineffectually sweeping eucalyptus leaves on the far side of the garden, near the corner wall. She was pushing the leaves in a circle, more than sweeping. After a couple of minutes, she stopped suddenly, as if listening to something, and looked intently into a glossy-leaved bush near the brick wall. She dropped the broom with a careless whack, and crouched into the pile of leaves. Shuffling clumsily into the bushes, she emerged a minute later holding a small, wriggling ginger kitten. Unaware of being watched, she smiled to herself, and rubbed her right hand over the top of its head and over the points of its ears. She put her fingertips in the soft fluff on its belly. The kitten leant backwards to grip at her wrist with the tip of its claws, and toppled over in an acrobatic backflip.

Despite himself, Max started laughing. Only now aware of his presence, Bea turned to the sound of the laughter, and smiled directly at him. She smiled completely, unapologetically, in a way that creased up the side of her scarred face. He forgot he shouldn't have been watching her. He felt an unfamiliar queasiness pass right through the lining of his stomach.

Max began to find excuses to visit her. To walk her around the garden, and goad her into practising her English. She never said much, but he found her sober and lovely. The vacant-eyed catatonia that had led Nurse Abilo to believe she was a lunatic cracked into sparks of temper, jokes, and a stoic innocence that, despite everything she had suffered, Max admired. He felt quite able to forgive her for all her previous sins, even her Catholic upbringing.

As time went on, and Max realized his visit was drawing to an end, he became increasingly worried about what might happen to Beatriz after he left. Would she be sent to some wretched asylum somewhere? It seemed the most likely fate for a woman with no skills, no money and, as far as he could tell, no family. Perhaps she could stay on at the hospital, and become a nurse, too? There were several ex-patients who volunteered their time at the clinic, in return for board on the east wing, and the soupy, unappetizing meals dosed out to the invalids. But Beatriz certainly appeared to have no aptitude for nursing. When enlisted to help in the clinic, she would prod the patient in question, wearing a blank expression on her face. She had little sympathy for others. She would become distracted halfway through a task, and walk away during the middle of a bandaging to pick absently at a loose thread in the sheets.

With surprise, Max realized the solution was rather

obvious. If she would have him, he would marry her. He could save her from all this. He could offer her a new life. After all, they both needed a healthy change of scene. A place where they could devote themselves to being useful in God's work, and repair themselves from the misery of the past few years. Neither of them had any family to object to their union. And so they were married, with little fanfare, by Gustav Horetz from the Empires of Christ, in the drawing room of his wooden cabin.

Not long after, Max set out with his new wife for the old world.

When the last of the trunks were dragged up the hill to Mission House, Jonson and Abel excused themselves to join Willie in the nakamal. Max and Bea rested their fingers on each box in turn, smiling at each other. Max caught Bea up from behind and swung her round as she squealed with happiness. In the trunks were the musty relics of their life, and they were lifted out carefully one by one.

Out came a box of black-beaded hatpins, and a grey wool housecoat which Bea held up to the candlelight only to find it punctured by moth holes. Bea sighed, deciding it would make a good bed for New Dog. She certainly didn't have much use for wool in the rainforest. She uncovered a small cellophane bag of barley-sugar candies, and a full sewing set with reams of coloured thread and a crochet hook. A tiny kit for repairing eyeglasses was wrapped in brown paper, although neither she nor Max wore glasses. She picked up a handful of Paper Mate pens, a box of rustproof brass safety pins, and a carton of Derwent colouring pencils. Bea slid open the cardboard box, and rolled them under her fingers. They were so impossibly new and uncorrupted. A few incongruous items she placed carefully back into the box. This included a pack of stockings, and magnolia-scented hand lotion. She looked at her hands. They were calloused and freckled on the back. Her fingernails were rimmed with red dirt and thin slivers of cuticles hung in shreds from her thumbs. She felt a tremulous unhappiness, a sort of squeamish culture shock. How had she thought these objects would be of use to her? She had been so stupid and naive.

In one of the crates was Bea's most treasured possession – a green Singer sewing machine. Bea hoisted it out on to the table and pressed at the pedal tentatively until it gave a little cough and a smart series of rotations. Bea's face hurt from smiling. What things she would create with her new machine! She looked around the room for inspiration. Perhaps curtains for the windows? Cushion covers for the stools? A new dress! Bea felt feverish with the urge to start one of these projects straight away, when she became aware of Max's voice from underneath the lid of a crate.

'My commentaries seem to have made the journey well.' He was fingering through a hardback book, and Bea knew he was making a deliberate attempt at understatement, as his face was pink with joy.

The next day, while Max was at church, Bea sat by the machine and stroked it like it was a beloved pet. She brought forth *101 Things*, and luxuriously turned through each page, relishing how many new beautiful projects were now within her reach. She would transform Mission House into a modern home; Max would be astounded at her skill. That afternoon, Bea walked the miles up to Aru's store, and bought a ream of plasticky pink fabric she recognized from the generous ruffles that bedecked many of the island dresses she had seen in church.

Over the next few weeks, Max noticed with initial amusement, then pride, and then some concern, as the pink fabric populated itself. At first, Bea produced a perceptibly asymmetrical tablecloth for Mission House, which, he had to admit, did rather cheer up the place. Then came a lampshade, which Max found perplexing, since there was only one hurricane lamp, and the last thing they needed was to 'shade' the paltry light that dribbled from it. A ruched bedskirt came next, which mostly served as a climbing aid for the cockroaches. Max rolled it carefully up into the frame of his bunk as an anchor for the mosquito net. Then came the plague of handkerchiefs.

Before the week was out, scores of people from all over the island were knocking at Mission House, asking for their own small scarves. They became something of a fashion hit, and were stuffed in pockets, worn on the front of clothes, tied to bushknives, and used for redistributing sweat around the face. Santra and Bea began a workshop on the Mission House table as Santra painstakingly embroidered villagers' names on to the handkerchiefs from Bea's alliterations on an old envelope. Max suggested Bea and Santra should charge for production, but Bea shrugged. 'It's goodwill, Max, you should know – you can't expect repayment for good Christian charity.'

9

The airstrip in the south of Advent Island was constructed during the last years of the war. Inspired by Ragrag Charley's airfield on Malekula, fifteen members of a local cargo cult had cleared a rectangular strip of rainforest parallel to the ocean. The project took over two months, and cost the lives of three men when a rotten tree fell on them. To curry favour with the gods, an even-sided wooden cross was planted by the coast, and was coloured with red dye. A small pandan hut was built at the top left of the strip for staging ritual incantations.

The project had been abandoned only six months after its construction, when, impressed by their entrepreneurial spirit, Garolf Sugarcraven offered to relocate the worshippers and their families to work on his Dadavoki plantation. A year later, the mock airstrip was repurposed as an actual airstrip, and put into use to bring in DA agents from Santo. Without the benefit of a small community to obsessively tend to it, the strip deteriorated into a shabby, pockmarked ribbon of grass. At the bottom of the runway there were 200 metres of thick bog left uncovered when the bush was cleared. The stinking mud greedily sucked at anyone who attempted to cross it, and after a rainy spell, it often swallowed Max up to the waist. The airstrip was unusable during the rainy season, when the endless days and weeks of monsoon turned the whole area into a gummy orange marsh.

During the dry season, on the last Friday of the month, an aeroplane from Port Vila made attempts to land on the island. The pilot would call ahead to the radio that lived on the site of the chief's hut, and Old Mobe, who now lived in the shack, would give a quick account of the mud, surrounded by snotty-nosed kids who assembled to see the monthly miracle of the plane arriving. On those Fridays, Max would set off at dawn for the five-hour walk to the strip, and wait all day for the tell-tale whirring sounds approaching from the west. No one was sure what time the plane was supposed to land, since even aviation seemed to operate on 'island time'– that frustrating consequence of life without clocks.

When Max and Bea had first arrived in Bambayot, even the schedule of the church services had been baffling. According to the laws of 'island time', worshippers turned up whenever they had decided it was 'morning' and therefore time for church. This entailed a steady trickle of people into the church between 6 a.m. and 2 p.m. Max started his services promptly at ten, which meant that for the rest of the day, doleful late-comers would be knocking on Mission House and peeping dejectedly through the window.

In fact, the only person in the village who could tell the time was Moses – Knox and Joyce Turu's eleven-year-old son. Five months before Max and Bea's arrival, two WHO workers had come to the island as part of a yaws eradication pro-gramme. Housed in Noia Saruru, their arrival had incited excitement all along the south coast. Chief Bule had called a meeting, and demanded volunteers to go down to Noia Sar-uru in kastom dress and dance around a bit, in the hopes of soliciting money which could be used to buy playing cards and cigarettes from Santo. Moses Turu was one of those 'volun-teered'. His poor lolling tongue and wayward eyes evidently moved one of the workers so much that they offered him his watch as a gift.

Moses was then granted the honour of custodianship over the Bambayot ching. The ching was a scraped-out, split tree trunk, carved at either end to represent bearded men. Max had no idea who had carved it – it was certainly far beyond Willie's capabilities. The ching lived in the centre of Bambayot village, and produced a loud, hollow booming sound when bashed with a wooden club. It became Moses' responsibility to work out what time the church singers should commence their practice, and run down to the ching to alert the other villagers. On the days when Moses was not in the village, practice slipped back into island time. After the first couple of misstarts, Max also enlisted Moses' support to announce the beginning of service.

Island time offered a lot of luxury for private contemplation. Nobody was ever in a rush. Nothing ever happened 'suddenly'. Meeting any villager, any boat, or any aeroplane, would inevitably require a lot of patient sitting around for a few hours either side of the appointed time. At first, Max carried books around with him in his island basket, ready to use the extra time productively. After a while, he rather got into the spirit of it, and began to do what everyone else did. Sit on the grass and stare off into nowhere.

Waiting for the aeroplane, though, was a special kind of excitement. His heart always leapt when he spotted its white body, a small tin can against the sky. It seemed anachronistic somehow, like a visit from the future. Max held his breath as the two-seater tentatively came in to land, glancing off the bumps in the grass and whining to a stop inches from the bog. On the days when the plane merely circled over the strip like a large gull, and headed back west again, Max felt a crochet hook of disappointment picking at the lining of his stomach. Standing at the strip with his shins coated in orange slime, another five-hour walk ahead of him, Max sometimes felt a horrible vertigo; that seen from the plane, he might be mistaken for a smudged and dirty villager, standing shoeless on a cult site, staring at the sky and praying. It was only post, he would say to himself. It would arrive eventually. If not this month, then next. After all, such inconveniences are part of the fun of living on the island, he would point out to himself.

All mail was handled through these flights, and in the grey months when no landing was possible, Max felt a deep longing, bordering on obsession, for the post. In the days before the landings, he would have brief, fevered dreams where he was holding a great bushel of letters in his hands, full of important information, and they would start to blow away with the wind, slipping one by one through his grasp. He tried his best to disguise his feelings in front of Bea. He knew it was a vain thing to worry over, and in the mornings before he walked to the airstrip, he made a point of mentioning the ten-hour round trips in the service of 'a bracing walk' or 'a chance to witness to the people'. But as Max trudged through foamy streams, between banyan trees, through swampy puddles, he rebuked himself for lying. It was obvious that Bea didn't care, either about the mail, or about his interest in the mail. And after all, who did she have to communicate with?

Any mail that did arrive was handed to him by the pilot, having been pre-sorted at Vila. Max then solemnly carried the bundle back to Bambayot tucked inside his shirt for safekeeping from unpredictable showers. Once back in the village, he locked himself inside the vestry. On the table, he set the mail out in a precise mosaic with a small, even margin around each one. Most of the letters were months old. All were soggy and rumpled, mournfully drooping, the ink dangerously close to seeping off the corners. Since his first parcel of post, Max had replied to necessary people, requesting they only address correspondence in ballpoint pen or in pencil, to make sure it would survive water damage.

Max filled his pipe with island tobacco, slowly shredding it into the bowl, enjoying the delayed gratification. When lit, he would start opening the mail with a bronze letter-opener Bea had bought for him the year before. The letter-opener did more harm than good to the distressed and sopping envelopes, but nevertheless, it was part of the fun. Normally, Max received two or three reports from the DA; requests for information or routine updates on the province. Included in this was usually a typed page with notes on news from the British Administration. He received polite postcards from women from his Boston church, promising care parcels – which never arrived on any plane, but would, he supposed, contain a handful of luxuries from home that frightened him to even imagine. He was also sent regular statements from his accountant on the remaining savings from the sale of Max's bar.

It had been named after his mother, Marybelle, who ran away from her mother's poky apartment in Providence at fifteen, cut off her hair, painted her eyes, and found her true calling dancing in a nightclub in central Boston. Max's father, also named Max, was the co-founder of Lucky Clover Ale, and before long, his parents' respective professions brought them together. Despite all the gloomy predictions from his mother's friends among the dancing girls, and the knowing eyebrows of his father's business associates, the two settled down to have an entirely conventional marriage, and a red-headed child. During Prohibition, his parents combined their talents to establish a small, but well-frequented speakeasy in the basement of an abandoned drugstore.

And so, Max grew up happily unchaperoned, inventing games under tables, keeping company with many shapely legs, abandoned cigar butts, shined shoes and overturned glasses of home-brewed Lucky Clover Ale. He entertained himself with a bizarre assortment of impromptu toys offered to him by bar clientele – glossy maracas, jewelled tie pins, collar stays. Max developed a detailed vocabulary of curse words, and the precocious pomposity of a child who has been treated as a tiny adult for his whole life.

At school, he wasn't much of a student, but he still managed an anodyne sort of popularity, aided by his embellished folklore about dancing girls. When he asked to go to Sunday School with a friend from his baseball team, his parents exchanged a glance, then helped him to comb his hair carefully each Sunday.

Max's parents regarded his growing interest in church as an eccentric character quirk. Marybelle would grimace in amused horror and toss her hands in the air. 'He's always been an old soul.' Max started staying late in church on Sundays, reading coloured storybooks about Noah's Ark to the toddler class. Then he spent Wednesday evenings at church as well, helping Pastor Robert to prepare mealy lamb stew for the homeless. When he begged to join the YMCA 'Juniors for the Lord' camp one summer vacation, Max Senior signed his permission slip with barely a word about his child's burgeoning holy conscience. Max returned from summer camp with poison ivy rash, an impressive spray of freckles, and a litany of robust songs about Jesus' enduring love.

His parents never went to church, although from time to time his mother turned up at a bake sale or fête looking incongruous among the pastel-coloured church ladies. Max would spot her instantly in the crowd, wearing a black velvet hat and scarlet lipstick, like a sleek tropical bird that had been accidentally released into the pigeon house at the zoo.

When Max graduated from high school, his parents were not at all surprised when he announced his decision to go into the Church, and his seminary fees were paid for with the profits from years of illegal moonshine. Max continued to live at home, and took the tram four times a week to central Boston, where he received lessons in Bible study.

Marybelle was killed in an automobile accident two weeks after Max's twenty-fifth birthday, and his home life was irrevocably shattered. After Marybelle's funeral, a tacit pact developed between Max and his father, and they never spoke of her. In the evenings, before he went to the bar, Max Senior read the sports pages in the hard-backed red armchair, while Max studied awkwardly on a small card table. And each evening as the house settled, with the gentle sounds of shifting wood floorboards and creaking door hinges, despite himself, Max would look up at each noise, fully expecting his mother to walk through from the other room. Then, catching the cocked, expectant expression on his father's face, they would both look down, pretending to read, cheeks burning at the inexpressible cruelty of their disappointment.

And so, Max became a missionary.

In 1946, after the war was over, Max received a telegram that his father was sick, and he returned to Boston to find impassable heaps of grimy snow piled against the front door. For the last four years of his father's life, Max nursed him with all the dedication of a son with an unseasonable suntan. He turned him to prevent bed sores, washed him twice a day with a sponge, and cleaned out his bedpan. Occasionally, he carried his father downstairs to sit upright in his red hard-backed chair with a blanket tucked around him. Max only left the house to buy groceries and attend church. He arranged Bible cell groups in the living room, serving hard shortbread cookies to his guests and checking on his father every half an hour. In his own childhood bedroom, Max cleared a space in among the tin soldiers of his boyhood, and tacked a simple map of the world. He looked at it before he went to sleep, wondering when he would next have the chance to follow God's missions abroad.

In 1952, after his father had passed, the bar was left to Max. He sold Marybelle's, and with more money in his pocket than he had ever owned, Max decided it was at last time to visit somewhere on his map. He had originally intended to go to Brazil, but changed his plans on a whim, when a now elderly Pastor Roberts put him in touch with an ex-cell member who was working for the Empires of Christ – a hardy, but quite mad group of American Protestants setting up missions in Venezuela.

Pastor Roberts was now a short-sighted, but still sprightly 92-year-old. Since they'd arrived in the New Hebrides, Max had even received a delayed Christmas card from him, dictated to his wife, slipped in with one of the newsletters from his old church in Boston. The newsletters contained spiritual readings, birth and death notices, and a featured hymn. Max cherished these newsletters and always saved opening them until the very last. He pored over them until his eyes stung from tobacco smoke, reading and rereading them until he knew each line by heart.

Their first mail packet had been disappointing. There was only one notice from the DA, and two letters to the former missionary addressed in pencil. Obviously, the last occupant of Mission House, 'Mrs Hardwood', had given the same instructions to her family or friends. They were back-dated from the previous year. He asked Aru if the last missionary had left any forwarding address, but Aru sniffed and shook his head. Max spent a couple of evenings idly wondering what he should do with them, before sending them back to her church – the address of which was stamped inside the Bibles in the church.

In June, yet another arrived. After the other letters had been consumed, with still no sign of promised parcels, Max, in a twitch of annoyance, swiftly tore open Mrs Hardwood's envelope, not bothering with the opener. He slid the letter out as far as 'Dear Marietta', and panicked, slipping the letter, unread, on to the fire that evening. Bea went to bed early, grumpily pecking him on his forehead and slipping away before he could get a hold of her waist and request a proper kiss goodnight. He propped himself awkwardly up in bed, and wrote a letter to her church, balanced on the back of *The Screwtape Letters*. He informed Mrs Hardwood that post was still arriving for her, and would she kindly notify her friends of her new address, as her clutter was still arriving on their doorstep.

Three weeks later, she turned up on their doorstep.

10

As fast as they could, Lien and Thieu made their way to Marietta. Nguyen had once told Thieu about a trail that led to the west coast. So, he reasoned, all they needed to do was cross the trail, and walk straight, tracing around the highest peaks until they reached the third large river. This would lead them down to Bambayot, where they would wait for the *Duchesse*. But these instructions were not easy to follow. The slopes were gushing with water from rainfall higher in the hills, and new streams simply appeared from one day to the next, so it was impossible to tell which ones were 'large' until they had seen enough to judge. And there was no such thing as 'walking straight' in the forest. They meandered in incremental gestures, corralled by impassable ledges, and then walked back on themselves for hours to pick up the route at another pass. They hiked through thickets of wet leaves, over craggy hillsides, and trudged through steamy, treacherous marshes of sodden earth. They were besieged by clouds of gnats and mosquitoes, and Lien bundled Minh in the net to protect him from the bugs, winding it over her back to carry him in a sling. To stay hidden from islanders, they had to travel only in tabu areas, dashing through open land at night. This quickly became another difficulty – deciphering where 'tabu' ended and the village paths began. They stuck to the densest, most awful parts of the jungle. Any time they came across a boar trap, or a line of trampled plants, or notches in the boughs from machetes, they retreated back into the unloved heart of the forest.

One morning, they broke through a rank of sturdy bamboo poles into a small clearing that was fluttering with hundreds of butterflies. Black and blue stripes flickered in the air as the butterflies nipped at the surface of a shallow rock pool. Lien and Thieu sat gratefully in the glade, and Lien unwound Minh from his chrysalis of mosquito netting to bathe him in the warm water. He bounced on his knees and clapped clumsily at the butterflies. The bamboo waved in the breeze, knocking together in hollow chimes. Lien took off her jeans, rinsing the rash on her thighs. Thieu leant over and kissed her on the chafed red flesh, and then washed his hair in the pool. They ate a handful of peanuts they had picked in the bush, and Lien recited Tan Da poems while Thieu drowsed, Minh chewing his own feet on the blanket.

In the early afternoon, three wild pigs snuffled in between the trees and slurped the pond water, then climbed over the rocks and urinated into the stream. Thieu pounced on the animals, but they scattered with a snort. He chased the largest for almost half a mile until it turned back and charged at him the other way, baring razor-sharp tusks. Thieu hid in the lower branches of a lime tree until it lost interest, and returned to the clearing, bruised and humiliated. They decided not to camp in the glade that evening, in case other, larger animals came to drink there at night.

They walked south of the clearing, and came to a curtain of oozing thorns crowned with purple orchids. They circled round, looking for a break in the thorns, and eventually wriggled through the cavity of a fallen tree trunk, passing Minh through between them. They looked out on to a narrow gorge carved into mossy rock. The bottom of the valley was a little muddy, but Thieu declared it a lucky find – no wild boars would be charging them in their sleep. Lien built a fire in the bottom of the crag, and they covered the aperture with a sheath of leaves to sluice off rain. Thieu hooked their hammocks between the rocks, and they slept in a ribbon of smoke from the embers to fend off mosquitoes.

In the middle of the night, Minh began shrieking. Six inches of foaming, murky water was lapping at their feet. A swarm of frogs had clambered into the groove while they were sleeping. There were hundreds of them, leaping and flashing in the moonlight like tiny green gemstones. Lien gripped Minh in panic, and he wailed even louder. She plucked a frog from the soft baby folds of his neck, whispering, 'I'm sorry,' over and over. Thieu ripped their hammocks down, and Lien clutched at their scant supplies with her one free hand. With a bubbling gurgle, the water rapidly surged up to their knees.

'Get out, get out,' Thieu shouted, and they scrambled for the bank as the water surged up, and up again, a metre in five minutes, and they clutched Minh and leapt over fallen logs and crashed through oozing thorns, as ice-cold water swirled around their shins. They walked slowly for an hour until the sun rose, then collapsed on a rocky outcrop at the base of a papaya tree and stared at each other in a daze.

'It's fine,' Lien said, 'it's good – we travelled so much ground. We'll be at Bambayot in two days, maybe even tomorrow.' She rocked Minh. 'It's good, it's fine.' She patted his back.

Thieu reached for her hand. 'You're OK?' She hadn't mentioned the measles even once while they'd been walking. Her face was swollen with mosquito bites, and she looked exhausted.

'Of course,' she said, frowning. 'I'm fine. Will you stop asking?'

Thieu didn't remember asking her. He gave her a weak smile. 'Nearly there,' he said.

Lien kissed Minh on the cheek. 'By this time next week, Marietta will wave us goodbye on the *Duchesse*,' she said. 'Will you wave back, Minh-Binh?' She picked up his hand and waved it for him. 'Say "*bonjour*, Port Vila"?' she crooned, in a singsong voice. Minh just squealed.

After the hottest part of the day, Thieu left Lien and Minh to nap, and followed a cackling echo to a huge banyan, where pot-bellied marmosets were scampering around the branches. He lurked at the base for two hours, and threw pebbles into the tree until he hit one of the creatures in the back of its head with his slingshot. Since they couldn't risk a fire until they were safely deep in the forest, he tied the carcass over his shoulder with his belt, and carried it on his back. Lien shuddered to see its limp head lolling horribly on Thieu's shoulder, and its skinny limbs trembling with his every movement. A nest of fleas evacuated the animal's fur and bounced around on the back of his neck. When they lit a fire that evening, Thieu stuck the whole body inside the flames and its fluff singed away in a sharp blaze. Lien looked away from the tiny, scorched hands of the marmoset, and refused to eat it. Thieu took the body discreetly out of her line of sight and hacked it into less recognizable pieces, tossing its hands and feet into the earth.

The next day, they rose early, and struggled through yet another close bracket of bamboo, and broke through into another dappled clearing, but this time, there were no butterflies. Lien grabbed Thieu's arm and pointed at a footprint baked into the clay by a shallow rock pool. He pushed her roughly behind the fringe of bamboo, and peered around them for the villager.

But Lien tapped him out of the way, squeezed her foot out of her sandal, pressed her own toes perfectly inside the print, and fell to her knees and wept.

They were lost.

II

Max was aware of Bea wriggling to the edge of the bed, and the pressure on the thin mattress lifting as she weaselled her way through the mosquito net. He stretched out his legs into the warm spot left by Bea's body, and fell straight back to sleep. It was only a little later, when he heard her returning footsteps on the gravel, that he realized Bea had left the house.

The front door opened, and the hurricane lamp twinkled through the other side of the thatch. Max rubbed his eyes, and clicked out his stiff shoulder. He shuffled over to make space for Bea in the bed. She opened the door to the room, carrying the lamp high under her chin. She had pulled a shawl over her nightdress, but her arms were bare. Above the elbows, they were coated in rings of dark brown mud.

'Maxis,' she hissed, approaching the bed.

'What on earth?' He sat higher up on the pillows, looking at the muck smeared over her dress. 'Please tell me you haven't been gardening,' he said.

Bea put the lamp on the ground, and pulled up his mosquito net. 'Max, you need to come with me, it's a woman.'

'What do you mean, a woman? Is someone ill?'

'Yes, no, yes. Please.' She looked over her shoulder. 'I don't know what to do.' She pulled the shawl around her chest, jiggling her arms up and down.

Max dressed quickly, as Bea hopped from one foot to the other.

'Should I fetch the supplies?' he asked, shaking a cockroach out of his sandal.

'I already took them,' she said. 'But, I don't know. I can't help.'

Bea left before he could get both his sandals on. She began crossing the hill down towards the ocean. Max grabbed the torch from the bushkitchen, and followed her. He switched it on, but the batteries were damp, and the light kept stuttering out.

'Bea, where are we going?' he called, louder than he had intended.

'Noia Saruru,' came her voice from lower down the hill.

Max slipped over a stone as he picked up his pace. 'Who is ill?'

'You don't know her,' Bea said abruptly, half turning her face towards him. 'You wouldn't know her. I don't know her. Santra's friend. Or cousin, or something.'

'Bea,' Max grabbed her elbow from behind so she had to stop and look at him. 'Bea, calm down. Tell me what's wrong, and we can talk about it on the way.'

Bea gulped. 'The baby is coming,' she said. 'But it's stuck. I don't know what to do.' Tears were running straight down her cheeks. She sniffed and wiped her face with her forearm. The lamplight swung drunkenly as its frame clattered against her elbow.

Max felt himself flinch. 'The woman is pregnant?'

Bea nodded.

'Ah, Beatriz,' he grimaced. 'In that case, I'm not sure I'll be able to help much.'

Bea sniffed. 'I know,' she said, nodding. 'I know, I know. But I don't know what to do, and I couldn't do nothing.'

'Sweetheart, don't worry. It probably looks worse than it is.' Max put his arm around her shoulder. She was shaking slightly. He pinned the torch under his arm and took the lamp from her.

They walked carefully towards Noia Saruru. As they approached the village, Max saw one of the houses was lit, and its bushkitchen was smoking.

They stopped by the doorway, and Max gestured Bea to go in ahead of him. She ducked under the low beam, and Max wavered by the threshold. The room was full of people. Even from the doorway, he could smell coppery blood. A woman was squatting in the right-hand corner of the room, braced either side by two other women. Despite her dark skin, Max could see her lips were grey, her eyelids pale. Her head was drooping to one side, and her face was covered in spit and mush. Another woman was sitting on the floor, with her hands between the woman's thighs, her forearms covered in blood. She was talking to the pregnant woman quietly in Language.

A man he didn't recognize was sitting cross-legged to the left, holding a small white bag, turning it over and over in his hands, humming. As Bea entered, a couple of women turned and noticed Max standing in the doorway. There was an exchange of voices. Max recognized Santra as she crossed the room. An older woman with short grey hair and wiry bristles on her chin came over, blocking the doorway with her tiny frame. She started saying something to him in Language.

'I don't understand,' he said in Bislama. A conversation was still going on in the back of the room.

Bea gently eased the older lady out of the way, nodding at her, as if she understood what she was saying. She looked over her shoulder at Santra, then back at Max. 'I guess you can't come in. No men, she says.'

'But *he* can?' Max pointed at the man on the floor. 'I'm the Pastor, did you tell them that?'

There was another exchange between Bea and Santra and the older woman. Santra came to the front of the door. 'He is very skilled in leaf magic,' she said.

'A leaf doctor? Oh, for heaven's sake.' Max wiped his hand over his face.

'Call the whitewoman,' Santra said, taking the lamp from Max's hand.

Max pointed into the hut at Bea, but Santra rolled her eyes. 'The old one,' she said.

'Marietta?' he asked.

Santra nodded.

About half an hour later, Max brought Marietta back to the hut. She coughed and panted and wheezed the whole way. The torch had completely died, and without any lamp to guide them, he had been forced to take her warm hand in his to guide her over slippery roots and pebbles. The grey-haired woman was squatting outside the hut now, ready to ward him away before he even drew close. She stood as soon as she saw them, and, turning one shoulder in his direction, held out her hand for Marietta. She started saying something, and Marietta answered her. They both looked into the hut. Max tried to catch a glimpse of Bea. Marietta went inside, directly to a bucket in the corner of the room, and began to wash her hands with a slab of soap. The grey-haired woman turned around in the doorway and fixed Max with a look. He sighed, and sat down in the wet grass. From outside the hut, he could hear a low moaning, mixed with the humming of the witch doctor. After maybe forty minutes, Marietta came back to the doorway.

'Go home, Max,' she said, wiping her hands on a pink handkerchief.

'Absolutely not.' Max stood up.

Marietta sighed. 'Look, honey, it's not going to do any good you being here. Go light a candle in the church, and pray. You can't help us.'

'Perhaps not, but I can wait for my wife.' Max crossed his arms.

'I'll bring her back to you, I promise.' Marietta gave him a faint smile.

★

Max woke up in the vestry. The sun had risen, and a cockerel was scratching in the dirt outside the window. The candle had burned out. Max walked up to Mission House to clean up, but when he opened the door, he saw Bea boiling water in the kitchen.

'Is that for the baby?' he said, pausing in the doorway. Didn't they always need boiling water for babies?

Bea gave him a look he couldn't decipher. She turned back to the pot. 'No,' she said. There was a bowl of rice on the side, and beside it was a small pile of rat droppings. 'It died. They both did,' she said.

'Oh, Bea.' Max walked to her, and embraced her from behind. She leant her head back into him and closed her eyes.

'I'm sorry,' he said.

Bea nodded silently.

'Why don't you go and get some sleep. I can do this.' He breathed into her hair, pressing his cheek against her forehead.

'It's fine.' Bea slipped from his grip, and recommenced picking through the bowl of rice.

Marietta came back to Mission House around noon. Her tunic was dark brown with mud, or blood. She sat on her stool with a sigh, sliding her feet out of her sandals and putting them up on the tablecloth.

'How was it?' Max whispered, not wanting to wake Bea. He wasn't sure what 'it' was, but there was bound to be something gruesome.

'It's done,' Marietta said. 'The funeral was just starting as I left.'

'What, now?' Max stood up. He looked towards his room, regretting he would have to wake Bea.

'Oh, sit down, Max,' Marietta said, blowing the hair off her face.

He did not sit down. 'Shouldn't we be there? Who is doing the service?'

Marietta chuckled. 'They're not Christian, Max. There is no service.'

Max sat down.

'They're burning the body. The bodies. There'll be something with the bones up top, once the fire has died down.' Marietta stretched her arms upwards and pointed her breasts towards him.

Max suddenly felt exhausted. 'What happened?' he asked.

'Oh, the child was stuck sideways in the birth canal. We couldn't turn it around.' She mimed a twisting motion with her hands. Max looked away.

'Masineruk lost too much blood, so, that was that. It's not as if there's anything we can do for blood loss,' she said.

'I suppose not.' Max watched Marietta as she inspected the grime streaked across her smock. 'How is Santra?' he asked.

'Santra?' Marietta wrinkled her brow.

'The young girl with the tattoo.' Max made the sign of a cross over his forehead.

'Oh, she's quite all right.'

'She's not upset?' Max asked.

Marietta scratched at a bite on her ankle. A tiny fragment of scab dropped to the floor. 'Everyone cried for an hour. But she's not unwell or anything.'

'But wasn't Matambe –'

'– Masineruk –' Marietta corrected.

'Yes, well – wasn't it her cousin, the woman who died?'

'Ah,' Marietta nodded her head, inspecting the open sore on her bite, 'yes. But she said she has plenty of other cousins.'

'Good grief.' Max rubbed his forehead.

*

The next day erupted with such fierce heat that the under-brush was quivering. When the morning service had finished, Max and Marietta stood outside the church, receiving their usual line of feeble handshakes and averted eyes. He had left Bea to sleep late, but when they went back to Mission House for lunch, she was nowhere to be seen. Max thought she might have gone to the waterfall at Noia Saruru to cool off. After a handful of peanuts and three warm slices of papaya, Max tried to convince Marietta to walk up to Masineruk's village to pay their respects.

'No one walks at this time of the day, Max.' She picked up Bea's little wooden fan from the table and began fanning herself.

'I don't know where it is,' he said. 'Please?'

Marietta sighed. But still, she put on her hat, and they started walking. It took around two hours to reach the village. It was a steady climb uphill, made even slower because Mari-etta's feet were swollen from the heat. Max's fingers were plump and tender, and he had to curl and uncurl them every few minutes, holding his hands upright to drain the blood. The path wound through fringes of manioc between allot-ments, and in and out of tiny villages. The mud was so dry that, as they walked, they kicked up red dust that settled on their clothes. Half a kilometre from the village, the sound of crying could be heard.

'Is somebody else ill?' Max asked, rubbing dust out of his left eye.

'Really, Max,' Marietta raised her eyebrows, 'you haven't been to any local funerals?'

'I absolutely have,' he said.

Marietta wiped her face with her pink handkerchief. 'You clearly haven't, if you can't tell the difference between illness and grieving.'

Max thought back to the first night he had heard the dark prayer in the church. How he had thought then someone had taken ill. He didn't say anything.

As they approached Natsulele, Max saw a small crowd gathered by the fallen log in the centre of the village. They had linked arms, and were wailing softly in unison. It almost sounded like a song. Chief Bule was standing on the far side of the log in the shade of a lime tree, wearing a red kastom mat tied around his waist, instead of his trademark pink blouse. Aru stood further back in the shade behind Bule. He was rocking someone's baby gently back and forth in his arms. In his navy serge trousers and collared shirt, Aru looked distinctly out of place, like an accountant at a rodeo.

Marietta began talking to a young boy who ran from one of the huts to greet her. He pointed to a large earthenware pot in the centre of the clearing in which, Max assumed, were the ashes of the deceased. Max wiped a sticky red paste of sweat and dust from the back of his neck, and went to join Aru in the shade. He skirted the nasara by a wide margin – one never knew about tabus. As he passed by, he discreetly peered into the pot sitting in the centre, and was horrified to see two skulls sitting in a pile of coal and black wood. The bones were a waxy yellow colour, with fragments of dark tissue stuck all over in patches.

Max climbed over the log, and shook Chief Bule's hand.

'Now we have all the whitemen together,' said Bule, grinning.

Max smiled. He took a long slug of warm water from his canister, resisting the urge to splash it all over his face. He nodded at Aru.

'Good afternoon, Pastor,' Aru said.

'Who is your friend?' Max asked, smiling at the sleeping baby.

'This is Abel. But he is a child, not my friend,' Aru said.

Max suddenly felt tired. 'Yes, fine,' he said, lifting his hat off.

'Mrs Anlon,' Aru said, 'she has become much better at making simboro.'

Max nodded vacantly.

'It is a shame, though, Santra Matan is the one to teach her.' Aru gestured towards one of the huts, and Max followed the direction of Aru's nod. And there was Bea, squatting in the doorway of a hut at the back of the village.

Max immediately approached her. 'Beatriz?'

She looked up, and gave a small wave. Max felt uneasy – he hadn't even noticed her. Her skin was so tan now, she barely stood out in a crowd.

She stood. 'Hello,' she said.

'Hello?' Max repeated weakly. 'What are you doing here?'

'This is Santra's hut,' Bea said, picking her sandals up from the ground. 'Look –' she pointed into one of the trees, where a half-dressed man was knocking fruit out of the branches with a bushknife. 'There's Charles,' she said.

'Hello, Pastor,' came a voice from the tree.

Max muttered something polite towards the tree. Was she casually hallooing him from across the charred skeleton of a baby? 'How long have you been here?' he asked quietly.

'Not sure,' she said. 'I came up to help Santra make simboro. Also, they have to cook this sort of stew, or potion or something. It smells awful –' She wrinkled her nose.

'You couldn't have mentioned this?'

Bea's eyes widened. She put her hand on his arm. 'Oh, I'm sorry. I thought you would have church duties today.'

'This *is* a church duty, Beatriz,' he said.

When the wailers had tired of crying, the men started to walk to the nakamal in Rangiran, an hour north. The women were congregating in Santra's bushkitchen, to stir the soup which was to be sprinkled over the place of her cousin's death. Santra would walk Bea back to Bambayot before conducting any vodou, so Max reluctantly left Bea to her potion-making. He began the walk back down to the coast with Marietta and Aru.

'Is that normal? With the skulls?' Max asked.

Marietta thought for a moment. 'No, not really. It's probably to ward off bad luck. Although for a revenge killing, the person is buried sitting up with their skull sticking out of the ground. Now I think of it, when I lived in New Guinea, often Bubu funerals —'

'But we can help,' Max interrupted. He was not in the mood for a lecture on Bubu rituals.

Marietta looked at him. 'Help with what?'

'With this situation. This is awful.'

'In what sense?'

'These circumstances.' Max's chest was fluttery. 'Is there even a midwife on the island?'

'Well, yes,' said Marietta. 'There's Naumu, in the North. And Chief Liki had two midwives.'

'But here. Here where we need them.'

'I don't know,' Marietta said. 'Filip, what do you say?' She raised her voice to Aru.

'No, Pastor,' he said quietly.

'Well, we should. There should be someone. A girl, with an aptitude for nursing. We can send her to Vila, for training.'

Marietta and Aru were silent.

'I could write to Jonson. Get him to contact the DA, send us some medical assistance.'

Marietta gave a short laugh. 'That man? He's nothing more than a colonial hangover, Max. Decorative at best.'

'Well, then I can write to the LMS. They might be willing

142

to provide the funding. How much do you think it would cost? With lodging, and food?'

Aru looked down at his sandals.

'I don't know, Max,' said Marietta.

'Maybe not even board, she could be hosted by one of the representatives. A living stipend, then.'

Marietta said something to Aru in Language. He replied, smiling and showing his little white teeth.

'Excuse me?' Max said.

'Oh, nothing.' Marietta flapped her hand. She cleared her throat. 'Look, Max, that's sweet. But it would never work,' she said.

'Whyever not?' Max stopped in his tracks. 'How often must this happen? It's lunacy not to be prepared.'

'There are kastom ways,' said Aru.

Max looked at him in astonishment. Of all the people in the village, surely he would know best the cost they were paying. 'With all respect, Mr Aru,' Max said, 'the kastom ways do not appear to be working.'

'Nobody would want to be trained,' Marietta said. 'No girl's family would allow them. She'd be shunned.'

'Not a girl, then –' Max pressed on '– a woman. A widow.'

Marietta scoffed, 'Even worse!'

'Pastor,' Aru said, after a moment of silence, 'for these matters, the new religion cannot help us. We have kastom. Any other way – it is tabu.'

'That's right,' Marietta said. 'Tabu.'

12

A storm blew in from the east. Lumpy purple clouds curdled in the atmosphere, and water poured from the sky, churning the soil into a grainy orange slurry. It was impossible to leave Mission House. Max, Marietta and Bea were stuck indoors looking out on to white steamy mist crawling the hollows in the hills. Even inside the house, it was damp and chilly. The wood was too wet to catch properly, and the fire sputtered thin grey smoke back into the building. The moisture in their clothes and hair merely leached vapour into the atmosphere so the house smelt like musty fabric and spent matches.

Marietta had caught a cold. She was keeping to her bedroom, but her hoarse tuneless droning was still audible through the walls, now complemented by zealous bouts of coughing and sniffing.

Bea sat on Marietta's stool, and watched the rain pummelling the soft earth in the garden. She was worrying about her vegetables. It had never rained quite so emphatically before. Bea imagined the roots might come loose, and start slithering down the hill and into the ocean. She longed for a hot bath. Her feet were cold.

Max and Marietta had intended to go on a walkabout to Kalu-kalu. It was apparently an arduous, week-long hike up into the hills, and they had planned their route carefully for days. But the village was high up in Central, round woozy hairpin turns over sharp drops. It was an impossibly dangerous voyage in the rain, so they were stuck in Bambayot until it cleared. Bea wasn't especially sad they couldn't go. Let them both feel what it was like to be trapped in the village for days on end. It would be nice, she thought, to spend some time with Max. It might be like it was when the two of them were starting out together, their early days of nervous camaraderie as a newly-wed couple, riding the tram into Boston arm in arm, playing backgammon after supper. But since the rain had started, Max seemed so dejected she couldn't gain much pleasure from having him around the house. He was glum and listless, and was barely speaking.

They had packed one deck of cards in their crates from Boston, but by now it had become distinctively worn from use. Max could identify most of the cards even from their patterned backs – how the ace of diamonds had a smudge-print of mud, how the jack of hearts was ripped in one corner, and the bend in the centre of all the queens from when he offered them to Lorianne to play with. They had spent two hours on the first day of rain playing rounds of Whist, keeping score on the back of an old envelope. But he had this awful feeling he was cheating, when he could more or less already tell what Bea and Marietta held in their hands.

Max was half slumped over the table. He had set the green mug in front of him, and was dolefully flicking playing cards one by one, trying to land them inside the rim of the cup. Bea was staring out of the window and twirling a piece of hair at the end of her plait, over and over, in her fingers.

The fire took a long time to catch, and dinner on the first night was barely-cooked rice, and wet, raw hedge. They ate it round the table in silence, punctuated only by Marietta's sniffs, and the ineffectual dabbing she made at her face with her pink handkerchief.

More rain rained. First one, then two, then three days. On the third day, there was a break in the weather. Marietta declared it the appropriate time to do her washing, and sat on the front porch with the bucket, scrubbing, singing and sniffing. Bea fled into the garden to inspect her crops. It wasn't as bad as she had expected. Several of her kindling fences had been knocked down, but there were no apparent victims of the flood. She lopped off the head of two cabbages and cut down a struggling snake bean.

Max announced he had to rescue some books and tobacco from his desk in the church, and trampled quickly through the squelchy grass down the hill. Alone at last, he stretched out his arms and breathed deeply. Only a few minutes later it began to rain again.

Marietta had barely fished her washing out of the bucket before the rain started. She had hung blouses, brassieres and underwear throughout the living room on a string tacked to a piece of wood inside the front door. Bea gave Max a murderous look when he entered. She made a great pantomime of stepping underneath the clothes, and over the fresh puddles they were making on the floor.

'I'm going out,' Bea said, meeting his eyes in what she hoped was a deliberate manner.

Max brushed the water drops from his hair, standing aside as she passed. 'Bea –' he started.

'I feel sorry for New Dog,' she said over one shoulder, pushing the door open so a shower of drops scattered across the stoop.

'You're not bringing it in here, are you?' Max asked. The only thing Max could imagine that could possibly add to their misery would be bringing the stinking, whinnying dog in there as well.

The door slammed behind Bea. 'No,' she called as she walked into the rain.

Max watched her disappear into the drizzle. Maybe he

should have offered to help? He could go after her, but it might look like he was avoiding Marietta. Instead, he retrieved the tobacco from inside his shirt, pulled his stool over to the wall, and began to pack his pipe.

Marietta cleared her throat, sniffed, and started to read out loud from the Bible.

How he wished he could tell her that he didn't want to hear anything from the Bible. He merely wanted to sit in silence, and smoke. Maybe drink a hot cup of coffee. If only he could lie down in bed, with coffee, listening to the wireless. They had brought a transistor radio with them, but the island was too far out to catch any frequencies. Soon after they first arrived, he had enlisted Lorianne to climb up into a tree with the radio, to see if they could find any signal up there. But it still hadn't worked. Secretly, he thought Lorianne might have meddled with the dials. It was not like she had ever seen a radio before.

When Bea returned later, sopping wet, Marietta was sitting at the table alone, reading the Bible out loud to herself.

'Who are you talking to? Is Max still here?' Bea wrung water from the bottom of her plait.

'Yes, dear, he had a headache, so he went to lay down. We don't want him to catch my cold now.' She held her handkerchief in the air, as evidence of her suffering.

Bea raised her eyebrows. No doubt the source of his headache was obvious.

'Did you find the dog?' Marietta asked.

'Yes, I found her. I wanted to make her a shelter. From the rain.'

'That's kind of you. It's not common for animals to survive long round here. Most of the time they end up being supper.'

Bea wasn't listening, she had noticed an empty tin of Spam lying next to Marietta's Bible.

'Oh, you don't mind, do you?' Marietta said, following Bea's eyes. 'Meat is good fortification for the health.'

Bea shook her head, swallowing hard to disperse the ridiculous ache of grief in her throat.

The next day, the rain was still raining. Max tried to stay in bed for as long as possible. He felt like if he even had to hear so much as Marietta's breathing, he might lose his temper. It was quite peaceful, lying in bed late into the morning. The sky was dark, and it was gloomy inside his bedroom. Bea had left hours ago, to do goodness knows what – more animal rescue missions, he supposed. When his stomach twinged with hunger, he held his breath deliberately to see if he could hear Marietta in the house. But there was no Bible reading, and no coughing. He decided to risk it.

Max crept out into the living room, to find Bea sitting on his stool. She was grating plantain into a bowl between her legs. The 'grater' was a dangerously sharp piece of equipment, one of Willie's inventions. After Max had explained what a grater was, Willie had cut open a tin can with an axe then, using a hammer and a nail, punched through the can, so sharp shards stood up along one side of the tin.

Bea looked up at him. 'Good morning,' she said, continuing to grate.

Max shushed her. 'Is *she* here?' he asked.

Bea nodded, gesturing her eyebrows towards Marietta's room. Max crept past Bea into the kitchen on exaggerated tip-toes, and Bea couldn't help but laugh. Max sat at the table while Bea grated, and looked out at the rain. He sipped from his mug of tepid rainwater, and crunched on another dry cracker. The wood was so wet he couldn't face even trying to light the fire.

'Fresh milk,' Max said, still staring out of the window. There was a quiet pause, as Bea looked at the blank expression on his face. Max could see it clearly, a small blue pitcher of milk, with a thin coating of cream on the top. He would pour it over cereal, and the skin would lift as the milk poured.

After a pause, Bea said, 'Cocoa.' She continued to grate. Bitter, hot cocoa. There were cocoa pods on the island. She had seen some on top, near the big, six-pronged waterfall. But it had to be ground, and roasted. Or was it roasted first? Bea caught the corner of her nail on the grater and quickly sucked at her thumb. Santra might know, she thought.

'Omelette, with ham,' Max continued.

'And okra,' Bea added, examining her thumb carefully. She heard him laugh.

'OK,' he conceded, 'with okra.'

Bea wondered, could she grow okra on the island? Maybe it already grew somewhere in the forest, but it was called by an island name. She could draw Santra a picture. Bea tried to remember where she had left her coloured pencils.

'Steak, with French fries. And tomato ketchup.' Max was in a sort of daydream. 'A hamburger, with cheese. Milkshakes. Malted milkshakes.'

Bea felt weak. She didn't have the heart to continue. Something small was breaking inside her. 'Oh, Max, please stop. It's too awful,' she said.

But Max was barely in the room. The half-eaten cracker in his hand sprinkled crumbs on to the tablecloth. 'Coleslaw. Walnut cookies. And devilled eggs. Bacon, with biscuits,' he said.

Bea wrapped her arms around her stomach. There was an unidentifiable pain pulsing there.

'Fresh orange juice. Meatloaf with mashed potatoes. Liquorice drops,' he continued.

Bea didn't know what liquorice drops were, but they sounded impossibly refined.

And then Marietta was standing in the doorway, shaking her head. 'I don't know what you two are talking about,' she said loudly.

Max turned to her. He had almost forgotten where he was. He could virtually taste the hot meatloaf. Hot meatloaf and cold orange juice. His stomach was throbbing. He put the half-eaten cracker down on to the pink tablecloth.

'All that junk is no good for you,' Marietta continued. 'Junk. That's what it is. Spiritual junk.'

Bea stood up from the stool, and carried the bowl of grated plantain into the kitchen, without looking at Marietta. Max felt his eyelid trill. He placed his fourth finger on the tic to see if he could slow it.

'The Lord should have washed all that nonsense off you by now. Honestly, Max, I'm surprised at you,' Marietta continued, blowing her nose on her handkerchief.

Max looked at Marietta without really seeing her. He felt a little sick. Why was she still here? In their house. What was she still doing here? Who was she to judge the importance to the Lord of Max eating damned rice and hedge for the rest of his life? The first thing, the very first thing he would do when he left this place, would be to eat a meal of meatloaf and mashed potatoes. With ice-cold orange juice.

13

Max and Marietta walked from Kalawoki in the dark. They
had spent a long afternoon talking to the chief there, and witnessing in a muddy clearing at the centre of the village.
Marietta gave a brief sermon, and a small crowd of about seven
villagers had gathered to hear her speak. No one had chosen to
come forward to accept the Lord, but Max was certain some
seeds were sown. The next time they came to Kalawoki, there
would undoubtedly be more questions, more curious parties.
The next village on their itinerary was high in the mountains
of Central. Max had never been there, but Marietta claimed to
know the route. After a quick meal of boiled taro in the nakamal, they had set off again. Marietta had insisted the village
they were heading to, Kalu-kalu, was a long, difficult hike, so
it would be best to spend the night at the nakamal in Salabot,
then continue on climbing uphill to Kalu-kalu at daybreak.

Max saw the sense in this, but he hated walking through
the bush at night. It was hard-going with only the light of the
moon as a guide. And the darkness played tricks on the mind.
Sounds that were commonplace during the day became agitat-
ing at night. A low growl circled in the trees as a howler
monkey defended its territory. Unplaceable suckling and snuf-
fling noises whimpered in the undergrowth. The limbs of
trees creaked and cracked and shifted, even though there was
no wind to speak of, and the soil bustled with stirring insects.
No one on the island walked at night. Admittedly, this was
more to do with superstitions about dwarves and vampires in
the forest. Still, it made his hackles rise.

The path to Salabot nakamal was narrow, and they were forced to walk uphill in single file. Leaving Kalawoki as the light dropped, Marietta had pushed straight in front of him. For the past two hours, he had followed her slow pace doggedly as she paused to huff and cough. He stared at her back through the dim moonlight, seething. It was so like her, to assume the front position. Without even asking him. Now he was forced to look at her bulk while they hiked. He couldn't even enjoy a few moments of his time without having her in the way. He was convinced she manoeuvred in front of him deliberately, so she could enjoy the unencumbered view.

At the first clearing in the path, Max picked up his pace to stride in front of Marietta. He was only doing it out of spite. Truthfully, walking first in the bush was miserable work. The trail leader was the one to put their foot down on a loose stone, or to step into a track of soft, knee-deep mud. It was often impossible to see where the path wound. The person in front was the one to walk straight through spiderwebs, with the inevitable ensuing moment of panic to locate the resident of the web as it tried to flee inside a collar. Marietta hummed atonally as she walked. Somehow, this was even more infuriating while she was behind him, like a bee just within his peripheral vision.

At one point, Max saw a huge creature creeping out on to the path in front of them. It was hard to make out through the darkness, but its long legs were moving sideways, one after another. It was crawling slowly, probing its way along with tentatively raised legs. It was a spider. A colossal spider, perhaps two metres across, with the body the size of a dog. Its joints made a smart clicking sound as it skittered across the path. Revulsion flooded through him, his chest grew tight. He couldn't move. It was as if he had stepped directly into a nightmare.

'What's the problem?' Marietta said, stopping short behind him.

Max snapped out of his hysteria. Of course it wasn't a spider. It was a coconut crab. He and Marietta watched as the enormous beast crept across into the bushes on the other side of the path. What had he been thinking? He rebuked himself as they continued their journey. Whatever creature he had imagined seeing didn't even exist. But, he caught himself thinking, if it were to exist anywhere, it would probably be here – in some unexplored corner of jungle.

They slept in Salabot nakamal up in Central, Marietta on one bench, Max on the other. He fell asleep almost immediately, although the bench was narrow, and barely accommodated the whole of his back. In the night, he woke with the distinct sensation that someone else had entered the hut. It was as if the room had suddenly grown a fraction of a degree warmer. A few moments later, he heard the rustling of a rat, before the animal scrambled over his shins.

These bush rats were not like the chubby little things from the tramway in Boston. They were foot-long, flea-infested monstrosities. There were several families of rats living in Mission House. He could hear them on the roof most nights, and they made the most colossal racket, scampering from one end to the other. It sounded distinctly as if they were rolling a large ball between them. They sauntered through his room at night to source materials for their nest. It was a couple of months before Max realized that the large grey rat he had named 'Monster' had developed a particular penchant for his underpants. He had come across it one night in the process of dragging a pair back into its nest under the pandan screen by the shower. Max stabbed his bushknife into the underwear with a yowl of annoyance, and the rat had held on to it with its teeth, tugging in the opposite direction, like a dog playing Tug of War. Disgusted, he had released his knife and resigned himself to losing yet another pair. The rats chewed on everything. They seemed to have developed a particular taste for anything white – candle wax, paper, and even their precious supply of penicillin. Max had taken to hanging his penicillin tablets in a burlap sack nailed to the rafters of his bedroom. One evening, coming back to his room after dark, he had seen an acrobatic little s.o.b. leaping from his bedside table on to the bag to get at the pills, making it swing pendulously from side to side.

When Max felt the spiny toes of the beast in the flesh of his shins, he yelped out loud. The cool weight of its tail slithered over his trousers as it scuttled to the floor.

Marietta sat up on the bench. 'Max? What is it?'

'A rat!' he shouted, leaping to his feet. 'It crawled right over me.'

Marietta lay back down, sighing in exasperation. 'Golly, Max, it's only a rat. Leave it alone.'

'I'm damned if I'll leave it alone. The thing will have my face off while I'm sleeping!' He rocked the bench from side to side to try to scare the animal out of the corner of the room. Its tail flickered under the bench. Marietta groaned, and sat up on her elbows. She stood, grabbed Max's bushknife from his hands, and turned towards the scuffling noise.

'For goodness' sake, Max, I'll get it. Stop your fussing.' She pushed past him to face the corner, and as she passed him she gave him a little shove in the process.

He was overcome with the sudden urge to hit her. The side of his shoulder where she had pushed him felt as if it were burning. He jammed his knuckles into his forearm to distract himself from the rage. He wanted to shove her right over. To knock her face against the edge of the bench. For that rat to climb all over her. His whole body was rigid. If she so much as touched him again, he might slap her. He had to get out of that room. He walked straight through the door and out into the moonlight.

As soon as he was out of the nakamal, he wanted to shout and break something. He kicked at the stump of a tree lying in the grass and it crunched softly, a flurry of translucent mites seeping out of the hole. He shook off the insects in irritation and cursed. He started to walk blindly on the path, just to be moving away from Marietta. He walked down the path for nearly an hour. The sun began to rise. He realized he was tired now, and headachy. He was embarrassed about his behaviour. Storming off like a child having a tantrum. It was absurd. Imagine if someone had seen him. It was the sort of behaviour he most deplored in Bea, and yet here he was, out in the bush without his machete, without any food or water, because Marietta was annoying. It was ridiculous. He would have to walk back and raise Marietta. With some breakfast in him, and a cup of hot tea, he would feel better.

When he walked back to the hut two hours later, he heard Marietta's snoring from outside the building. The rat was laid by the front door. It had been killed by a blade across its head, and its mouth was open, its two front teeth exposed. Max shuddered. It looked so human, lying there with the tiny tip of its tongue lolling out of the corner of its mouth. A nest of brown ants was swarming over its stomach. He shouldn't have made such a fuss. It was only a rat, being a rat. It wasn't doing him any harm. Now it was dead.

He sat down in the grass in front of the nakamal and put his head in his hands. The island was doing things to him. He was supposed to be here to set an example. He was supposed to be the level-headed one, not a little girl flapping about mice in the middle of the night. It was shameful. He was ashamed of himself. Marietta made him ashamed of himself.

*

In the morning they walked for hours without talking. There was no food at Salabot, and Marietta insisted they would arrive at Kalu-kalu before sundown, so they may as well push forward. Max had a headache from tensing his shoulders, and his calves were tight from jolting downhill during his night-time outburst. The day was heavy with humidity, and billows of condensation rippled through the grass. The closeness of the air made it difficult to breathe. Sweat dripped down his body, crawling between his thighs, gathering in the hair on his chest, soaking his shirt to his back. He longed to take it off and walk shirtless, as the villagers did. Distracted by his misery, he trampled through a thigh-high patch of Devil's nettle, realizing his error only when the skin at the back of his knees began to burn and blister.

They climbed higher and higher, winding up alongside a steep drop on to a sort of municipal garbage pit. Max looked over the edge of the path at the heaps of rubbish. The rusted frame of a truck stuck out from piles of garish plastic trinkets that must once have washed up onshore. The trash was mingled with rotting vegetables, dying grass, nangalat cleared from the bush, mouldering creeper vines. Clouds of flies thrummed over the waste, and banana palms grew here and there from the refuse. With so little wind, the wretched stink of decay from the dumping ground squatted over them. As they climbed, Max could hear the distinct hush as a sheet of rain from the hills crept closer to them. And it started to rain. Slowly at first, then dark grey clouds rolled across the sky like marbles and split open. Water fell in one continuous flow. He could only see rain in front of him. He could only hear rain in his ears. Within seconds Max's clothes were stuck to his body. He could barely move one leg in front of the other, the fabric was stuck between his thighs where it chafed and clawed with every step. He looked ahead for Marietta, but she was gone. He couldn't even see her.

He was suddenly filled with a bolt of rage. He was always waiting for her. But she never waited, she never, ever waited for him. How was he meant to know where he was going? What was he supposed to do – sit and wait for her to realize she had left him behind, like a child in a department store? Well, that's what he would do. Damn her. He would sit here like a child and wait for her to realize. She'd have to puff all the way back to get him. Maybe she would learn to wait. For once in her blasted life.

He sat down in the sopping grass. It made no difference, he couldn't have been more drenched with water. He crossed his legs, and scratched at the rash spreading across the back of his knees.

He heard her calling for him from somewhere. Typical. She was too lazy to even walk back for him. But somehow, the noise was coming from below – how was she below? And then Max realized. She wasn't up ahead of him. She had fallen.

He called out for her, but the rain muffled his voice. Like when it snows, he thought aimlessly, it's quieter somehow. It soaks up all the sound. He edged along the path where she had last been.

Through a thick fringe of manioc leaves he saw Marietta two metres beneath the path. She was balancing on a slimy, dripping mud ledge over the garbage pit. Her elbows were hooked over exposed root nodules, she was grasping at the slope with her hands, tearing clods of mud, wet leaves. One foot was wedged into a shallow divot in the slope, the other was dangling over the edge of the garbage pit.

'Oh!' she yelled.

Max looked down at her foot. It looked so small against the drop. His hands began to shake. He thought he might be sick. He tried to move towards her, but he couldn't. Somehow he couldn't move. She's going to fall, he thought. But it was as if the words were typed as a subtitle, he saw them visualized as letters at the bottom of his vision.

'Help, damn it,' Marietta was saying.

Max stared at the back of her hair turning dark with wet mud.

'Max,' she yelled.

Max's arms were trembling.

She stepped backwards on to the crumbling ledge. With each tread, more earth tumbled below. She twisted her belly, her neck craning. The roots began to splinter. She turned around to face him. More earth rolled from under her feet.

He should stab his bushknife into the mud so she could hold the handle. He should drop down, and hold out his hand. He should.

He took one step forward.

And then she was gone. And there was a noise. Or maybe there wasn't a noise. He thought he heard her, cracking against the ground. But he couldn't possibly have heard it. Not over the rain. It wasn't like in the movies. He didn't see her eyes growing wider in her head. She just dropped. He stepped forward again and peered over the edge. There she was, lying in the pit, amidst the plastic rubble and rotting compost. Her right leg was crookedly out to one side, and her right arm was moving a bit, only a bit.

He stood and watched. Her arm flailed and flailed, it was grabbing pointlessly at something. He couldn't see her face. It was too wet. There was too much water. He backed away from the edge.

He backed away, and he left her.

PART TWO

14

Bea had waved Max and Marietta farewell from the porch, but didn't even wait until Max's red hair was out of sight, before she slammed the door to Mission House and sighed deeply. The house seemed extremely quiet without Marietta's sniffing and spluttering. She didn't envy them their witnessing trip. The walk to Kalu-kalu would be tough and slippery, and it was only a matter of time before it began to rain again.

Bea changed out of her island dress so she could garden. She decided to risk the tabu of trouser-wearing, since most people were sheltering inside their huts. She put on a pair of damp linen trousers and pulled the belt buckle. Given the nutritional poverty in which they lived, Bea felt rather disappointed she could wear the same notch as before they came to the island. She reasoned that a diet of white rice was not great for the waistline. Bea stretched out her shoulders, tied her hair back into a tight bun, and picked up her bushknife.

The garden was in bad shape. The earth was soupy, and the new seedlings were nowhere in sight. Bea wondered if during the next storm, she could find a way to pot some cabbages and carry them into Mission House? Although Max might think her truly nuts, if she began populating the house with pet vegetables. Bea started to pull sloppy weeds out of the earth around her carrots, but within a few minutes, she heard a low grumble of far-off thunder in the north. It grew colder. Soft drops of water began to fall.

Without Max and Marietta in the way, Bea decided to get ahead on the housework. She swept and washed the floors, and wiped the window frames. Max always told her to leave the spiders alone, but when he wasn't around, she instituted a ruthless cull of anything hairy-legged. In the top right corner of the wall in the corridor, she found a silver spider with a body the size of a plum. It was carrying a white egg sac on its back. Bea shuddered in anticipation before swatting it with one of Max's boots. The legs twitched underneath the sole, but as soon as she raised the boot, a flurry of tiny translucent baby spiders spilt from the burst sac and scattered over the wall. She leapt back in horror, squeaking, before attacking the newborns with the shoe. But it was too late, they had escaped.

After scraping the bottom of the boot on the front step, Bea retreated a safe distance into the living room, and washed some of her own clothes in the bucket. Out of spite, she hung them to dry in Marietta's room. Bea sat back at the table and darned her blue skirt and two pairs of Max's socks. The light was dim, and she was concentrating so hard she was getting a headache. She didn't dare light a candle before nightfall, since their supply was running low. No cargo ships had come by the island since their trunks arrived, and no doubt the bad weather would delay the next shipment even further.

Three weeks previously, she had walked up to Aru's store, hoping she might be able to buy extra candles to carry them over until the next boat. But there was a chalk notice written on the sheet metal inside: 'No Candles. No Flour. Please fast and pray.' It wasn't only candles and flour in low supply. With the garden in such a state, there wasn't much to supplement their bag of rat-rice. Bea's fingers lingered on one of the tins of corned hash in the pantry. It wouldn't be fair to break into their stash without Max and Marietta, but it hurt her stomach to think of it. Bea regretfully put the can back on the shelf.

That evening she climbed into Max's bed, and tried to make herself as cosy as possible. She picked up Max's Bible, intending to allow herself enough candlelight for one page of Song of Songs, since Max wasn't around to spoil her pleasure with exegesis. But her eyes fell over the shape of the words instead of reading them. Idly, she opened the book to the blue-bordered note of his prayer list glued to the back page. His parents' names were written in black ink in Max's neatest handwriting. In pencil underneath: Beatriz, Filip, Leiwas, Mabo-Mabon, Willie, Charles, Santra, the people of the New Hebrides. She stared at the list for a few moments before blowing out the candle. Why was her name in pencil? It hardly seemed fair to be scribbled in alongside Leiwas and Willie. Surely, he could have taken the time by now to go over his own wife's name in ink? Would he notice, if she wrote over it with a pen, before he got back? She blinked into the dark, thinking of the prayer list in the back of her own Bible: Max. She pulled the sheet over her shoulders and fell asleep to the sound of rain dripping from the eaves of Mission House. During the night the squalls picked up again, and she slept fitfully, waking to the noise of rainfall crackling and hushing, as if the jungle were full of radio static.

The next morning, the rain had temporarily stopped, though the air was humid and the clouds low and broody. Bea walked around the shallow bush behind Chief Bule's hut to look for food. She tried all her usual spots, but the storm had knocked the ripe fruit off the branches, and the earth smelt sweet with rotting pulp. Up on the left behind the ridge, there was a young banana palm that looked almost ripe. She held it steady with one hand, and inexpertly chopped down the heavy head. A large drop of plasticky sap fell on to her shirt, and she tutted in frustration at her own clumsiness. Banana sap stained clothes like nothing else – it would never come off.

Bea carried the bananas to Othniel and Jinnes' house. She

hoped that out of Christian duty, they might offer her some food in return. One person could not possibly hope to eat all the bananas before they went bad. The bushel was heavy, and a stripe of brown ants crawled from the suckers and over her forearms. She rested it by the front of the house and called in through the doorway. But there was no one there.

Bea looked around her at the village. The bushkitchens weren't puffing out smoke. It was oddly quiet. There weren't any children squabbling over the ching. She pulled off three bananas to eat later, making sure to pick them at the root, so they would preserve for longer. She lifted up the rest of the bushel and walked through the mud, peering at each house in turn. The whole village was empty. She made her way towards Willie's nakamal, and spotted Edly Tabi sitting on the branch by the bottom of the hill, playing with a piece of twine. She manoeuvred down the hill towards him.

'Hello!' She smiled at him.

Edly nodded by way of a reply.

'Where is everyone?' she asked.

'Funeral in Bavete,' he said, pointing to Central.

Bea nodded. Perhaps she should be offended that she hadn't been invited. She offered Edly the bananas, and he took them. He put them down in the sand beside the branch, and continued to examine the fishing line. He didn't say thank you, or even make eye contact.

She walked back to the house. She gobbled the three bananas while sitting in Max's bed, and threw the peels out of his bedroom window. There was a nervy, hollow feeling in her stomach. She tried to read, falling into an uneasy sleep in the early afternoon.

The next morning, Bea walked around the village in the drizzle, to see if Jinnes and Othniel had returned. Truthfully, she was hoping for Lorianne. But there still wasn't anyone there. She could hear a new, odd wailing sound echoing in the hills. It was a low, musical moaning that rose and fell, and seemed to be echoing all around in the forest. It wasn't until later she realized it was the sound of mourners at the funeral.

Bea took another tour through the shallow bush. Eventually, she spotted a single ripe pomelo high up on a tall, young tree. It was far too narrow and straight to climb. She collected rocks from around the hill, and threw them up at the pomelo, hoping the tough skin would protect the fruit when it fell. It took almost half an hour for it to swing and drop. Bea gratefully gathered it up in her arms. It was almost the size of a soccer ball. She ate half of the pomelo for lunch, half for supper. It was sour and acidic, and produced jabbing pains in her stomach. But at least it wasn't rice. The crying sound went on and on and on through the night.

The next day, while touring the village in search of more rogue fruits, Bea became convinced she could hear someone calling her name. But when she paused to listen, there was nothing. She thought the crying from the funeral was playing tricks on her mind. She haltingly circled the huts in the village. There was still nobody there. She lingered on the hill, hoping even to catch sight of Edly Tabi, but he was nowhere to be seen. Bea began to feel afraid. Where was everyone? Where was New Dog?

She had a horrible thought, that maybe she didn't exist. Maybe she wasn't real. Maybe she had died, and not noticed, and this was the afterlife. Maybe she was a ghost. She shook her head to dislodge the thought. Imagine how disappointed Max would be if he heard her say such things. She lowered her imaginary screen, and apologized to God in her head.

Bea walked towards the stream at the north of the village, hoping the fast-moving floodwater might have dislodged coconuts from the palms on top and washed them down-stream. What if, she thought, everyone had moved from the village? They had started a new village somewhere. Or per-haps an infectious disease had swept through, and they were all lying dead inside their huts. She turned towards the village, wondering if she should go back, and check inside the houses. But this was madness! Edly had told her they were away for a funeral. With all the rain, nobody would have tried to make the journey back until the streams subsided. First, she thought to herself, she needed a proper meal. She would find a coco-nut, then she would light a fire, and cook some rice, even if it took all day.

Eventually Bea came to the stream. The sides had burst the banks and flooded the grass either side. She looked up and down for coconuts that might have rolled into the water. The sound of her name began again. But now it was louder, and coming from the right. Bea waded through the sludge until she could see the caller. On the other side of the water, there was Santra. Bea was never so happy to see anyone in her whole entire life.

Santra shouted to her. 'Come –' she beckoned Bea across.

Bea looked at the stream, which was running with frothy torrents from the mountains. There was no way she could walk through that. Santra pointed further uphill, and Bea walked back up the slope, where a papaya tree and a frangi-pani tree had fallen into the water and become lodged against the rocks, forming an impromptu bridge across. A thatch of mushy twigs and leaves had collected against the tree trunks. Santra gestured for her to cross, and Bea felt compelled to be on the other side of the stream – to be anywhere away from the village.

She steadied herself on a bush, and stepped cautiously on to a tree trunk with one foot. It was squishy, but not in any danger of disintegrating. She squatted, and brought up the other foot. Santra watched her from the other bank. Bea took a couple of steps forward, and in the middle of the stream the trunk sank by two inches, its soft crunchy centre imploding. Bea hovered, then rushed across as fast as she could, not looking ahead, but down at each individual step. She leapt from the last root, trying to appear as graceful as possible.

Santra looked her up and down, 'You look really, really bad,' she said.

Bea couldn't help but smile. 'I'm sure you're right,' she said.

Santra's village had also been affected by the relentless rain, and she was running out of food. 'I heard there was a market in Ranvoki,' Santra said. 'No one else wants to go.'

Bea's stomach contracted. A market! She felt into her trousers for the coin in the pocket, and patted it. At least she would eat well tonight. Santra and Bea walked the three hours up to Ranvoki. It was tough walking, the mud was so wet that every so often one of them slid sideways and had to clutch the other. The day was overcast and almost cold. Charles apparently had a bad headache. He'd been in the hut moaning and vomiting for days, and Bea suspected the market rumour was merely an excuse for Santra to leave the house.

When they arrived at Ranvoki, there was no one in sight. No one in the centre of the village, certainly no market, and judging by the lack of smoke, most of the houses were empty.

'Let's go back.' Bea heard herself whining, pausing at the edge of the village hill. She didn't want to waste energy hanging around if there was no food to be found. If they stopped, if she sat down, she would feel a lot worse getting back up again. The only thing to do was to turn around straight away and walk back to Bambayot. Without saying anything, Santra disappeared into one of the huts. Bea lurked outside, unsure whether she should join her. She had just made up her mind to go inside as well, when Santra reappeared, holding a single onion, the size of a ping-pong ball.

'That's it?' Bea's mouth opened.

Santra nodded.

Together they walked back to Bambayot. Half an hour away from the village, the dim groan of thunder rose from over the ocean. Long tails of lightning cracked through the clouds and dipped into the water. It began to rain again. Heavy pellets of rain dropped so vigorously they bounced off their skin in silver plumes. Bea tucked the onion into her brassiere. It began to rain even harder. It was like being pummelled. Drops of water hung from the tip of Bea's nose. They walked in silence, not looking at each other. The last big hill before Bambayot had turned into a slow-moving sheet of mud. Bea and Santra had to climb up on all fours and ease themselves down the slope sitting on their behinds, slathering their clothes in red slime.

The tree trunks at Bambayot stream were still there, now fortified by more detritus from upriver. Bea selfishly went first, figuring it was more likely to break for the second person across. And anyway, Santra was better at swimming.

At Mission House, she lit the fire while Santra squatted underneath the window, smearing mud on the wall and dripping puddles on to the floor. It took half an hour for the wood to catch, but after a few minutes, it stopped burning completely. The water in the pot was warm and it had barely cooked the rice. They ate bowlfuls of hard rice with palm oil and half a raw onion each. Bea put her spoon down. She didn't feel hungry any more. She gave the rest of her food to Santra.

The following day, Bea experimented with crime. Max had locked the door to the church, but Bea broke in by climbing up one of the lime trees and squeezing through an open window. She hoped she might find some leftover breakfast crackers that were used for Communion. On the table in the vestry, she found a plastic wrapper punctured by small holes where it had been gnawed by a creature. There were two soft, droopy crackers left in there. She put them in her island basket anyway. Nearby, on the wooden table, Bea spotted an upside-down cookie tin. She touched the corner of the tin. There was no way it could still contain cookies. If there had ever been cookies in it in the first place – more likely it had contained Marietta's sermons at some point. But she couldn't help herself. She turned the tin over.

Immediately, a rat leapt out and jumped straight at her. It was frantic, skinny, its mouth snapped. Bea shrieked, and hit out wildly with the bushknife. She swatted at it, and somehow managed to slice partway through its head. The rat squealed. Bea backed away, and it lurched on to the floor, dripping blood and squeaking before it crawled to a stop. Bea squatted on to her haunches and inspected the rat. A pink sliver of brain glinted through the gash. She examined the scrawny body lying on the floor. Could she eat this? She looked carefully at the rat. It would have to be skinned, and gutted. Bea rubbed the back of her hands over her face. She let out a groan of frustration. She couldn't do it. She couldn't. She picked it up by the tail, which was a horribly ropey texture under her fingers. She swung it out of the window into the long grass. Standing up, she looked back at the cookie tin. There were deep grooves in the wood under the tin where the rat had tried to claw its way out. God knows how long it had been trapped in there. It had been starving, too.

The next day, when Max arrived back at Mission House, he found Bea in his bed. She was fully clothed, wrapped up in the sheets, whistling a tuneless rendition of 'In The Garden' to herself.

She sat up from the covers with a start. 'Maxis!' Her face was a picture of joy. 'Did you get back just now? Oh, Maxis – I'm so hungry, do you have any food?' She stretched one hand out of the mosquito net towards him. 'And where is she?' she added in a whisper.

'Marietta?' he asked, taking the island basket from around his shoulders and setting it on the floor.

'Of course!' Bea beckoned him closer with her fingers.

He lingered in the doorway, 'She's – gone. She went back East.' He said it quickly, all in one breath.

'No?' Bea sat up on her knees in the bed. 'For how long?'

'I don't know.' Max picked up the island basket again and walked out the doorway.

Bea called his name, but he kept walking.

15

Beatriz was sitting outside Mission House on the sawn-off palm stump. The washing bucket was on the ground next to her, a foamy slab of wood resting inside the rim. Bea had twisted up her skirt, and tucked the knot underneath her thighs. Even from the bottom of the hill, Max could see the slope of her leg muscles, and their gradient from dark to light brown over the tops of her knees.

He felt suddenly irritable. She knew how much he hated it when she lounged around like that, with her legs exposed. What must the men of the village think? It was hardly any wonder her only friend was the heathen girl with the tattooed face, dear Lord!

As he came closer to Bea, he noticed something and stopped. Bea was leaning back against the wall of the house, looking off at nothing. She was aimlessly worrying a muddy piece of pink fabric between her fingers. It had crumbled little bits of earth on to her calves and her left ankle.

Bea watched Max. He looked like he was drunk. His lips had gone almost completely white, and his forehead was shiny. He groped uneasily around him for something to hold, and landed on one of the dwarf banana palms. As he leant his weight on it, the shrub shifted in the earth and started to tilt away from him. He was looking at the ground, muttering, one hand on his chest. Bea suddenly thought he might be having a heart attack.

'Maxis? Are you having a heart attack?'

His expression wasn't reassuring. He released the banana

tree and stumbled towards her, finally kneeling awkwardly in the wet grass. He shook his head in response to her question, but said nothing. He leant his head forward, so it almost rested on his knees, exposing pink sunburnt skin at the back of his neck. When he spoke, his voice quavered like a scratched record.

'Beatriz –'

'Yes?'

'I . . .' He trailed off.

He was squinting his eyes to see her against the sun, but it made him look ugly, she thought. His face was all sweaty and white and scrunched up.

She held up the small square of pink, and rubbed her thumb over its embroidery. 'This is Marietta's. It had blood on it.'

When he was a child, Max's parents had once taken him to Coney Island to visit the amusements there. He had insisted on getting on one of the rides alone. It was shaped like an orange and golden bird, with large iron wings which flapped ponderously as it swooped up and down. As soon as the sharp little door swung shut, he had regretted it. His parents smiled at him encouragingly, his mother popping her cigarette in her mouth to wave more enthusiastically with both hands, her bracelets clacking back and forth. And since they were watching, and smiling, he had to pretend not to be scared. But as the ride started to move upwards and away, Max had a horrible feeling. He was all alone, and it was all his fault.

'Maybe it's from when Matambe . . .?' He couldn't finish the sentence.

'No.' Bea swapped the handkerchief between her hands, and the excess material flopped over the tops of her fingers. 'I boiled everything after that. Remember – I had to cut a piece out of my nightdress?' She was looking at him carefully.

Max felt an odd shiver pass through all the usually

anonymous parts of his skeleton – it rang in his kneecaps and his toe joints and his eardrums.

'It's –' He felt as if his mouth were filled with sludge.

'Maxis,' she said in a quiet whistle, throwing the handkerchief into the bucket of soapy water, 'I know there is something you are keeping from me. You've been so strange since your trip. Tell me now.'

'I –' Max felt his face burning. His eyes watered. He felt dizzy. 'I – she fell. I pushed her. I pushed her. I could have helped. I didn't help. I don't know. She's dead. It was all my fault.' He put his face in his hands.

Bea watched him in silence. His shoulders were moving heavily. For a horrible moment, she thought he might be crying. Bea drew a deep breath. 'Maxis, you're overreacting. So, she fell? Up top?'

Max's head nodded.

'Well then, that's not your fault. It was an accident. She fell over – she died?'

Max's head nodded again.

'So are you supposed to carry her up the mountain? Why didn't you tell me?'

He looked up at her, and his eyes were swollen and bloodshot. 'No – you don't understand. I could have helped her. I didn't. I didn't help her – she's dead because of me.' His voice was hoarse. He twisted his arms up around his side.

'Maxis, stop this!' she almost shouted.

He was being ridiculous. It at least explained why he had been acting so oddly recently. Since he came back from the trip to Kalu-kalu, he'd hardly been at home. He was always in church, praying, or walking around by the shore in circles. He had barely spoken to her. It was almost a relief. She had thought maybe he was tiring of her, that he was feeling disappointed by the practicalities of married life.

Max was rocking from side to side. 'Are you – what are you going to do now?'

Bea didn't answer, but motioned towards the bucket. She was going to wash off the blood, obviously.

'Are you going to – will you leave me?' His voice wavered.

Bea let out a high laugh. 'Why would I do that?' She shuffled the bucket in between her legs, and began to scrub at the little square. Dark water sloshed over the lip of the bucket and dripped on to her foot. Max watched as the little drop of water gathered the crumb of earth there, and softened it into a tiny puddle in the hollow of her ankle bone.

'What I've done – what I did.' He said the words as if he were moving a handful of boiled candies around in his mouth.

Bea blew a strand of hair off her face, and continued scrubbing. 'So what?'

Max looked up at her and his mouth opened with a half-formed question mark on his lips.

She met his eyes. 'She fell. It was an accident. You aren't going to push me off the mountain –'

'How can you even –' Max stuttered, the whites of his eyes showing. A frail web of spittle formed between his lips.

'Well, then –' Bea said, thinking it a bit unnecessary for him to act so terribly offended '– I don't care.' She shrugged again.

Max was speechless. Was she making a joke?

She raised her eyebrows at him.

'I –' he began, not knowing even how to finish his own sentence.

Bea shushed him impatiently, scrubbing harder at the strip of fabric. 'It is done,' she said.

Max sat back in the grass. He felt quite unwell; the sky was shimmering unsteadily. He didn't know this woman at all. His wife. That she could be so capable of accepting and forgiving him. He felt a rush of confusion and joy all at once.

She understood! She didn't care! She still loved him, she would not leave! She didn't think he was a monster. Acid caught in his throat.

'You were careless, do you know that?' Bea wrung out the cloth over the bucket. 'Why did you say she went back East? Someone could have seen you with her. She's dead. People die all the time.' She gestured around them to the hills with the wet rag. 'If anyone else found this –' she shook the handkerchief in her hand '– they would think you did leaf magic or something on her.'

Max felt the sick, reeling feeling again. How *had* she found it?

Bea read the panic on his face. 'New Dog,' she said. 'She left this outside the house.'

'But how?' Max stuttered, realizing it was a stupid question.

'I don't know,' Bea said. 'It must smell of her – or you.'

Max felt the blood bubble back up into his cheeks. He should shoot that dog.

Bea traced his wandering eyes, the rise and fall of colour from his face, as he mouthed silent words to himself. She stood up off the stool and knelt on the grass in front of him, looking at his face until he met her stare. The hand with the wet handkerchief mopped damply at his shirt. 'Don't worry. We will be fine,' she said.

And they would. She was sure of it. Nobody would miss Marietta. She certainly wouldn't miss her. People slipped, and fell, and died all the time. Or maybe worse – people slipped, and fell, and survived. And then spent weeks sweating to death with pus dripping from their eyes like Santra's friend Lorifer.

Max nodded dumbly, mechanically reaching to clutch her to him. She smelt like onions and ginger. The handkerchief bled a wet patch over the back of his shirt. Bea's use of 'we' rang in his ears. She would not leave him.

*

That night, Max lay awake. Bea had crawled next to him in the bed, her left leg tangled awkwardly in the mosquito net, one arm sprawled across his stomach. She'd fallen asleep almost immediately, and he listened to the faint snoring catching in the back of her throat. A cicada in the room was humming in a high buzz. He eased his arm out from underneath Bea's neck. How could she drop off to sleep as easily as that? It was almost disturbing how she wasn't worried about him at all, he thought. Then he corrected himself, she wasn't worried about *them* at all.

And Bea's faith in him was reassuring. He had not married an idiot, he thought. Max turned to look at Bea's face in the shadows next to him, feeling a strange vertigo, as if he were looking at her from a great height. It was odd, he thought, how easy it was to assume the person you love is the same person as you. But she was someone else entirely. He said her name clearly in his mind. Beatriz, he thought, is a different person to me.

16

Jonson took a deep breath and dived under the surface of the water. It hadn't rained in days, and the ocean was clear and still. Jonson bobbed in place and tried to keep his movements as small as possible, so as not to scare the fish. Grey with orange stripes and dappled faces, they flickered through the ruin of the plane. Its rusty frame was painted with darts of light, and through the busted door of the cockpit Jonson watched the fish nibbling on the algae-coated walls. He swam closer to the skeleton of the machine, keeping a wary distance from the tangles of pink coral. Coral cuts took months to heal, and his ankles were already lumpen with scarred tissue. He kicked to the surface and caught his breath, wiping the salt-water from his eyes.

'Mr Jonson!' A village man was waving at him from the beach.

Jonson recognized him as Titus Garae and waved back. 'Go away,' he muttered through gritted teeth. 'Go away, go away.'

'Mr Jonson, come please!'

'Why?' Jonson yelled.

'Come to see!'

Jonson sighed. He had been watching the grey-and-orange fish for days, in an effort to work out what kind of vegetation they lived on. His previous experiments with exotic goldfish had failed miserably, and after the sixth black-and-orange fish died, he had decided to switch species, and try a different sort of stripe. The next trial relied on careful reconnaissance missions to observe their feeding habits. Jonson paddled to shore, conscious of Titus's eyes on him. Although he swam every day, his stroke was still poor, and he loathed spectators of his sloppy form. He scrambled to stand as soon as the beach grew shallow, plucking his shirt and shorts away from his body.

'Mr Jonson, Fritchard was hunting flying fox in Central, and he caught the Tonks,' Titus shouted from the treeline.

'From Sara?' Jonson hobbled in the waves.

'Yes! A family of them! Come quick, they're in the nakamal.'

Jonson hesitated. His thighs were outlined by the fabric of the shorts, and his nose was painted with zinc oxide. His sandals squelched water. 'They're in the nakamal at the moment?'

Titus lifted his eyebrows.

'And who's with them?'

'Fritchard, of course.' Titus licked his top lip. 'He'll get his reward now?'

'Mr Sugarcraven will be responsible for that. Not me.'

Titus waited as Jonson crossed the beach, watching his feet with an amused curl to his lips. Jonson was aware swimming in sandals made him an object of ridicule in the village, but his pride did not go so far as to volunteer the soles of his feet to water spiders.

'You were out by the plane?' Titus glanced sideways at him as they waded through the slow water of the stream and down towards Bwatapoa. 'The other day I heard the ghost drowned someone there.'

Jonson's wet shorts dragged on his stride, and irritably, he blamed Titus for his bedraggled exhibition in the centre of the village. 'It's perfectly harmless,' he snapped. 'That Jap's ghost has better things to do than hang around drowning people. It's probably in the forest settling down with a ghost family.'

Titus's eyes grew wide.

'Where were they found anyhow? The Tonks?' Jonson said.

'On top.' Titus pointed up into the mountains. 'Taking taro from a garden.'

Jonson stopped. 'They didn't eat it, did they? Raw?'

Titus shrugged. He pushed ahead of Jonson, and stooped through the nakamal door, then stuck his head back out and gestured for Jonson to enter.

Fritchard was crouching on the left of the doorway, listlessly probing his hair with a wooden comb. The runaways were huddled on the bench in the back right corner. The man was bare-chested, one arm clamped around a young woman. On her knee she was jiggling a baby of perhaps a year old. The exposed skin of the two adults – their faces, necks, forearms, his shoulders and chest – were covered in scarlet mosquito bites. The man was filthy and downcast as a flat tyre. He was deeply tanned and smeared with mud, his fingers black with dirt. He was so thin the bones in his breastbone rippled with each breath. The woman was less dishevelled, but her eyes were rimmed with purple circles. They looked up at Jonson, then exchanged a glance he could not interpret. Jonson tapped Titus aside and took a step into the middle of the nakamal, dripping water on the floor. His sandals squeaked under his weight, and his sodden shirt was clinging uncharitably to the round flesh on his belly.

'My name is Mr Jonson,' he said, trying to muster as much gravitas as was possible while wearing Hawaiian print. 'I am the British Administrator on Advent Island.'

The couple exchanged another glance, and the man chewed his lips.

Jonson addressed him. 'Are you feeling well? You didn't eat any taro, did you? Any taro leaves?'

But the man just kept chewing and looking at the floor.

Jonson turned to Fritchard. 'Did they eat anything from the garden? Have they been ill?'

Fritchard shook his head. 'I gave them oranges.'

'Anything else?'

'Only oranges.'

'Would you like some water?' Jonson asked, but the man didn't meet his eye. Jonson mimed drinking from a glass, and the woman gave him a brief nod.

Jonson turned around to address Fritchard and Titus. 'OK, you two are to guard them from now on,' he said. 'And find somebody to walk to Sara. Fritchard, can you ask Tole to go?'

Fritchard plunged the comb in his hair, and stood up to leave. Jonson called after him, 'And get a girl to bring them drinking water.'

Jonson inspected the baby. Other than three pink scratches across its cheek, it looked healthy; cheerful, even. It opened its gummy mouth and blew a spit-bubble. 'Is it a boy or a girl?' he asked the woman, enunciating slowly.

She shook her head.

Jonson lost interest – it hardly mattered anyway. Polite niceties with Garolf's delinquents would earn him no favours with anyone. 'What do babies eat?' he asked Titus.

Titus grinned, and cupped his own breasts.

'All right, thank you, that's quite enough.' Jonson waved him to stop. 'Ask Fritchard to find it a banana or something.'

'Shall we take them now?' Titus leant against the doorway.

'Take them where?' Jonson realized he was about to play host to a family of scabby fugitives in his spare room. 'No, absolutely not, they can stay here until they're collected.'

'And then we'll be rewarded?' Titus said.

'When Mr Sugarcraven arrives, we'll see what kind of mood he's in.'

17

With the worst of the weather finally exhausted, Bea began to tend her garden in earnest. Santra came by nearly every day to help. Mostly, that meant Santra told stories while Bea worked, and Lorianne listened nearby, scratching her scalp. Bea couldn't help but feel as if a strange pressure had been lifted from their home. With Marietta gone, Mission House seemed so much larger. She cleared Marietta's belongings from her old bedroom, and started sleeping in there again. Sometimes she missed Max's presence in the evenings, but he was a lot less grumpy now they were both sleeping properly.

Bea decided she would begin the project of sourcing some of the food she had been dreaming about during the rainy weeks. She showed Santra her book of botanical sketches. Santra was not used to looking at pictures, and Bea had to stand behind her, explaining the drawings to her in words, until Santra could see the image. She had once made a quick doodle of a carrot in her notebook, to explain to Santra the lacy fronds growing around Mission House.

Santra had stared at it for some time before handing it back to her, saying, 'I don't know who that is.'

First on Bea's list was to collect some of the cocoa pods she knew they had passed on one of their trips on top, while catching crayfish. She had no idea how the seeds turned into the food, but the first thing was to get hold of the raw ingredient. For the chocolate mission, Santra and Bea travelled uphill, north of Bambayot, then took a right through a slow river. They walked for an hour upstream through the shallow water, cutting overhanging plants away with their bushknives. They left the river, and scrambled up slippery rocks in dense jungle dotted with tiny chestnut-coloured orchids.

They crossed into fields of soft white grass in the shadow of a vast overhanging crag. They climbed over the dead body of a huge strangler fig tree, and joined another stream to wade up to a waterfall, split to form six thin spouts, which flowed in a slow trickle into an ankle-deep pool. They stood with their backs against the sharp rock, and let the water wash over their heads like an icy shower.

Near the six-pronged waterfall, Santra pointed out the cocoa trees. The pods looked gorgeous, like tapered mangoes. Santra had no idea which ones were ripe, so they gathered a couple of green, red and orange ones for experimentation. Bea felt excited. If she could get this to work – she could make her very own Mission House chocolate.

They turned back on themselves and followed the stream up even higher to a waterfall Bea had never visited before. Almost hidden behind a crack in the stone, the pool was shallow around the edges and extremely deep in the middle where the water changed to dark blue. The waterfall came over the south-east side in a heavy, noisy rush of white water. Santra put down her island basket and bushknife, and looked around them. In one motion, she ripped off her dress. Bea looked away. Santra was impossibly thinner than the billowy folds of the island dress had suggested. She took a couple of steps to the side of the pool, and jumped inelegantly into the water. She splashed around, cheering. This had to be beyond tabu. If Max had any idea, he would be horrified. Bea deliberated for a moment. She should really sit by the side and keep watch, in case anyone came by. She could put her feet in the pool. But the temptation of sunlight over the bare skin of her body was overwhelming.

Bea peeled off her own dress, and holding her hands over her breasts, she crept over to where Santra had jumped into the water. Santra was watching her naked body, with a horrified expression on her face. Before she lost her nerve, Bea leapt. The water was icy. The temperature knocked the breath out of her chest. She struggled to the surface, coughing, to see Santra splashing around in circles. Santra paddled over to her.

She nodded her head up and down towards Bea's body. 'So you're not black under your clothes,' she said in mock disappointment.

Bea giggled, trying to concentrate on keeping her head above the water.

Santra waved her closer to the falls, and shouted over the noise, 'Let's go under – there's a cave.'

Santra took a deep breath, dived under the water, and vanished. Bea waited for a few seconds, then copied her, hoping she was kicking in the right direction. She kicked as hard as she could through the turbulence, and looked up to see Santra's legs in a still ceiling of water above her. When she broke the surface, they were both bobbing in a shallow cave behind the waterfall. Bea looked around it nervously, expecting a new range of special and monstrous cave spiders. But to her eyes at least, it was bare. Santra helped Bea to hoist herself up on a sharp ledge which ran around the back of the cave. It scraped over Bea's buttocks, and she tried not to wince. It was too noisy to talk, so they sat and shivered, watching the blue light shining through the falling water. This was the South Pacific of *South Pacific*, Bea thought.

While Bea was busy gardening, and gossiping, or whatever she was up to, Max recommitted himself, whole-bodied, to his spiritual mission on the island. He rose early to pray, and practised fasting two days a week. He went witnessing in Central, careful to be back in Bambayot long before dusk. It was on one of these witnessing trips that he heard Bea's dog had been eaten. Some boys in Kumuvete had apparently captured the beast and cooked it up. He walked from Rangiran to Kumuvete to investigate the rumour, where the boys' father offered Max the dog's thigh bones to take home with him. Max politely declined. He arrived back at Mission House later than usual that evening, as Bea was preparing their meal of rice and island cabbage.

'Beatriz,' Max sat down at the table, 'I have something to talk to you about.' He gestured for her to take a seat.

Bea perched on the stool, straining to listen for the water boiling in the kitchen.

'It's about New Dog.'

'Oh.' Bea felt relieved. He was wearing the serious expression he usually reserved for admonishing parishioners.

'I'm afraid, I think – she was, she has passed on.'

Bea cocked her head to the side. 'Oh, that's a shame!'

Max felt taken aback. She looked as if she had just been informed her train was delayed. The ugly urge to provoke her bubbled in his chest. 'She was captured last week, and then killed.'

Bea reviewed the most enthusiastic practitioners of smacking New Dog in church. 'Was it Othniel?' she asked.

Max shook his head. 'No, a couple of boys in Kumuvete, and –' he paused, grappling with the conflicting desire to comfort and upset her '– I'm sorry. I know you enjoyed having a pet.'

Bea shrugged. 'She lived a good life for an island dog. Did you know Rainson told Moses to bash her with that club – instead of the ching?'

Max watched Bea in amazement. How many times had he seen her feeding that dog scraps from their table? How many times had he heard her whistling for the beast? She had spent a full week cutting her wool coat and restitching it into a dog bed. 'I'm afraid to say it was killed for meat.'

Bea wrinkled her nose. 'Yuck. I bet that would taste awful,' she said, offhandedly, standing and crossing to the kitchen where she peered into the simmering water.

Max watched her through the doorway. 'I went from village to village, trying to find out what happened. It took all day.' He could hear the whiney cadence in his voice. Why had he wasted the whole afternoon if she didn't even care? Wasn't she going to thank him?

'Poor you,' she said, picking through the rice. 'You should have said – I would have come with you. Did you see Santra? Or Charles?'

'Beatriz,' he said, so sharply she turned to him. 'You're not upset?'

She put the bowl of rice down. 'What do you mean?'

The expression on her face was irritable, accusatory, as if she were being harassed. Her pet had been roasted and eaten! Who on earth would shrug that off? Did she have no ounce of sentimentality? He thought of how grateful he had been for her forgiveness, after what happened with Marietta. He remembered how he had knelt, clinging to her in the garden – and felt suddenly squeamish – as if he had embraced an automaton. She was still looking at him.

'Why do you want me to be upset?'

After a beat he said, 'Nothing, never mind.' Then petulantly, he added, 'You wouldn't understand.'

But she was staring at him. 'Understand what? Did you do something?'

'What?'

'Did you do something – to New Dog?'

He felt himself flinch. 'Good grief, what? Of course not!'

Bea hadn't moved. 'You're sure?'

Max blinked. 'Did I eat your dog? What are you saying?'

Bea rolled her eyes. 'No, not eating. Just – you always hated – and with the handkerchief – maybe?' She gestured vaguely.

To his horror, Max felt his lower lip wobble. 'I'd never –' But he swallowed the rest of his remonstrations.

Bea resumed picking through the rice. 'Because if you did, you should tell me now.'

Max shook his head, silently. A thread of frustration tugged around his throat. It wasn't fair, to bring up Marietta, so casually. As if he were as bad as those boys – running around in the bush, killing other people's pets, throwing their bones to rot in the jungle. Eating a dog!

She looked up at him. 'OK, Maxis, it's OK. Don't worry.'

He swallowed. 'I'm sorry about New Dog.'

Bea exhaled through her nose. 'Me, too.'

He lingered in the doorway. The water in the pot began to bubble and Bea gave the bowl of rice one last shake. 'You are careful, though, aren't you?'

She frowned at him.

'When you walk around the bush? You don't go too far, too deep? I mean –' and he stopped, not knowing what he meant. For some reason, he recalled the spider-crab, the clicking sound of its joints across the path, the vivid moment he had believed it a real mutant creature from deep in the forest.

'Oh, I'm fine.' She tipped the rice slowly into the boiling water. 'Santra's the careful one. I just do what she says.'

After the issue of New Dog had been resolved, Max turned his attentions to the Bambayot church. There was a broken window, a hole in the roof, and a spongy fungus had spread all over the side of one of the walls. He enlisted the help of Edly and Willie with repairs, and after some thought, Max also asked Willie to carve a new stool for Aru, which could be left in the vestry. Willie said he would do it 'next week', which in island time meant Max could expect it within a month or so. But it was a start. Max was convinced that, with time and mutual respect, he and Aru could come to an understanding. And he would need a new comrade, now, on the island.

Between Marietta's return, and the interlude of Chief Tabi's funeral at Bavete, there hadn't been a single incident of dark praying in the last two months. Leiwas' wedding had taken place shortly after the deluge, and after a teary farewell, she had been sent off to Central to build a new house with her husband. Perhaps, Max thought, that had something to do with the lessening tension. It might have been Leiwas' fears that had driven the whole nonsense forward in the first place.

Max enlisted Aru's help with Marietta's Language dictionary. Aru flicked through the pages quickly, before asking for a pencil. He went through it page by page, correcting and crossing words out. Max was delighted. Why had he never considered asking Aru to accompany him as a translator? After their first session with the dictionary, Max asked Aru if he would consider acting as his tutor. He desperately needed help improving his Language, and he would need someone to navigate him around the villages, now Marietta was gone.

Aru looked down at his knees and said quietly, 'Pastor, I will help you.'

'You'll come with me, on witnessing trips?'

'Of course.' Aru smiled.

Max clapped his hands together. 'Great. I'll be so glad to have the company.'

'Mrs Anlon won't be with you?'

'Hanlon,' Max said, gently. 'And, well, probably not.'

'She's with Santra Matan?'

Max rolled his eyes, good-naturedly. 'At least her dog is gone.'

Aru shook his head. 'That dog smelt so bad. Eating it must have –' He pulled a face.

Max laughed. 'You'll help me, then? You and me – we can rely on each other?'

'I will help you,' Aru said. 'You and me.'

That night, Max awoke to an urgent knocking on his bedroom door. He half started out of bed, fumbling for matches.

'Hello?' he called.

The door opened, and Bea emerged, cupping her hand around a candle, her nightdress slipping over one shoulder. There was a pink crease from her pillow across her right eyebrow and cheek.

'Maxis!' she hissed. 'Can I come sleep in here?'

He blinked. 'Well, sure – what's wrong?'

She approached the bed, climbing in and spilling a hot drop of wax on to his kneecap. 'They're standing outside,' she whispered, settling back on his pillow. 'Max, please make them go away!'

'Who's outside? Sweetheart, you were dreaming,' he said softly, patting her on her shoulder, and taking the candle from her, placing it on the floor by the bed. He brushed back a wisp of hair from her forehead. Her face was warm and puffy from sleep.

'It's not a dream! They're out there, look for yourself!' She pulled his sheets over her chin and gestured for him to go into her bedroom.

He picked up the candle, and walked across the corridor to Bea's room. As soon as he approached her doorway, he blew out the candle. She wasn't wrong. He could hear people talking in the garden. How had he not noticed the noise before?

Through Bea's bedroom window, he could see the half-illuminated figures of a dozen people standing in a line. One of them was carrying a hurricane lamp, several others held candles. It was some girls from the church. They were singing a hymn, and a girl's voice was chanting monotonously from the right-hand side. He saw, through the cracks in the bamboo, faint glimmers of light extending almost all round the house. He backed out of Bea's room and into his bedroom, where Bea sat with her knees drawn up to her chin.

'Did you see? Are they still there?' she asked.

Max shut the door to his bedroom. 'Yes, they're still there. Don't be frightened, though – they're praying for protection.'

'Are you sure? Why aren't they praying for your protection, then?' She gripped her knees.

'They're doing it for us all in turn – don't worry!' He did his best to smile a light-hearted smile.

Bea breathed out, screwing her nose up. 'It's a very inconvenient time.'

Max laughed, and climbed into bed next to her. He unfolded his knees to allow her cold, muddy feet into the inside of his thighs, for warming up.

'I don't like it,' Bea said, holding on to him like a vice until she fell asleep.

Max lay there while she slept. He listened to the sound of the hymn die out, as Aru's voice clearly and carefully cast Satan out from Mission House.

18

Max's fever came from nowhere. He had complained of a headache one night, and gone to his bed early, before it was even dark outside. Early the next morning, Bea found him there, lying flat on his back. He was very still, and for a few ghastly seconds, Bea thought he was dead. She pulled back armfuls of his mosquito net, and put her right hand on his cheek. He opened his eyes a fraction, and she breathed a great hiccup of relief. His face was flushed, coated in a polish of sweat, and the sheets over him were wet to the touch. Bea twisted the mosquito net into a rope, knotted it as high as she could reach, and sat gingerly on the edge of the bed. She held his hot wrist and felt his pulse, but its dim beating didn't mean anything to her. It was just something the nurses used to do.

'Maxis, are you ill?' she said, peering at his face.

His eyebrows pulled together in a wince. 'It's quite hot,' he exhaled.

She stood up again, stripped off the top sheet and dropped it to the floor. Leaning over him, she coaxed off his shirt and trousers while he lay there listlessly. When he was naked, she pressed her hands to his chest and thighs. His skin was scalding to the touch. He gave a quiet moan of relief at the coolness of her fingers. Bea brought her laundry bucket from the front porch, and filled it at the well. She grabbed a handful of pink handkerchiefs from her basket and laid them down next to the bed. She wrung the handkerchiefs out, and dabbed them over his face, neck, armpits, his chest, his groin. His feet were icy cold. She took each one between her hands and rubbed them vigorously. Wasn't that meant to bring a fever down from his head? Or was that something she'd read in a novel?

After a couple of minutes, the heat rising from his body warmed the handkerchiefs through, and they were hot between her hands. Max had fallen asleep, and his quiet snoring comforted her. She didn't want to leave him lying naked and damp like that, so she brought through a fresh sheet from her own room and laid it over him, just to his stomach. She rubbed the gingery trail of hair under his navel, and looked around the room. What was she to do? Max had never even caught so much as a cold before.

Max lay there for almost three weeks. Bea washed him with the handkerchiefs, and left the laundry bucket in there so he might relieve himself into it. Sometimes, she climbed into the bed with him, and brushed his hair, while his clammy hand gripped her other arm appreciatively. She left a canister of water next to him, propped up on a pile of books by the bedside, so he could help himself. Whenever she went into the room she checked the canister to see how much he had drunk. She force-fed him ladlefuls of the stuff at a time, propping his head up with one forearm while the lukewarm water dribbled into his beard. He seemed to be sleeping all the time. Bea tried to keep the room neat and clean, since that was what she would have wanted in her illness. She swept the room each morning, and cut a ginger flower from the garden to stand in a glass on the green stool.

Max watched this flower from his bed. There was nothing else in the room to look at. He watched as glossy brown ants teemed out of its cells, streaming along the stem, across the floor. They marched in columns up into the bed. They crawled on his face, they crept inside his ear canals. He could feel this exquisite itching he couldn't reach with his hands or his tongue. He rubbed his face up and down on the sheets, trying to dislodge the ants. But the ants had spread; they had multiplied into a thick sheet on the wall opposite his bed. There were so many, they made a rustling sound like a summer wind. He called out for Bea, but his throat was hoarse and she couldn't hear him. When she came later that evening, she kept telling him there were no ants, patting the walls as if they weren't there, plunging her arms wrist-deep into the ant thicket. He couldn't trust her after that. He didn't want to drink the water she left for him. There were ants in there, too – floating, dead clots on the surface. She pretended not to see them. In the night he could still hear the ants in the room, rustling and ticking like a colossal clock. They swarmed around the feet of the bed, and it listed from side to side.

Bea checked on him as often as she could, but there was so much to do. There was never-ending weeding and clipping in their garden. She had to strip switches to mend fences to protect their seedling cabbages from rats and hungry children. There was the hot, heavy work of drawing rainwater from the well. She had to fish out drowned, distended rats with the 'rat stick', an instrument she had invented by inexpertly hammering a nail into the end of a bamboo pole. There were hours spent collecting and chopping firewood. She had to walk miles to Aru's store twice a week to try to buy candles, as Max, in his illness, had developed a fear of the dark. There were the normal duties of the Mission House. Children knocked on the door to have a tooth pulled, teary-eyed mothers turned up with swollen-bellied children in need of yaws injections. It was hard trying to look after Max with all those distractions.

Max was barely eating anything. She boiled tea for him, but he refused to drink it. She hacked down one of the ripening banana stalks from the garden, and tried to cajole him into eating one of the warm, soft-bellied fruits, but Max gagged so violently she gave up on that completely. She had to eat mainly bananas for three days. Bea tried to think of other ways to fortify Max's diet.

She walked through the forest to collect fallen coconuts, and took them back to the village to husk. There, she screwed Max's penknife through the dark eye of the shell, and drained out the water into a bowl. Then she cracked the shell around its circumference with her bushknife, until it could be prised open. Next she sat on the uneven stool, holding the coconut-scraper under her thighs, grating out all the flesh. When the scraps of flesh were scored out of the shells, she soaked the strings in rainwater until it turned cloudy. This she mixed with grated manioc, and boiled it to a sort of custard, sweet-ened with sugar cane. She spooned it into his mouth like a baby, while he eyed her furiously. She mopped the floors with a wet cloth, she scrubbed his clothes and sheets every day, and hung them to dry outside. She boiled the handkerchiefs she used on him, afraid of contamination.

Bea asked Aru to send for a doctor. And three days later, a hunched middle-aged man knocked on the Mission House door in the early hours of the morning. Dressed in a red-and-white striped soccer shirt over his nambas, with 'Oldham Athletic' embroidered into the shirt collar, the sorcerer intro-duced himself as Varu Garae. He brought from his basket a tiny white bag filled with dried seeds. He nestled a seed in the groove above Max's top lip, stretched out his arms, cracked his knuckles, and pushed his thumbs into the base of Max's stom-ach. Bea winced involuntarily as Max groaned and swiped at his arms.

Through Aru's translations, Varu instructed Bea to make Max drink a cupful of water with bark in it to help his fever.

Bea didn't much trust leaf-water, and decided to send a message to I. A. M. Jonson. She had no idea what else to do. Jonson was no doctor, but he was a man, a man who spoke English and wouldn't expect her to fix Max with leaves. Sending a message to Jonson amounted to little more than waiting around until someone wanted to walk to the North, and asking them to take a message. And praying.

Bea worried Max's mind was turning. He almost wept when she tried to take the hurricane lamp out of the room with her each night. He croaked constantly about insects stirring in the room. At first, she tried to reassure him there weren't any, but he became so frantic that she appeased him. She brought the broom into the room, swept in every corner and declared victory over all those pesky ants.

She thought he might need something to occupy his mind – anything else but ants. She tried reading to him from the books on his shelf in the study, but they were mostly Bible commentaries or biographies, and she found them so inexpressibly boring she couldn't bear to read more than a few pages out loud. She perched on the green stool in the corner, and tried to read to Max from the Bible, but she was conscious that as loopy as he was, he might notice she said all the names wrong. Nothing seemed to relax him – he would just scratch and sweat and stream. She thought about reading out 'Adam and Eve', but Genesis seemed to be long names and endless begetting. After the first three days, she gave up on the Bible, and asked Santra to come and tell him stories. Each night, Bea lit a candle for him, and placed it carefully in a saucer of water out of his reach.

Max lay awake most nights. It wasn't so hot then, it was easier on his eyes. He had to stay vigilant anyhow, or the ants would crawl through his eyelashes and into the corners of his mouth.

He lay awake listening to the screaming from the church as it continued, long, long into the night. The screams knocked around his brain. He would hear the sounds retained in perfect pitch, even hours after they had stopped. Song refrains drilled into his skull and were trapped in there, like a small bird in a hat. He sang 'Jesus, Mi Lavem Yu Tumas', over and over in his head until he felt nauseous. He craved peppermint, he ached for it. Just a taste of peppermint, he thought, and all the sickness would be over.

One night, he heard a tapping at the window frame. They were deliberate taps, a fingernail against wood. Max struggled up on to his elbows and squinted at the window. Perhaps it was one of the girls from the church, playing a cruel game. The tapping grew louder. Someone was pushing against the frame with the palms of their hands. Someone was trying to break into the room. The wooden frame fell through into the room with a clatter. The open window let in a humid breeze. But there was also a dark shape moving outside. Somebody was standing there. All the hairs on Max's scalp began to twist in their pores. Two white hands and a shoulder gripped the splintered frame. And the shape edged through the window, and into his bedroom. Max knew instantly who it was.

It was Marietta.

Marietta struggled halfway through the window, her hands placed flat on the ground. She was looking down in front of her, breathing unevenly. She was moving slowly, inelegantly, her legs hooked over the frame of the window as she lowered herself on to her forearms and knees. She was still fat, after all. It was dark, too dark to see her properly. But that grey lock of hair was all in front of her face. She took another breath, and looked up, suddenly, towards the bed.

The eye he could see was milky white all the way through, like that of an old man. Max couldn't move. He could smell her, warm and nasty, a dog after the rain. Her face was turned towards him now. She looked at him curiously, the way a child might look at a stranger. On her hands and knees, she began to crawl towards Max's bed. Max tried to call out against her, a prayer, an exhortation. All that came out was a high whine like a calf. She crawled closer, until her face was almost level with the bed. The dog smell moved his stomach. She lingered for a moment, then perched up into a squat on her haunches. Max heard the cracking in her knee sockets.

He couldn't move. The room was so small. His legs were shaking under the sheet, his heart felt like it was climbing. Marietta took a few heavy breaths, and pressed her face against the folds of the mosquito net at the end of the bed. A cross-hatch pattern fell on her skin from his only candle. The shaking spread to his arms; he could hardly keep up on his elbows. And then, all in one movement, she turned and scuttled back across the room. For a moment, Max thought she was leaving, but she clambered unsteadily up on to her old green stool. She leant her head back against the wall, and with those cloudy eyes, she watched him.

When the sun rose, Max saw Marietta was still there, sitting on the stool. She had been there, watching him, all night. But then he realized it wasn't Marietta. Santra was there instead, for storyan. She was shuffling pandan leaves together, braiding a basket. She nodded to him expressionlessly.

'In the old days, people never died. When your outer skin grew old, and heavy with wrinkles, you could take it off, and leave it somewhere, dropping your age behind you. One day, an old woman took her children to wash clothes in the river. She left her old skin upstream and walked down to take the children home. But her daughter didn't recognize her. She cried and wailed. "Don't worry," said the mother, "it's me – your mother. I've only removed my old skin." But the daughter was afraid, she was suspicious of her newly young mother, and refused to leave the river with her, calling for her real mother to come and chase away this stranger. Her mother pleaded with her. For if she put her old skin back on, she wouldn't be able to take it off again. She would stay old, and die. The child wailed and cried until the mother had no choice. She sighed, and went back upstream, heaving her lined old skin back on to her body again. And from then on, people could not remove their skins, but stayed old and died.'

Max dreamed he was walking uphill in the bush, going up to Central. It was not long after the rain, and the slopes were tacky with orange mud. It was hard walking; he had a cane with him to help push off the sides of the hill. It was a warm, bright day, with high white clouds brushed up on to the blue. He saw himself, walking along beside him. This seemed normal at first. But then he realized, it couldn't be himself, for he was already himself. He looked at his other body, and saw it was only a mask, a dead skin. It was crawling with a black, seeping network of veins. He saw the thing wearing his skin had failed to cover its feet. They were grey and cracked, with long toes that tapered into points. Max remembered he had taken his skin off and left it by the stream behind him. Now a demon was wearing his face. The demon had put his skin on all lopsided. Its pink tongue left a trail of white spittle on the corners of its mouth.

Max woke with a yelp. He looked for Santra, but she was gone. Aru was there instead. He had pulled the stool up by his bedside. His Bible was open on his lap. Aru put a finger inside his Bible, and put a hand on Max's forehead. His palm smelt clean and a bit sickly, like that pink soap. Max felt a pawing inside his stomach. He knew suddenly Aru would know what to do about Marietta creeping around in the corners of his bedroom. Aru would understand. His own wife was some dark thing now in the forest as well. Max tried to explain that Marietta was in the bush, or somewhere close, and also in the house, by his bed. But his tongue was thick, he couldn't get the words out. He felt his eyes burning with frustration. A cold slimy queasiness licked up and down inside his chest.

Aru said nothing. He looked carefully at Max in silence. He pulled his finger from the pages, closed his Bible, and he left.

Max fell asleep again, exhausted, alone. No one could help him. He wished he could burn the room to pieces – leave her nothing to creep through. But Aru came back sometime later – a day? He didn't know, it was dark again, maybe it was the same day. Aru dropped his island basket by the left wall, and from it brought a small sack of crystal salt. Max wept with relief. He didn't even care that Aru would see him. Aru understood. He had understood him, after all. Max wept thin tears as Aru whispered soft words, and traced a circle of salt around his bed.

Marietta couldn't come into his room now. But she was still lurking around. She came up to the house from the forest at night. She sat against the wall of his room outside the house, looking up towards the hills. He could smell her hot, wet dog smell from the bed. It made him gag small pitches of liquid on to the sheets. Sometimes she sang. Sometimes it wasn't her singing but it was the girls at the bottom of the hill, in the church. In the daytimes, Aru was there. Aru knew about Marietta. He cast her out of the house, he cast her out of the village. He prayed over Max's body. He pressed his Bible down to his forehead, and Max felt relieved, utterly relieved that he was taking charge.

Aru knew about the demons in the forest.

Aru knew about them creeping and crawling into houses, and also into souls.

Max understood now. He understood that one had crept into his body in the night. It had come creeping in from the dark and crawled inside his mouth. He hadn't killed Marietta because he was evil. Aru told him so – he wasn't evil. He wasn't evil, but something evil had taken a hold of him.

And Aru was right, there was something evil.

There was something dark in that forest and it had crept inside his body. It was wearing his face as a mask. It had used him to kill Marietta, and now it was trying to kill him. His body was trying to burn it out. But only God could burn it out from his soul.

19

Jonson rose early to the sound of parrots fussing in the bushes overhanging his porch. They weren't exactly squawking, so much as singing in poor voices. When he opened his front door, they gathered in a bouquet and fluttered into the sunlight. The sky was an unapologetic blue, so solid and ceramic-looking it seemed as if he could reach out and crack it with the tip of a hammer. He could tell it was going to be a scorcher. Even by 7 a.m., sheets of hot air were rising from the grass.

When Garolf tapped at the door frame of the kastom bank, Jonson was sitting at his desk, absent-mindedly running the back of his hand over his face, wondering if he needed a shave.

'Good morning,' Garolf said.

Jonson rose to shake his hand. 'Surprised you didn't send Ephraim,' he said.

'I need to go to Noia Saruru anyway, Leen has a calf he's going to sell me.'

'A cow? For what – milk?' The image of fresh cream spread across scones flashed before Jonson's eyes.

Garolf sighed. 'How am I going to use a calf for milk if its mother is in Noia Saruru? And you think I want to drink the cow's milk? I thought you were well educated.' He gestured towards the wooden desk burrowed with wormholes, the notebooks warped and rumpled with humidity.

'Fine,' Jonson said, snapping his ledger shut. 'Anyway, don't you want your employees back? They're in the nakamal.'

They walked east through the village to the nakamal. The

day was now brewing fierce heat and it pulsed from the earth in waves. Jonson heard the audible plunk of a drop of sweat rolling off the tip of his nose and landing in the dirt.

Garolf pulled his shirt away from his skin and shook it in billows. 'Today's going to be a bad one. There'll be a storm later.'

'I hope so. Your workers are going to roast otherwise.'

When Jonson poked his head into the nakamal, he could smell the runaways before he could see them – unwashed human, and soiled baby linens. He was also surprised to see Patro Tarileo perching on the stool. Patro was bouncing the baby up and down in his arms, making whistling noises.

'Those are them?' Garolf gestured at the bedraggled captives.

Jonson leant against the door frame. 'Who else would they be, for goodness' sake?'

Garolf looked them up and down. 'The *Reunion* is passing soon. Be ready,' he said. He stared at the baby a beat longer, then walked out of the hut and nudged Fritchard, who was lying in the shade under the nakamal thatch. 'Get them a bucket of water.'

Jonson nodded at Patro. 'Good to see you.' He looked around the base of the stool to see if Patro had brought any deposits for the kastom bank.

Patro pulled his thumb out from in between the baby's fist. 'The whiteman in Bambayot is sick,' he said.

'The Pastor?'

Patro raised his eyebrows in a 'yes'.

'How sick?'

'Bad sick. He's got a fever.'

'Has he any medicine?'

'The Pastor's wife said no to leaf medicine. She asked for you to come quickly.'

Jonson rubbed his forehead with his knuckles. If the man

had malarial fever, and no medicine, he would most likely die. And if he didn't die now, he would probably die during the next bout, or the next. There wasn't much he could do, other than take him Atabrine tablets, and hope for the best. Still, if his wife had called for him, it was his duty to go. As an administrative officer, but also as a gentleman.

He blinked out into the sunlight. 'When is the *Reunion* passing?'

'Two, maybe three days,' Garolf said.

Jonson gestured back towards his house, and Garolf walked beside him. 'I'll join you on the boat. The Pastor in Bambayot has fallen ill.'

Garolf wrinkled his nose. 'Not another one. You'll need your tweezers.'

Jonson sighed. 'I think it's more likely malaria. His wife asked for me to come to help her.' After a moment he added, 'Urgently.'

Garolf raised an eyebrow. 'Urgent like DeWitt?'

'I think if we'd reached DeWitt levels of urgency, Bule would have said something by now.'

Jonson had maintained a polite distance from Reginald DeWitt, a paunchy, balding American with a glass eye. When DeWitt turned up at weddings with a copy of *Baebol Long Bislama* in lieu of a gift, Jonson would hide in the nakamal until he'd given his speech and left. When DeWitt married a thirteen-year-old girl from Wansan, the family made no objections, and Jonson bit his tongue. When DeWitt declared his pregnant wife was carrying the prophet John Frum, Jonson left him to his incarnate messiah, assuming the happy couple would soon be taking their progeny to Tanna where he could be worshipped with the proper adherence. But DeWitt began leading hectic parades up and down the coastal path, adorned with a frangipani crown, and reciting Isaiah 53, over and over.

At that point, even his generous bride price wasn't enough to quell local gossip. His wife was kidnapped by sympathetic locals in Kumuvete, and returned to her aunt and uncle. DeWitt hanged himself from an outcrop below Pilgrim's Rock, in Central. His body was partially buried under a sparkling pile of guano before anyone found it.

'And are you ready for tonight?'

Jonson snapped back to attention with difficulty. 'What's tonight?'

Garolf frowned. 'The hunt! Best eating of the year!'

'Oh, the hunt's tonight? Damn, and my generator's out.'

Garolf threw a damp arm over Jonson's narrow shoulder. 'There wouldn't be any meat left for your stupid cooler once I'm finished, anyway.' He patted his belly with his free hand.

They waited in Jonson's house for the hottest part of the day to pass. Jonson sat in his bed trying to read his latest Dorothy L. Sayers, *Gaudy Night*, until the sweat trickled down his arms and he left moist thumbprints on the paper. He spread a towel over his thin mattress and lay prostrate for an hour, scratching at the drops crawling over his brow. Outside, the three empty petrol canisters on his porch expanded with the heat, pinging and clattering. He closed his eyes and fell into a somnolent daze, conscious of the muggy air against his cracked lips.

When he felt his own brain was baking in his head, he rose, the room swirling, and knocked on the door frame of the spare room. Completely nude, Garolf was leaning against the window frame, fanning himself with a woven pandan fan usually carried by old ladies on their way to church.

'Swim?'

Garolf nodded, heavily pulling on his shorts. 'But –'

'What?'

'Not in the cove – we might scare away the dugongs.'

Jonson sighed. 'Stream, then.'

They trudged through the village, passing villagers napping under trees and dogs sprawled dolefully under hedges. Jonson had left his sandals outside his front door and the soles were scorching, the rubber stiff and tight from the heat. The stream at the top of the village had thinned to a trickle, drawing back to viscous mud around the edges. Jonson crossed into the middle of the stream bed and lay flat on his back, fully clothed. The mud was glutinous and sticky as warm custard. An icy gurgle of water splashed over the top of his head and sprinkled his neck and shoulders. Garolf spread out in the coarse grass under a breadfruit tree and waited his turn.

'Wait –' Garolf sat up on his elbows.

Jonson opened his eyes just enough to gaze through his white lashes. 'Wait for what?'

'Listen! I knew it would rain.'

Jonson heard the distant grumble of thunder, and smelt the faintly chemical smell of electricity.

'Come on –' Garolf knelt and offered him his hand.

Half coated in mud, Jonson squinted up into the hills of Central, where a grey mist zipped through the forest. Within minutes, it was raining bullets of warm water that splattered crowns of mud in the air. Jonson and Garolf stood gratefully in the downpour until they heard whistles by the shoreline. High up on the verge overlooking the ocean, three teenage boys in tattered shorts were pointing out over the water.

'The dugongs! The storm's already brought them in, I told you it would,' said Garolf.

'You said nothing of the sort!'

Villagers woke from their naps, ventured out from their shelters, and ran through the stream to the shore to watch the hunt. Jonson saw Titus splash past, his T-shirt tucked into the back of his shorts like a diaper. 'Who's watching the Tonks?' he shouted.

Titus shrugged. 'I put a namele leaf on the door – the tabu will stop them from getting away.'

'Oh, for heaven's sake.' Jonson tugged Garolf's arm. 'No one's guarding the nakamal.'

Garolf groaned.

Jonson jogged down to the nakamal, expecting to find it empty. As he approached, he saw a namele leaf had been nailed into the thatch above the nakamal doorway. But when he put his head through the doorway of the hut, the couple sat up groggily from the benches where they had been dozing.

'They're still here,' he said, as Garolf arrived behind him, breathing heavily. 'We'll have to take them with us to the hunt.'

Coughing, Garolf rapped against the door frame. 'Come out,' he shouted. First the man, then the woman filed out of the hut, the baby napping against her shoulder. They were limp with sweat, their faces shining. The woman cupped her hand over the baby's head against the rainfall.

'All right, move along,' Jonson said, 'to the coast.'

The couple stood still, looking deferentially at Garolf.

Jonson sighed. 'What's his name again?'

Garolf chewed his lip. 'Probably Nguyen.'

'Nguyen,' Jonson said, loudly, 'come along. It's manatee for lunch.' Garolf opened his mouth to correct him and Jonson threw up his hands. 'I know – they're not the same thing. He's hardly going to know, is he?' He pointed at the Vietnamese man, who was wiping raindrops off his brow. Jonson clapped his hands. 'Go, go!'

He ushered the couple through the village, watching the twitching face of the sleeping baby bobbing up and down over the woman's shoulder. They waded through the slimy mud in the rising stream, then down the shingle path that led to Bwatapoa's grey pebble beach. Hermit crabs disturbed by the rain crawled along the shoreline rocks. A crowd of villagers had gathered by the spit of land at the north of the beach to watch the dugong hunt, and two teenage boys were knee-deep in the water, fussing over Dyson Bule's dugout canoe.

In the front of the canoe, Dyson was tightening the vine tied around his spear. His son, Wistly, was crouched in the back, bailing out water with a rusty tunafish can. Dyson nudged the boys away from the canoe with the handle end of his spear, and Wistly paddled the boat through the channels in the reef and out into the deep water.

Garolf ordered his runaways to the back of the beach where a crop of mango trees framed a boulder. He took a seat a few metres in front of them, in the shelter of a banana palm. Jonson walked down to the shore and waded ankle-deep into the surf, where grey worms were wriggling in the sand. He shielded his eyes from the foggy haze of rain on water, and watched Wistly manoeuvring the canoe around the plane wreck.

Wistly paddled further north, then lifted his oar and let the boat float. Dyson was crouched at the prow of the canoe, peering into the water. Wistly turned and hissed towards the shore. The boys crowded on the beach shoved each other until silence fell. Dyson stood, and raised his harpoon. He hurled it into the water, losing his balance momentarily. The spear struck something below the surface, the handle bobbing above the waves. Dyson pulled on the rope attached to the catch, then lifted the tail of a dugong from the water. Wistly shuffled forward in the canoe, and together they grappled with the tail, holding the animal down in the churning grey until the tail grew limp.

From around the lip of the cove, another canoe paddled into view. Jonson didn't recognize the fisherman, but he was grinning in victory. Trailing behind his canoe was the body of a second dugong. Cheering, the two teenage boys swam out towards the boat to get closer to the victory, only to turn around and swim back to shore again alongside the canoe. In the shallows, the fisherman of the second canoe wrested his spear from the animal's flank. Jonson stepped back as six men ran forward to lug the dugong out of the shallows and up on to the beach, where they laid its blunt head across a makeshift bridge of flat stones.

'It's definitely pregnant,' Jonson shouted to Garolf, scrutinizing the protruding curve of its belly.

Garolf gave him a thumbs up. 'How many kilograms?'

'How should I know?' Jonson yelled. 'Come see for yourself.'

Garolf grimaced. 'I like my meat cooked.'

The fisherman jumped out of the canoe to a chorus of appreciative whoops. Striding up the beach, he approached the animal and raised his bushknife. He smacked the dugong once across the head. A spurt of blood ran from its tiny eyes and from a white gash in its neck.

Garolf winced, averting his head.

'They're going to ask you next,' Jonson called to him in a sing-song voice.

Garolf looked around. 'Where's Chief Tabi?'

'No idea. Haven't seen him in weeks.'

'Damn.'

Sure enough, once the fisherman had made the first cut, a young boy ran up to collect Garolf and then, overcome with shyness, averted his face and giggled. Garolf sighed and walked over to the beast. He straddled the glistening body of the dugong. At six foot long, it wasn't even as tall as Garolf, but its swollen stomach gave it the bell-shaped heft of a submarine. Its grey hide was scored with nicks and scratches, its dog-like snout crusted with black sand. Garolf put his hand on the mound of its still-squirming belly, and pulled out his hand-knife. He felt for the top of the animal's ribs, then stuck in his knife between the bones. Its fat was so thick, he barely sliced through the creamy white flesh. Garolf wiped off his hands on his shorts and gestured for the fisherman to continue his work.

As women gathered round to help carve up the animal, Dyson's canoe paddled to the shore and he shouted for help. Jonson felt rather sorry for him; after all the ceremony for the first animal everyone had forgotten about Dyson's catch. A group of teenagers and clapping children ran down to drag Dyson's dugong to shore.

Now the air pressure had dropped, Jonson was growing chill from the rain, and he joined Garolf crouching under the banana palm. He turned behind them to inspect the couple and the baby, which was mewling softly. The man had pulled a pile of leaves from a mango tree, and was wiping the baby's behind and throwing the leaves into the brush.

When a young girl collected Garolf to attend to the next dugong, he performed a cursory incision and returned, frowning. 'Second one's not so fat.'

'Don't sulk, there's plenty to go around.'

Garolf picked at his fingernail. 'I suppose. And the bulls haven't even arrived yet,' he said cheerfully.

The rain sluiced diluted blood from the two dugongs down the beach, running pink loops between the pebbles. Dyson's wife, Cynthia, knelt by the larger of the animals and plunged her hands into the cavity, pulling out the white ropes of its intestine on to the beach. Using her bushknife, she cut beneath its ribs, and lifted from the body the quivering sac of the calf. Carrying the jellied bundle down to the water's edge, she rinsed it in the surf until it leached yellow.

'They should save some for the Tonk,' Garolf said,

gesturing behind him into the bushes, 'the fat's good for nursing mothers.'

Jonson turned to the Vietnamese couple. The man had the baby across his shoulder, and was licking his lips, over and over. As Jonson watched him, he crossed himself. When he glanced at the woman, he realized she must have already been looking at him, since she met his stare directly. Her eyes flicked to the squirming caul of the dugong calf, then back to meet his. Her expression was cool, evaluative, her gaze steady.

'I get the feeling she's lost her appetite,' he said.

20

On one of Aru's visits to the invalid in Mission House, Bea was busying herself in the kitchen, spooning weevils out of the powdered milk. She heard Aru's footsteps cross the living room as he left through the front door. Seconds later, there was a knock on the frame.

Bea approached the door in disbelief. 'Mr Aru – but please come back in!'

He took a step away from the front door.

'Mrs Anlon, the Pastor has requested I take over the church duties until he regains his health,' he said, into his sandals.

Bea wiped her hands on the sides of her dress. 'Well, yes, of course, that would be splendid of you.'

Aru nodded and looked over her shoulder towards Max's room.

'Would you like to come back in?' Bea put her hand on the door to open it again.

'No, thank you.'

Bea dropped her hand. 'I can't begin to thank you for visiting the Pastor. I know it brings him great comfort.'

Aru lingered in the doorway. 'Will you be attending service on Sunday?'

'Of course.'

Aru fingered the lintel. 'And your friend?'

Bea looked around her hopelessly, thinking of New Dog, before she realized he meant Santra. She laughed. 'Oh, no. I doubt it.'

'You should bring her,' Aru said.

'The next time I see her,' Bea smiled, 'I'll ask her to join us.'
Aru nodded again, and turned to walk back to the village.

That Sunday, Bea kissed Max on his hot forehead while he struggled and muttered. She collected her fan and her Bible, and took her customary place in church. The service began much as normal. Aru strummed his ukulele on the front right-hand side of the church, accompanied by several rounds of hymns, courtesy of the church singers.

Then, Sousan was given the honour of distributing the 'altar wine' for Communion. Except, of course, there was no wine. Instead, there was a Vietnamese rose-flavoured cordial incrementally watered down with warm rainwater, and passed about in one large plastic beaker. Each villager took a sip from the cup, and, in lieu of bread, helped themselves to a fragment of SAO breakfast crackers from a 'plate' of banana leaves.

At the end of each row, Sousan handed the beaker on to the next row of churchgoers. Since the cupbearer travelled anti-clockwise, and Bea sat right at the front on the left, she was always the last recipient of the cup, and she always dreaded the moment when she must sip from it.

Bea looked around her at the room full of elderly women with luxurious beards, young children dribbling mucus down their chins, toothless teenagers chewing betel nut. Absolutely the last thing Bea ever wanted to do was to press her lips against the cup that had already been sucked and spittled on by every last person in the village. When it was her turn, she rested the cup gingerly above her top lip. She tipped it so the red cordial lapped up against her skin, and mimed swallowing while trying to maintain an appropriately holy expression on her face.

*

And then, Aru began his sermon. At first, Bea was grateful he was speaking in English. But as his service continued, she began to wish she hadn't been able to understand.

'The End of Days,' Aru bellowed, swaying side to side, on the tops of his toes, as if stepping on hot sand. Then, more quietly, 'The End of Days has come upon us.'

'A-men,' a woman at the back of the room replied.

'Praise be to Jesus!'

'A-men.'

'And right now, now, even as we sit here in church giving thanks to the loving Holy Father and His son, Jesus Christ –'

'A-men.'

'– the Beast walks among us.'

'Oh Lord!' The woman shook her head sadly from side to side.

'Yes, sir. The Beast walks among us. And it is the will of the Beast that the body of the church be split up!' Aru pointed his finger to the sky, leaping on to his toes as he did so. 'Yes, indeed. It is the will of the Beast that the believers, the body of Christ in the church, be divided.'

'Oh, Jesus! Oh, Jesus!' the woman moaned softly.

'The Beast is the enemy. Anyone who is not in the body of Christ, is against the body of Christ. Any man, woman or child, who is not with the body of Christ, his believers, seeks to destroy us. To tear us up!' Aru raised his voice to a yell, punching both his fists in the air.

The women in the church fanned themselves more quickly, to a muttered chorus of, 'Yes, sir,' and, 'A-men.'

'And how do we recognize this danger, you may ask?' Aru said in a stage whisper, half-crouched on the stage, beads of sweat shining on his top lip. 'I'll tell you how. They are the weak of spirit, the weak of flesh. And the mind controlled by the flesh is hostile to God. Their weak bodies are wide open to evil. Any enemy of this church is an enemy of God!'

'A-men.'

'For too long, we have kept the weak amongst us. The weak of spirit are the enemy of God. It is their unbelieving ways that lets in the darkness.' Aru paused, holding eye contact with the congregation, not making a movement. Barely a breath was drawn. When he spoke again it was a thundering roar. 'It is our job, our holy obligation, to seek out these unbelievers and cast them out of the body of Christ. We *have* the power of the spirit and the Lord Jesus Christ –'

'A-men, Lord Jesus!'

'We have the blessing of the Lord!'

'A-men.'

'Praise be to Jesus!'

'Hallelujah!'

'And in these sad times, we see what dangers threaten the community of God.' Aru strolled across the platform, shaking his head. 'We must be grateful God has spared us, that Jesus has died for us, and we, we will be saved.' He raised his hands to his face, his voice breaking with emotion.

'Oh, praise Jesus,' the woman muttered, the 'Jesus' foaming together like one hiss under her tears, 'Praise Jesss, praise Jesss.'

'We must search out the weak. The unbelievers. They may not even know their own weakness. They may not even know – they are under the power of Ukunu – that they work for *Satan himself*!'

A chorus of whooping went around the congregation, with more flapping of fans, more whispering of A-mens.

'We will come together as one body, one body of believers, one body in Christ!' Aru continued.

Several drops of sweat fused together at the base of Bea's neck, trickling down her back to the strap of her brassiere.

'And cleanse them of their weakness! By the power and the spirit of Jesus Christ our Lord!' Aru shouted, almost drowned out by the noise of so many A-mens.

Bea felt her face flushing with the heat, her tongue stuck to the roof of her mouth. Nod, she told herself. Say, 'A-men.' She was gripped by a wave of paranoia, tinged with a sudsy, nauseous rim. Why was everyone looking at her? They couldn't be talking about her? She was the Pastor's wife.

She gripped her fan and waved it furiously under her nose. Whatever happened, she mustn't faint. She must not faint in front of these people. They would only think it was the devil in her trying to escape, being affected by the power of their Holy Spirit. Bea pushed a thumbnail into her left thigh, hoping the tiny nag of pain would distract her from the green splotches popping on the corners of her vision. Close your eyes, she told herself, close your eyes and say, 'A-men.'

21

On the day of the christenings, Bea walked north to Hot Wata with the other women. Max, Edly Tabi and Aru had gone ahead hours ago. There were about six women walking all together, dressed in their finest island dresses, with hibiscus flowers tucked behind their ears. The day was shimmering with heat, and as they walked, Bea could smell the clay cooking in the mud along the coast. Bea watched the flower wilting in Morinda's hair.

Bea had already been baptized, of course. In her father's house there had been a small photograph of her in her white baptismal gown in her mother's arms. As a scrawny, frowning baby with unusually thick eyebrows, Bea barely looked related to the slim, glamorous woman in the short-brimmed hat and white gloves.

But Max had said this was a different kind of baptism. Aru held a yearly ceremony for any members of the surrounding villages who wished to recommit themselves to the Lord. And this year, Max was in charge. He hadn't exactly asked her to participate, it was just implied. He had been especially excitable in the days leading up to the ceremony, whistling in the house. She hadn't thought it a good idea. He had barely recovered from his fever – surely, she'd told him, the baptisms could wait. Aru could do them, she offered, and Max could be in charge next year. But he hadn't even replied to her suggestions. He hadn't spoken to her much at all. One day, he'd just been out of his bed, bright-eyed and jittery. He'd become so thin, Bea was perplexed he even had the strength to sustain this rush of sudden energy. And he'd shaved off his beard.

He and Aru had drawn up a list of the names of the people who had received baptisms over the past few years, as well as those participating in this year's ceremony. Beside each name, Max had drawn a tiny cross. Bea had seen this list tucked inside Max's Bible on the kitchen table of Mission House. She had unfolded it to find her own name written carefully in pencil along with the others. There was no cross beside her name.

An hour or so after they left Bambayot, a boy appeared on the coastal path, running towards them holding a huge stick. He had almost reached her skirts before Bea realized it was Moses. He grabbed his mother's hand, beaming, and started speaking in rapid-fire Language that Bea couldn't understand. The women nodded between themselves, before following him down to the beach. In the shady part of the sand, near the tree-line, there were two other boys about Moses' age sitting on the roots of a huge mango tree. The commotion seemed to be directed somewhere behind the roots.

Bea approached warily. It wasn't the first time Moses had enthusiastically steered her towards one of his finds – a dead parrot with its brains unspooled, or a trail of ants carrying a severed bullock's tongue halfway up a papaya tree.

But cornered behind the tree roots was a huge turtle. Its shell was the size of a small bathtub, and its long head bobbed slowly up and down. Joyce and Moses began bickering behind her, and a couple of the women broke away from the beach, ambling back up towards the coastal path. Bea took a step towards the turtle. Its head was tapered and scaly, and it was wearing a strange half-smile on its face.

The boy on the root closest to her was watching her carefully. 'Whitewoman,' he said, whistling.

He was sitting astride the roots, one pink foot dangling. He offered up his stick, and gestured towards the turtle. Bea shook her head, recoiling. She knew in theory turtles were slow-moving, but this was a monster. The boy chuckled at her and, with a swift jab, poked the turtle in the chin. It drew its head partway back into its body. The boy looked at Bea again. She felt some kind of reaction was expected, so she smiled and nodded in appreciation of his bravado. Moses had stormed off down the beach. He threw his stick on the shore, and kicked up a flurry of sand. Joyce turned to Bea and rolled her eyes.

'He loves to eat turtle –' she pointed at Moses '– but this is a Mama Turtle. It's tabu to kill them.' Joyce raised her voice in quick admonishment to the two boys guarding their prize, and walked back up to join the others.

It took another three hours to walk to Hot Wata. No one said much as they walked. Bea had hoped there might be singing, or gossiping, but the mood was sombre. Finally, as they approached Hot Wata village, Bea saw a small crowd had gathered by the path to watch the spectacle, smoking and swatting flies with their bushknives.

A chubby teenage girl wearing an island basket tied around her forehead stopped nearby. She touched Bea lightly on the inside of her elbow. 'Do you know the Pastor's wife?' she asked, her eyes wide.

Bea was taken aback. 'I am the Pastor's wife,' she said, looking around her for validation from Joyce.

The girl nodded, and stood staring at her in silence until Bea awkwardly walked away.

By the shoreline, Max and Aru had set up an impromptu table on a wooden crate. On it were placed a plastic beaker and a Bible. An archway had been created from large twigs, bound together with vine, which was wound with more hibiscus flowers and palm fronds.

Bea had been expecting a sermon of some kind, but instead, the singing began, and one by one, each woman walked through the arch, to join Max and Aru. They both waded into the ocean. There, Max and Aru exchanged words, pressed the Bible against the woman's forehead, and submerged her in the water.

When it was her turn, Bea walked extra carefully. The last thing she wanted was to lose concentration and slip and fall in front of all these people. As she waded into the ocean, a swell rose against her legs, and the hem of her dress lifted. Bea quickly clamped it between her shins, struggling to get into the water past her knees.

Max and Aru said their prayers. Bea wasn't listening. She had heard it all before. She turned towards Max, as the others had done. Despite the ocean, she could smell the sweet smell of Max's sweat. The water had lapped up over his shirt and it was translucent over the muscles in his arms. When he reached forward to push her under, his expression was unreadable. She realized it was the first time he had come close to her in weeks.

After the baptisms, the women stood to the side, dripping, while Max and Aru led them in more prayers. There was more singing. And then people began to disperse. Someone laid a banana leaf filled with slices of taro into Bea's hands. When she looked up to say thank you, she didn't know who had given it to her.

Max walked over to stand next to her. 'Today was success-ful, I think,' he said, looking around the small crowd of dispersing villagers.

Bea nodded, quickly swallowing a crumbly mouthful of taro in case he expressed an opinion about fasting or feasting.

Aru came to stand by them, then he and Max began to walk away north along the coast. Max half turned to her, raising one eyebrow, which Bea took to mean she should follow him. They walked along the shore for about ten minutes until they reached Hot Wata spring. Bea could smell the sulphurous, eggy water before she even saw the trickle. They stopped on either side of it.

'This is a holy spring.' Aru pointed at the water.

Bea looked up at Max, who nodded generously.

'This was the landing place of the first pilgrims to come to the island. It was the site of the very first church on the island,' Aru continued.

Beatriz looked around her.

'Before the earthquake,' Max added.

Aru pointed at the spring. 'This is the water of life.'

'Beatriz,' Max turned to her. 'I ask you to cleanse yourself in this water.'

'But –' Bea pointed out into the ocean '– I've already been cleansed.'

Max looked at her. 'Your spirit has been cleansed, but your will must also submit.'

'My will?'

'Your stubborn will.'

Bea looked down at her own ankles. Her face felt hot. She did have a stubborn will. But how could Max say such personal things in front of Aru?

'You are special to me, Bea. I have to take a particular care of your spiritual health,' Max said.

Bea peered up at him. He had never said anything like that before. Special? She felt her throat grow tight.

'I have a special responsibility for you,' he continued.

Bea nodded, pressing her left big toe into her right big toe, until the nail went white.

'I can't rest until I know you are safe – that your soul is safe.'

'You must practise obedience,' Aru said. His eyes were downcast.

Bea tried to keep her face neutral.

'Yes,' Max said, 'obedience to God. How can the Lord do His work through you, until you admit your sins?'

'I have, I admit my sins, I do!' Bea looked around her, blinking back tears of shame. She wished Aru weren't there.

'We are all sinners. And we must all practise obedience. It is not enough to say the words. You must demonstrate it in your actions, in your spiritual life. Only obedience to the Word can drive out the sin – the evil of the soul.'

'I will, I shall. I do.'

Aru gestured towards the spring.

Bea looked up at both of them. The sulphur water shot out of the ground in a spitting stream. 'Oh, no.' She shook her head.

Max exchanged a look with Aru. 'I have taken responsibility for your spiritual well-being. Do you understand?' Max said.

'I do.'

'I can't stand by while you continue to reject God's grace. It is not your fault. We are all sinners. I was once like you, too. Vulnerable. You must practise obedience until you are truly clean.'

Bea stepped back. 'No, I can't. It is too hot, I can't – it will burn me!'

'Beatriz,' Max said, gently, 'it is only flesh.'

Bea felt shaky as she walked towards the water. The spring was little more than a muddy puddle, bubbling over in a rolling simmer. There was barely enough water to reach her ankles, but the stink was overwhelming. She stood with her face towards Max. Despite the months of walking across coral without her shoes, her feet were prickling and itchy in the searing heat of the stream. Max laid a hand on her shoulder and pushed lightly downwards. She crouched in the water and her knees dipped into the bubbling spring. The dress soaked up the smell. She wobbled, and put her hands out to steady herself. She heard herself gasp. The water was scalding. It pierced all her bites and scrapes. The sore on her right hand stung and throbbed. The water was silty and gritty at the bottom, it felt almost greasy on her skin.

Aru prayed, and Max cradled her head back in his hands, so the egg water splashed over her scalp, trickling down the sides of her face. Bea held her breath, and closed her eyes.

It was only flesh.

22

Ten days after her baptism, Bea woke up to the pressure of Max's hand on her left foot through the mosquito net.

She sat up on her elbows. 'Maxis?'

'My dear.' Max gave her foot another squeeze. He was holding the hurricane lamp. 'Sweetheart,' he said gently, 'will you come with me?'

Bea's heart started beating in her throat. 'Is there a storm? The garden?' She began to paw through the folds of mosquito net to find the opening.

Max chuckled. 'No. Nothing like that. I want you to come with me.'

She squinted at the floor for her sandals. 'Where are we going? Is everything all right?' Bea realized a glimmer of light was perforating the wall to the corridor. 'Is someone else here?' she asked. She shook out her sandals and leant against the frame of the cot to slip them on.

Max looked back over his shoulder quickly. 'Yes. Morinda is here.'

'Morinda?' Bea combed out her braid with her fingers and began to re-plait it.

'Don't worry with that now,' Max said impatiently, gesturing towards the door frame with his head.

Bea kept braiding her hair anyway. 'I don't understand. Why is Morinda here? Is Mabo-Mabon —'

Max took a step back as Bea peered into the corridor. Morinda was holding a candle, looking shyly at the ground.

'No –' Max put his hand on the back of her shoulder '– Mabo-Mabon is fine. We'd like you to join us for a prayer.'

Bea's stomach dipped. He wanted her to join them in the church.

Bea followed Morinda, watching the pale semicircles at the back of her bare feet as Morinda walked slowly out of the front of the house. Her candle blew out as soon as they stepped out of the door. Bea didn't look ahead, but concentrated on putting her footsteps inside the imprints left by Morinda's heels in the wet grass.

As they walked down towards the church, Bea could see a faint glow of illumination coming from within. There was already a group of people inside. She could hear low, soft singing coming from the building. A wave of adrenaline crested in Bea's stomach. She felt sick. She wrapped her arms over her chest. She wished she weren't wearing her nightdress.

As they entered the door of the church, Bea could see the benches had been pushed against the walls of the room. There were seven girls standing in front of Aru, who was strumming on his ukulele. Max put the hurricane lamp down on a pew on the left corner of the building, and pointed to the centre of the room.

'Stand there, sweetheart,' he said.

Morinda crossed in front of Bea, and stood against the back wall. Bea turned towards the group. She didn't want to look up, to catch anyone's eye. She walked towards the centre of the room. The girls around her took a step back. Bea stood still. She kept her head bowed, and her arms clasped over her chest. She looked down at her feet. They were wet and dirty from the grass. She could see the faint muddy footprints she had tracked across the wooden floor.

Aru began to play a new melody, and the girls started to

hum. It was a song Bea recognized. A sweet song, about the light of God. Aru continued to strum chords as the girls' singing dwindled. Over the music, he began to pray.

'Almighty Jesus. We call on you this evening to grace us with the power of your spirit.'

Murmurs of 'A-men' came from the girls.

Bea continued to look at her feet. But from the corner of her eye, she could tell Aru was shifting his weight from side to side.

'Lord Jesus Christ, we call on your powers of mercy, of justice, of righteousness.'

'A-men.'

'We call on your powers of healing. We ask you to come down, to bless all those here with the grace of your mercy.'

'A-men.'

'Oh Jesus,' Aru placed his ukulele down on one of the benches, 'we beseech you to fill us with your healing spirit! We ask you to send us your wisdom. We ask you to come down this night. To fill us with your healing *spirit*.'

'A-men.'

'We are only sinners, oh Lord. We are only sinners but for your grace. Fill us now with your power to heal! To purify! To reject the power of darkness!'

'Oh Lord, oh Lord,' began the chorus from the girls around Bea. They were rocking slowly from side to side.

The girls began to mutter.

'Oh Lord, we beseech you.'

'In the name of Jesus Christ.'

'Almighty Jesus, help us.'

'We pray, oh Lord! We pray you fill us with your holy *spirit*! We pray that you cast *out* the demon from within this child!' Aru continued.

'Oh Lord, help us, help us.'

'We ask you to help us purify this child in Jesus! To save her from the power of the Beast! By your mercy!'

Bea stood still, though she was disorientated by the movement around her. The girls were swaying. Some of them were whispering.

Bea kept her arms clasped over her chest. She was acutely aware she wasn't wearing any underclothes. Would they make her lie down? Could she somehow signal to Max that she wasn't wearing any underwear? Would they allow her to go back to Mission House and dress properly?

The noise grew louder. Aru was praying on his own now. Bea couldn't pick out the words. They all jumbled together in one hush of whispers, of prayers, of humming. Bea stood rigid. She felt as if the room were spinning, and her own feet were far away from her. If she clenched her legs really tight, nobody would know she wasn't wearing any underwear.

The girls began to move around the room. Someone was banging on the wood on the walls of the building. Someone was crying. Someone was shrieking, 'I cast you *out*!' over and over. Bea could see flickers of movement as people shook their wrists out at her.

Aru's voice suddenly shouted out above the din, 'In the name of Jesus, I cast out Satan and all his evil works.'

And then, Max's voice. 'Lord Jesus. We call on you to heal this weakness. Protect this child from the power of darkness.'

Bea felt unsteady. She had almost forgotten Max was even there. It was the first time he had spoken since they came into the church. Had he been there the whole time?

Bea clamped her knees together. She kept her head down. But someone was walking towards her. It was Aru. He was carrying something. A Bible.

'In the name of Jesus,' he whispered, and he put one of his

hands on Bea's forehead. He gently tipped her head back. He pressed the Bible against her forehead, and pushed her. Bea was forced to lean back against the brace of his other forearm. 'I cast you out –' he clamped the Bible tighter against her forehead '– in the name of Jesus!'

Bea felt tears dribble out of her eyes and streak into her ears. She closed her eyes. She could smell the damp leather binding of the Bible against her nose. And then it was lifted. She felt somehow as if there were still a pressure against her face. One of the girls took Aru's Bible from him, and handed him something. Bea's head was still tipped back by his forearm. She felt the lip of a cup against her mouth.

'With this holy water I cast out the powers of darkness,' Aru said.

Bea's arms were still crossed over her chest. She tried to look sideways at Max but her eyeballs hurt in her skull. She pressed her lips together. She would not drink from that cup.

Aru's hand gripped her at her waist, not unkindly. He began to pour, and warm liquid ran over her mouth. It dribbled down her chin.

'Drink, and be healed!' Aru whispered to her. 'Cleanse yourself from the power of evil.'

Bea's back and legs began to shake. More tears dripped towards her throat. She felt as if she might fall backwards. She raised her hands to push away at the cup.

Max came to stand by her. He placed his hand over Aru's on her forehead. He pressed one finger softly into the spot between her eyebrows. He leant his head down towards her. She could feel his stubble against her ear. She wanted to rub at where it was tickling.

'Sweetheart, please,' he said softly into her ear, 'it's for your own good.'

Bea felt her body shake harder. She turned to Max, her lips

opened, and Aru began to pour the warm, salty seawater into her mouth. Bea struggled for breath. She shook free of Aru's hand, and tried to take a step backwards. She doubled over, retching. A few grains of rice splashed on to the wood. She wiped the sticky corner of her mouth. Her tongue was crawling. She could feel the salt burning in her nostrils.

Max held her gently under the elbow. Bea looked up at him and he smiled at her. She leant against him. He brushed the hair away from her neck, and nodded at Aru. Aru came to stand by her, and placing his hand on her forehead, tipped her head back. Max cupped the base of her skull with his hand. Bea began to cry in earnest now. Her body shook against them.

Aru poured again. 'We purify you in the name of *Jesus*! In the name of the Lord we cast you out.'

23

Jonson and Garolf squatted on the corrugated-iron roof of the *Reunion* as it bobbed south. Garolf was an Advent Island celebrity, and alongside the whiteman and the family of Vietnamese captives, they made something of an impression on the boat. The captain came up on to the deck to greet them with handshakes and nervous smiles, as if they were visiting dignitaries. Jonson looked out at the white fingertips of coral poking through the green ocean, and wondered who was steering the ship. The runaways and their baby were shuffled into a sort of makeshift pen at the front of the boat, surrounded by wooden crates.

Garolf and Jonson crouched on a pandan mat under the awnings by the engine, fanning themselves and eating slivers of warm laplap. Jonson sniffed suspiciously at the fetid water in the drinking bucket, and instead resigned himself to Garolf's private supply of kava. Garolf explained to Jonson in a connoisseur's language the virtue of this particular vintage of kava, which had been fermented from top-quality roots, mixed with the most acidic water on the island, and chewed by the purest pre-pubescent boys. Jonson couldn't tell the difference between the good stuff and the usual putrid swill, but he drank it anyway. There was a reason nakamals were so dark, he realized. Drinking kava in the daytime splintered light through his skull and he felt perilously close to a glittering, ringing headache. He and Garolf lounged in the shade as the boat rolled through the rippling water.

Jonson thought of Beatriz Hanlon. What would happen to

that poor woman if the Pastor died? Would she go back to wherever she had come from? Perhaps missionaries received a form of pension for dangerous work in the service. Jonson ran his finger over the tip of his bushknife experimentally. Not quite awake, but not quite dreaming, he imagined Bea might come and live with him. She could live in the spare room, perhaps take on some of the housekeeping duties. Transported by this fantasy, he dozed in and out of consciousness for hours.

The boat finally crawled to a stop downstream of Bambayot village in the late afternoon. Whoops of appreciation echoed all along the coastline, as villagers celebrated their arrival. As the boat anchored, Jonson tentatively stood up, and brushed off a fine dust of white sand that had settled into the creases of his jacket. He took off his shoes and socks, and clambered down into the water, which was as warm as a bath in the shallows. It felt incredible. Slim silver fish sparkled in the still water. He looked back to Garolf, who touched his forehead in a pantomime of Jonson's own habit of raising his hat. Jonson walked unsteadily towards the shore, carrying his shoes in one hand, while Garolf helped to unload crates from the boat.

Jonson climbed the Bambayot hill, wondering where to look first. The Mission House, or perhaps the church? There was every likelihood he would find the poor fellow in a hole in the ground next to the stream, along with the other missionaries who had expired in the line of duty.

Before long, a circle of children had surrounded him, shouting hellos at him as if he were an animal in the zoo. Their motion was disorientating after the rise and fall of the ship.

'Where is Pastor Hanlon?' he asked one of the older children.

She opened her eyes wide and turned to the gaggle, as a flurry of consultation began in a mixture of languages.

Jonson thought perhaps the chap was dead, after all.

'Where's the whiteman?' the girl shouted up the hill, towards a pair of young twins sitting at the top of the bank. 'His brother is looking for him.'

'I'm not his –' Jonson began, before he stopped himself, shaking his head and sighing. Really, what was the point?

The twins came scooting down over the top of the hill, gliding on the soles of their feet in the dust, grinning with the jubilant responsibility of knowing more than an adult.

'The church, the church,' they chorused, unnecessarily pointing towards the church building. One of them gripped Jonson round the wrist, to escort him there even more efficiently.

Jonson peered through the doorway of the church, where the tall figure of the Pastor was bent over a book, absorbed in sewing the white pith of the pages back into the binding.

Max looked up, disturbed by the shadows of the twins who were excitedly scampering in the doorway, whispering his name.

Jonson felt himself deliberately compose his own expression, to hide his surprise. The Pastor had clearly only just about recovered from a serious bout of illness. His clothes were loose on his frame, and his eyes were puckered by red, puffy flesh. His beard had been shaved off – recently, if the pale smudges around his chin were anything to measure by. He looked gaunt and shiny and distinctly unwell.

'Pastor Hanlon, delighted to see you have recovered.' Jonson walked towards him purposefully, his hand outstretched.

Max stood up from the chair with a squeak, took the hand and gave it a firm pump. Jonson had forgotten how tall he was. Even depleted by fever, the man was impressively large.

'How on earth did you know? Yes, I am quite well, it's great to see you.' Max clapped another hand over Jonson's and held it there.

'Mrs Hanlon sent me word, through Tarileo. I thought

perhaps I could be of assistance.' Jonson removed his hand and discreetly wiped it on his trousers.

'How decent of you, truly!' Hanlon bobbed his head in time to his own words. 'I am fit as a fiddle now.' He beamed, outstretching his palms to the heavens. 'Praise be!'

'Praise be,' Jonson echoed meekly, unsure if that were the appropriate response. 'And Mrs Hanlon? I trust she is well?' Jonson was suddenly aware of how thirsty he was. He eyed the plastic beaker on the table.

Hanlon looked solemn, and dipped his chin. 'My wife –' He looked to the right, breaking off his thought.

Jonson shifted his weight from foot to foot. Perhaps he had made a dreadful faux pas, and the wife had since contracted malaria and died. He felt a lump of guilt in his throat, as if his covetous daydream had precipitated some tragedy.

'My wife is on the road to well-being,' Max completed, turning his head back to Jonson. 'She is in the vestry, praying.'

Jonson was relieved, although a little embarrassed, as if he had pried into an intimate revelation about her toilette. He supposed people did pray, but he preferred the details of it to remain private. He couldn't imagine Mrs Hanlon in the act of prayer. That woman was halfway to a wild heathen, with her demonic dog, and muddy feet. Perhaps she was overjoyed by her husband's return to health, and had experienced a grateful spasm of piety.

Jonson looked back through the doorway to the village. 'I say, where is that animal?'

Max looked at him in confusion.

'The beastly thing that loves visitors. By now it should be trying to pick my pockets.'

Max tipped his head back. 'Oh, New Dog. Well, I'm afraid there was something of a –' he coughed '– canine supper, in Kumuvete.'

Jonson grimaced. 'Ah. Well, probably for the best.'

Max put a finger on his lips. 'Perhaps don't discuss that with Mrs Hanlon.'

Jonson nodded. He gratefully accepted a beaker of water from Max, then left him in the church, wearily trudging back to the *Reunion*, to help Garolf with further unloading. After all that, it had been a wasted journey of sorts, and it would take at least a week to walk back to the North. He lasciviously imagined the spare bed he would receive in the Mission House that evening, safely protected from the bellows of Garolf's snoring.

Jonson was surprised when he came through the door of Mission House three hours later to find Hanlon himself stoking the fire in the kitchen over a steaming kettle.

'Good evening!' Max hailed him from the hearth. 'Would you like warm water for your evening bath?'

Startled by his easy domesticity, Jonson nodded. After three days on the water, his clothes and hair were faintly crunchy with salt spray. He carried a china jug into the spare room and sponged himself down. When he was freshly shaved and less saline, Jonson sat at the table in the front room of Mission House, while Max poked about in the fire. Max had been ill for so long he was vague about the latest news in the area, but they debated the possible fate of Garolf's runaways.

Half an hour later, the door swung open to reveal Mrs Hanlon. She gave such a jump her hand flew to her mouth.

'Mr Jonson,' she said.

He stood up, unsure whether he should offer her his hand. She stood in mute astonishment, and he watched, perplexed, as she stared at him. 'Madam,' he tipped his head at her. This seemed to break her reverie.

'You came?'

The childish gratitude in her voice made a flush rise into the tips of his ears. 'Yes,' he said.

She looked almost as dreadful as Hanlon did. She was much thinner, and her hair was tied back from her face in a severe bun that made her crooked nose even more pronounced.

The Pastor came through into the living room, and spooned boiled chouchoute and rice on to Jonson's plate. Mrs Hanlon sat down opposite them at the table on an upturned crate. She was watching her hands, which were poised in front of her as if she were at the piano. They were scaly and blistered, textured with patches of burnt skin. A black-and-crimson tropical sore across the fingers of her right hand forced her to hold it at an odd angle.

'Will you be dining with us?' Jonson asked, hoping she would stay and help to save their faltering conversation.

She didn't look up.

'Mrs Hanlon is fasting at the moment.' Max smiled widely at Jonson. 'It's good discipline for the spirit.'

Jonson looked back to the woman, who was pressing her fingertips into the surface of the plastic tablecloth. Every now and again, she lifted her fingers to examine the smudgy prints they had left behind. She raised her eyes to meet Jonson's. She looked at him blankly, as if she were a floating, dead fish.

Jonson suddenly lost all appetite. The rice sank in his throat. 'That's admirable of you, Mrs Hanlon,' he stammered.

She licked her lips, slowly, but said nothing.

Jonson pressed his fork into the pile of rice, his stomach squirming. These two were barmy. They had both caught DeWitt's jungle fever in their brains. He decided to start his travel back to Bwatapoa sooner than he'd anticipated, perhaps the next day. It could be contagious.

It was pitch black when Jonson awoke. A scream crawled through the darkness and scribbled itself into the centre of his stomach. He sat up, blinking cold sweat out of his eyes.

His heart was racing. Another, shorter scream rang out. His hands were shaking. He tried to light a candle, but he held the match too straight and it smoked out straight away. When it finally caught, he was aware the night was not as black as he had thought. Through the window he could see a white light flickering at the bottom of the hill. A refrain of girlish screams warbled across the village. Jonson dressed, too fraught to notice the cockroach that had climbed into his trouser leg. He swung open the door of the bedroom and stepped into the corridor, coming almost face to face with the Pastor's wife in the darkness. He let out a high-pitched yelp.

She was standing completely still, in a clear state of dishabille, clad in a loose nightgown with a large grey patch darned across the front. Her feet were bare. She was holding her arms across her stomach.

'Mrs Hanlon! You startled me.' He tried to look behind her into the room, in case the Pastor was in there, and had overheard his ladylike squeal. It appeared to be empty; a candle was burning by the bed. The howling grew louder. 'Can you hear – that noise? We must get help – the Pastor –'

She cut him off. 'That is the Pastor,' she said quietly.

'The Past–? But it must be two in the morning – has someone fallen ill?'

She shook her head. 'The noise, it's Max.'

He gaped at her dumbly, trying to half start a word or two.

'It's not my turn tonight,' she said. She turned to walk back into the room.

Jonson's mouth opened. A chill slunk over his skull and into his jawbone.

'Go back to bed.' She turned to look straight at him now, her right eye pulsing in its socket. 'Please.'

*

The next morning Jonson was jittery. He had barely slept. The Pastor's wife had disconcerted him further by climbing into her bed and lying there with her back turned to the door, the candle guttering in its frame. Jonson had ignored her request, and walked out to the top of the hill above the church, the warm breeze spitting ocean salt in his face. He listened to the noise for another ten minutes, half starting towards the chapel three times before turning back on himself. Eventually he went back to his cot in Mission House and lay awake, hearing Max come back in sometime around sunrise. He dropped off to sleep soon after, waking late in the morning. His mouth felt dry, and he was still wearing all his clothes.

There was no one else in the house, and in the light of morning, the madness of the night before seemed like a dream. Perhaps he had been overreacting. He found Max cleaning a gas canister behind the chicken coop near Willie Kakae's house. He was smudgy with grease, the very picture of normality. Jonson walked towards him until Max noticed and grinned.

'Good morning, Jonson! You slept late.'

Jonson nodded in reply and took a seat on a log to the left. After a minute of silence, Jonson cleared his throat. 'Pastor?'

Max gave an inviting, 'Hmm?' without taking his eyes off the oily rag.

'Last night, I heard some, sounds – of distress.' Jonson spoke slowly, choosing his words.

Max sighed and rubbed the rag between his fingers. He squinted up at Jonson. 'You certainly did, Jonson. We are undergoing a period of distress at the moment. But we are fighting a winning battle.'

Jonson waited a beat before asking, 'Against?'

'You know very well against what.' Max cocked an eyebrow at him, knowingly.

Jonson merely nodded, stood up, and walked away without saying anything. He made up his mind to leave Bambayot the next day. Mrs Hanlon, he thought, was she safe here? She was the Pastor's wife, after all. Perhaps all this seemed normal to her. But then Jonson remembered her face in the darkness, the pulse in her eyelid.

24

Later that day, Max took Bea to Chief Bule's hut, where the plantation workers were being kept. He collected her from the vestry, and together they walked to Rainson's bushkitchen, where Takataveti was boiling taro for the captives. After much back and forth, Rainson insisted on wrapping a rope under the lip of the pot, and carrying it with them up to Bule's hut. Max had never seen Rainson so much as boil water in all the time he'd been on the island, so his burst of domestic generosity was no doubt fuelled more by curiosity than altruism. Looking at the heavy pot, Max felt rather sorry for them, since it was not much more than animal fodder.

But they must have been hungry enough, because as soon as Rainson and his pot entered the hut, the Vietnamese man rose from the bench and stared at it longingly. Knox Turu, who had been guarding the runaways, stood up from the floor, and nodded to Max before slipping out of the door.

'Some food for you,' Max said in Bislama, motioning for Rainson to lower the pot to the ground. Bea was hanging back behind him near the doorway.

Lien watched the whitewoman carefully. She was not old. She seemed to be in her twenties or thirties, Lien thought. Her hair was brown. And her skin was brown. Could Trinh have been confused about the age of Marietta?

The hut was hot and airless, but Lien was shivery, and her skin tender with exhaustion. She and Thieu had sat awake all night, rigid with horror at the sounds from the bottom of the hill. Thieu thought maybe a battle had broken out between the villagers. After half an hour of sweating and pacing at the back of the hut, Lien had volunteered to wake Garolf, who was snoring on the bench. She nudged him gently, and he sprang up with fierce alertness and ordered her back into their corner.

'No bathroom until the morning,' he had said.

Garolf had nodded straight back to sleep. As though it was the most normal evening in the world. Lien and Thieu gripped each other, holding Minh between them, as if it would somehow cushion the terrible shouting in the hills. Minh bawled and bawled, but Lien hardly knew how to comfort him. She could still hear the sound of the horror ringing in her ears. Girls, young children, crying out in pain. In fear for their lives.

Bea called out, 'It's hot, watch out,' as the Vietnamese man advanced on the pot, but he didn't hear, or didn't understand. He put his right hand straight on to the searing lid. He drew back his hand and let out a string of rapid-fire words in a language Bea couldn't understand. He shook his hand in the air and clamped it between his knees, gritting his teeth.

Bea jostled past Max into the hut, and gestured to the man to follow her, but Max launched forward and clamped his hand on her wrist.

'Don't touch him,' he said.

Bea looked at him, dumbfounded. Was he so devout now that even Vietnamese curse words offended his ears? Rainson was whooping with laughter on the floor, trying his best to imitate the yelps.

'But he needs to put his hand in cold water –' Bea rotated her wrist in Max's grip, '– I should take him to the well, or the stream.'

Max tightened his hold. He turned to Rainson. 'You don't

touch them either. Any of them – not even the baby. They're tabu. Do you understand? Unclean.'

Rainson immediately stopped laughing. He looked nervously back at the captives.

Max yanked Bea outside the hut.

'What are you doing?' She brushed him off her arm. 'We have to help that man, his burn –'

'There's a measles outbreak in Sara, apparently it's been going on for months. Garolf said at least six have died. We can't risk an outbreak here. They could be contagious.'

'Measles?'

Max hushed her and pointed mutely at Rainson, who was using a banana leaf to scoop taro out of the pot.

'Maxis, he barely understands when you talk to him about the weather.' She rubbed the mark on her arm where he had grabbed her. The smell of taro lingered in her mouth. Maybe, Bea thought, if she crept back there later, Garolf would let her have some of the leftovers.

Max pointed down towards Mission House and started walking off. Bea had to break into a light trot to keep up with him.

'I don't want anyone to panic. So not a word, do you understand?' He bent his head a little closer to her. His face was strangely flushed.

'Yes,' she said.

Thieu examined his palm. It was still searing hot, and a white blister bubbled under the surface of the skin.

'Are you OK? Is it bad?' Lien touched him lightly on his shoulder.

'It's fine.' Thieu pushed his hand under his other thigh to trap the throbbing.

'You should have gone with her,' she hissed into his ear. 'We need to get her alone – to ask about the ship.'

'You heard what the whiteman said.' His words came out hollow. 'We're tabu. Untouchable.'

'He's a missionary. You know they're always saying things like that.' Lien squeezed his shoulder.

'It's the wrong woman.' Thieu coughed, he could hear his voice catching. 'She's too young to be Marietta. This is a crazy place – those noises – it's the wrong village. We must have come to the wrong village.' He dropped his face on to his knees and began to cry.

Lien looked up as the sunlight dimmed. The large frame of Garolf appeared in the doorway of the hut.

'Rainson, hello. Where's Knox?' Garolf said.

Rainson gestured towards the village.

'What's wrong with *him*?' Garolf asked, pointing at Thieu.

'He burned his hand.'

'Bad?'

'I don't know.'

'Get one of the girls to come look at him. Or the Pastor's wife.'

Rainson raised his eyebrows, and began to stand up.

'Wait –' Garolf sat on the corner of the bench. It sagged under his weight. Garolf nudged Rainson on the elbow with the tip of his foot, and gestured towards the steaming pot.

'You shouldn't sit there,' Rainson said, scooping taro out of the pot with a banana leaf.

Garolf half rose from the bench, looked underneath his buttocks, then back at Rainson, perplexed.

'The Pastor says to keep away from the Tonks.' Rainson nodded towards them.

'Because they're heathens?' Garolf sat back down. 'He has to save them first?' He pulled the banana leaf on to his lap.

'Unclean,' Rainson answered.

Garolf tipped his head back and laughed. 'I'm sure he can clean them. It's not him –' he waved his leaf at Thieu '– who should be crying. The woman will be crying tonight, if he gets them in the church. The baby, too.' He kicked Rainson gently on the shoulder. 'Think the Pastor can find enough space for them? Or is the demon not hungry today?'

Rainson shrugged defensively. 'The demons are always hungry. We need the Pastor to protect us.'

Lien cuddled Minh into her chest, smelling his soft hair. She pulled the leaf of taro on to the bench and balanced Minh on her right leg. She squeezed a crumb of yam into a paste and pushed the mush into Minh's mouth. He opened his mouth into a tiny 'o', but some of the mush dripped out and on to his belly. She scooped it up and poked it back in his mouth. Thieu's shoulders were still shaking, but she ignored him.

Her face was burning.

Demons?

Her baby?

25

Jonson stepped inside the nakamal that evening to find Garolf slumped against the back wall. Garolf was already heavy with kava, and nodded stiffly towards him. He sat beside him on the bench with a sigh, leant his head back against the bamboo, and closed his eyes.

'I trust you heard the commotion?' Jonson heard the question rise from his body, rather than consciously form it.

There were a few moments of silence before Garolf answered. 'Everyone heard it.'

'Care to illuminate me?' Jonson opened his eyes, feeling a twitch flutter in his cheek. He crossed his legs. Then he thought better of it, and uncrossed them.

'Dark prayer. They're all kranki in this part of the island. The new religion confused people,' Garolf said.

'You knew about this? And you couldn't have mentioned it before?' Jonson goggled at him. 'We were on that blasted boat for three days!'

'I heard some stories.' Garolf scratched his nose. 'I didn't think it would be this bad. It happens now and then.'

'What happens?'

Garolf waved a vague hand, dismissing the question. 'You heard it.'

'No – what exactly happens? I need to know precisely.' Jonson sat forward and pulled a shell of kava on the counter closer towards him.

'See for yourself,' Garolf offered, raising his eyebrows.

'Not a chance in hell,' Jonson replied, staring into the murky slime of the kava shell.

Garolf smiled, his gold tooth gleaming in the gloom.

Willie strolled into the nakamal, holding a plastic bucket of kava. Clearly he and Garolf were preparing for a long session.

'Did you hear this dark prayer last night?' Jonson asked him.

Willie inhaled deeply. 'I heard it,' he said.

'And what do you think? Is this normal? How long has this been going on for?' Jonson ran his fingers over the bare rim of the coconut shell.

Willie licked his lips and tipped his head to the side. 'A long time,' he answered finally.

Jonson slugged back the kava and spat on the floor.

'Aru, he thinks Ukunu is here,' Willie continued.

Jonson looked back at him in surprise, 'But I thought Ukunu was good? A sort of good spirit?' Jonson wiped his lips as the numbing effect of the kava began to slow down his mouth.

Garolf shifted in his seat. 'It depends on what part of the island. In the North, Ukunu is good, in the South, he is bad.'

'So Aru thinks bad Ukunu – he is here, in the village?' Jonson asked Willie.

Willie paused. 'Yes,' he said. 'Ukunu is here. Him, and the Devil.'

That night, Jonson couldn't sleep. He hadn't even bothered undressing. Just as the previous evening, he and the Pastor had eaten rice and boiled chouchoute while Beatriz sat on the other side of the table, her eyes glazed over. Jonson retired to his room as soon as the meal was over, claiming a headache, and climbed into the cot. Being inside the mosquito net helped to make him feel better, like he was a moth safe inside its cocoon. A couple of hours later, he heard the front door close as someone left the house.

A chorus of children singing began shortly after. And then the singing turned to muttering and chanting. The chanting turned to crying and laments, the laments turned to screams. The screaming went on and on, slithering around in the darkness. He heard gibbering and moaning, whispering, shouting and clapping, wails. It was a sickening din. He could hear it echoed in the hills above the village and spun back, distorted. It was even more of a frenzy than it had been the previous night.

He picked up his Delta lantern torch and jiggled it to settle the batteries inside the cartridge. It was shaky, but it was working. He crept outside the Pastor's bedroom and put his eye to the thatch in the door. His wife was in there, sitting up in the bed completely still, staring out of the window on the opposite side of the room. At least she was inside the house, and not down there in that tumult of madness.

He closed the front door carefully behind him and walked to the crest of the hill above the church. At first, he hadn't intended to turn the torch on, rather to quietly approach in the darkness. But thick cloud covered the moon and it was sheer black outside. He tripped on loose pebbles, and set his foot upon the tacky density of what he hoped was a slug. He turned the lamp on and lit the path. As he grew closer to the noise, he could see there were already a couple of people standing at the top of the hill. His courage paled, and he almost turned around. But they would have seen the torch. He walked towards the figures. Adrenaline rushed through his body so quickly his ears rang.

'Who's there?' he called to the two men, hoping he had simulated sufficient confidence in his voice.

'Turn that light off, you're hurting my eyes,' someone whined.

'Willie?' Jonson switched off the torch.

'It's us,' Garolf answered, but his face was turned towards the church.

'What are you doing here?' Jonson asked him, feeling inexpressibly relieved. He walked over to stand next to them.

'Couldn't sleep,' Garolf answered. Jonson could feel, rather than see, Garolf shrugging casually in the darkness, as if they had gathered for a midnight feast.

'This is –' Jonson broke off. He couldn't think of the right word. 'This isn't good.'

The three men stood on the hill watching the spectacle within the building. The church was illuminated by candlelight and in the low glimmer they could see a group of children inside. Their silhouetted shapes moved strangely, as if they were fitting. Some of the children lay on the floor, jerking and writhing, shrieking and sobbing. Yet other children stood over the bodies, praying and crying, chanting and calling on God to release their spirits from evil.

Two more men quietly joined them on the hill. Willie greeted them, but Jonson didn't know who they were. No one seemed in the mood to make introductions. Jonson turned his torch back on and flashed it over the building, trying to pick out the faces of those inside. He caught at least two adults, and one white face. No doubt this was the Pastor.

The noise coming from the church began to quieten. The screaming simmered down from frantic to fraught, and the sound of a grown man's voice could be heard. And then there was a distinct change in atmosphere.

The children began to whisper. Lying on the floor of the building, they started to crawl towards the window, creeping, like snakes. In the flash of the torchlight, Jonson could see the whites of the children's eyes reflected in the darkness. It sounded as if they were hissing. Jonson had to listen carefully for half a minute before he could comprehend the words. 'Ukunu,' they were whispering. 'Satan.'

Then Jonson understood. The children weren't invoking the Devil. Rather, they were identifying him. The children were staring directly at them, and naming them Satan. The children were talking about him. His wrist felt weak. He turned off the torch. Goosebumps on the flesh of his arms brushed against Garolf's warm skin. No one felt much like staying on the hill.

Willie took the two strangers back to the nakamal, and Garolf and Jonson walked in silence back to Mission House. Garolf bade him goodnight, and went off to Bule's hut to relieve Rainson and Knox, who were guarding the Vietnamese couple. Jonson went into Mission House, and knocked on the door frame of the Pastor's bedroom. Through a narrow gap in the doorway he could see a candle burning inside the room.

'Mrs Hanlon?' he whispered at first, before remembering he was actually trying to rouse her. 'Mrs Hanlon, it's I. A. M. Jonson. Are you awake?'

'Yes.' She came to the door. 'I thought I could hear someone in the house,' she said. She was pale in the lips.

'Are you all right?' he asked her, almost afraid of the answer. She nodded.

'Mrs Hanlon, we – is this – ? Are you quite content with this arrangement?'

She looked at him blankly.

'Will you permit me to assist you? I would very much like to accompany you back to the North.'

She flinched away from him.

He felt a blush rising. 'I give you my word, you will come to no harm. You can inform the Pastor, or you could leave him a note. It need only be for a little while –'

Her head twitched on its stalk. 'He'll hear you,' she

whispered. Her eyes were wide. She glanced towards the door of Mission House.

Jonson touched her, lightly, on the elbow. She looked back at him.

'I won't insist. But I will be leaving tomorrow. This environment is not healthy. Your husband is not well. We need to arrange medical attention for him. I invite you to join me while I make arrangements. I do not recommend you stay here.'

Jonson retreated back into his bedroom. He slipped off his shoes, and sat sideways across the bed. His limbs trembled as if he had been running. He reached through the mosquito net and lit a candle, picking up the copy of *Gaudy Night* he'd left under his pillow. The sounds of mewling and chanting ran through his head, and he couldn't concentrate on the shape of the words. Through the chorus of terrible screeching, he heard their infernal dog trampling around softly in the vegetables outside his window. But no, Jonson remembered, closing the novel, Max had told him the dog had been killed. Jonson blew out the candle and crept across the room. There were hardly any cockroaches in the room – a sure sign there was a rat nearby. He peered out into the garden. It was so dark, he could hardly be sure he had his eyes open.

But there was undoubtedly someone – a man, walking about in the garden and humming. Jonson could only make out the shape of his silhouette. He was sprinkling something on to the ground from a plastic bottle. Jonson swallowed. What if it was gasoline? What if it was one of the madmen from Hanlon's church – come to set the house alight? He sniffed the air, but couldn't smell anything other than the usual dank, honeyed smell of jungle. Perhaps the man was spying on him for the Pastor? Jonson felt himself colouring. What if he was dragged down into that nightmare at the bottom of the hill? He imagined himself surrounded by writhing village children, the whites of their eyes rolling in their heads, whispering, pointing at him, invoking Satan. Jonson left his room and almost jogged to the front door, catching sight of the man as he passed by the stoop. He paused in the living room, and peered out from a crack in the thatch as the man got down on his knees. The man was dressed in a white shirt and blue serge trousers, and Jonson vaguely recognized him. The man chanted under his breath, then got to his feet, brushed off his knees, and strolled back off into the darkness, still humming.

Jonson lurked by the front door until he was sure the man had gone. Then he tenderly crossed the sharp pebbles to where the man had been sprinkling. He knelt and touched the earth. It was barely wet. He sniffed the air again, but it wasn't gasoline at least – it must have been a potion of some kind. He glanced around in case the man was coming back, but the night was black, and still spinning with horrible wails. Through the sparse trees on his left, Jonson could see candlelight flickering through the weave of Chief Bule's hut. He felt a sudden yearning for Garolf's deep laugh and the musty scent of his coconut-oil pomade. He went back into Mission House and pulled on his shoes. An evening of exorcisms and potions and chanting might be totally normal for Mrs Hanlon. She was the Pastor's wife – she had a certain kind of protection against this nonsense. But he was an outsider. There was no such protection for him. There was every chance the praying man had overheard his suggestions to the Pastor's wife. No, he was not going to spend the night alone being circled and chanted over. Jonson crossed the village to join Garolf in Bule's hut. Even a night cramped on a bench with the runaways and a baby seemed less subtly horrible than a night peering into the darkness around Mission House.

26

Max woke early, and went to the church to pray while the day was still cool. Two hours after sunrise, there was a clatter against the door frame as Willie Kakae ran into the vestry.

'Pastor –' He was breathing quickly and he looked awful. The colour had drained from his lips and eyelids. He was shaking. 'Pastor, come quick, please.'

Max rose at once and followed Willie out of the church. He was concerned by his tone, but also strangely mollified, since it had been some time since Willie had confided in him. Max had made many attempts to encourage Willie to come to services, but Willie always nodded energetically along to whatever Max said, then ignored him.

Willie sprinted uphill ahead of him. Only half-dressed, Willie's body was hard in the sun and he ran with large strides. Max was feeling his age. He hadn't fully recovered from the fever, and his legs were stiff. When Max arrived at Bule's hut, Willie was already standing outside, impatiently shifting his weight between his feet. He pointed towards the door of the hut, his arm trembling.

Two dead bodies were lying on the floor.

Garolf was sprawled out on his back with a gaping slit over his throat. Dark blood had clotted in lumps across the wall and splattered over the gravel. Jonson was sitting with his back against the bench, as if he were merely dozing. His head had slumped forward, and the back of his skull was a splintered mush of pink and black. A circle of fat, buzzing flies were crowning his white hair. A broken pot was shattered on the floor, and there were livid marks on Jonson's forearms where it must have cracked against him. A chorus of ants swarmed over the bodies. The hut was filled with flies doing frenzied somersaults in the ripe stink of putrefaction. The men couldn't have been lying there for long, or the insects would have stripped them clean.

The Tonkinese were gone.

Max was breathless. He gripped the door frame. He closed his eyes as the room wavered. He thought he might be sick. How could this have happened in his own village – on his watch? His stomach twisted. This was an act of pure evil, committed during his guardianship of the village. All his efforts – everything he'd done – had been for nothing. He fished in his pocket for a handkerchief and covered his mouth.

Max swallowed, as tears burned in the back of his throat. He had let Jonson down. He had let Garolf down. He had let the village down. He had done everything in his power to protect them from the darkness – the breathing, lurking badness in the hills.

But Satan had found a way – found a chink in their armour – and slunk into the village.

Max tightened his eyes shut. His heart wrenched in pity. This was no way to die. Jonson was a Christian at least, thank the Lord. But Garolf – the poor man had been a pronounced heathen. Max offered a prayer for the man's soul.

Max left the doorway and approached Willie, who was sitting on the ground, rubbing his head, over and over. 'Can you find Chief Bule?' he asked.

Willie nodded, not meeting Max's eyes.

Max put his hand gently on Willie's shoulder. He knew Willie and Garolf had been friends. 'He was a good man. A great man. Let us pray together for his soul.'

Willie looked up at him with doleful red eyes. He dipped

250

his chin in soft acknowledgement. They were silent a moment, and Willie wiped tears away from the base of his nose.

Max gave him a pat on the shoulder. 'Find Bule,' he said.

Willie stood up, and took a step back. He half tripped over something lying on the ground, and Max caught him by the arm. Another pot lay on the path to the hut. A trail of red ants leaked from under the lid. Willie steadied himself, and looked back at Max once before running off into the bush to find Bule. Max crouched down and stared at the pot. It was their own kettle from Mission House.

Bea had been there.

What was he to do? She professed to be saved, but he knew. He knew, even if she was blind to it. After all, he had been vulnerable to those influences, too, once. And despite his best efforts, the darkness inside her persisted. It followed her into the village, into his dominion, spreading evil whispers in the hearts of the unsaved. Those murderers had escaped. Two innocent men, dead. And he could have prevented it. If only he had tried harder, to cleanse her. To drive out all things dark and lurking. He would have to take control.

Max strode back to the centre of the village, his heart hammering. Sale, Rainson's youngest son, was cantering around in the bush near Bule's hut, riding a stick.

'Pastor, look,' he squeaked, as Max walked towards the church, 'it's an aeroplane.'

'Sale, bang the ching,' Max called to him.

Sale dropped the stick and looked around him. 'But – Moses?'

'You do it.' Max nodded.

Sale broke into a grin, and ran off in the direction of the ching.

The hollow beats of the drum echoed in the hills.

27

Bea woke before sunrise, and saw that Max had already left for church. She knocked on Jonson's door, but there was no response. She wondered if Jonson had already gone back to his village. She boiled a pot of rice, sliced three bananas on top, and left it to cool while she dressed. She carried it to Bule's hut for the runaways, but the hut was silent, with no smoke from the bushkitchen. She tapped on the side of the pot with a stick to let Garolf know the food had arrived, and left it outside on the path in case she woke the baby.

As soon as the sun rose, Bea walked down the Bambayot hill towards the beach at Noia Saruru. The sore on her right hand had never quite healed after her baptism at Hot Wata, and the skin was puffy and hot. Her legs felt wooden, and her left kneecap kept locking up underneath her. She and Max had decided she should only swim early in the morning, so she wouldn't be spotted walking around in wet clothes. She passed Willie's nakamal on the left, and walked heavily through the sand near the mango trees.

She bunched her island dress between her knees and waded into the warm water. It was a gorgeous temperature, slightly below the heat of her body. The water was so clear she could see her long brown toes wiggling underneath her, and the sunlight catching in the folds of the dress. It was perfectly still, and a shoal of apricot-coloured fish spun around her in circles. She was too tired to swim properly, so she turned on to her back and floated. She could smell the mango blossoms on the shoreline trees. The flowers drifted in the air and landed on the water, sticking on the surface like sprinkles on a pudding.

She felt swollen and heavy from her plate of rice and bananas that morning. The past few weeks had not afforded her much chance to eat, and her stomach felt strangely tight after a full meal. As long as Max was watching her, she was supposed to be 'fasting'. But she took green oranges from the bush whenever she could invent an excuse to leave the house. Sometimes she ate raw beans from the garden. But still, all her clothes were horribly loose. Mabo-Mabon kept asking her if she had worms. Santra hadn't been by the house in weeks, or else maybe she could have brought her some food in secret.

Bea felt her face beginning to burn from the sunlight reflecting off the water. She paddled back towards the island, and waded back to shore. As she reached the sand she wrung the water out of the extra cloth around her legs, so it wouldn't stick to her body. She walked up the beach towards Noia Saruru. The sand coated her wet feet in gritty little socks. She wished she had her bushknife with her, feeling strangely naked without it.

She passed the couple of huts at Noia Saruru, and climbed up to the rock pool near the waterfall. She walked through the mud around the base of the pool, then with considerable effort clambered over the hot rocks fringed with green algae. At the top, she launched herself into the deep grey pool at the bottom of the waterfall. It was icy cold. A thick froth of white water from the falls surged over the edge and pummelled against her skin. She kicked herself vigorously around in a circle, unbraiding her hair and letting it float darkly around her. She imagined slipping out of the heavy dress and paddling naked.

Bea hoisted herself out of the pool, and avoiding her stiff fingers, pulled herself on to a ledge on the left of the waterfall.

She began to walk slowly back up the hill towards Bambayot. Max would be looking for her by now. He became worried when she was away from the village for too long. Perhaps he had always been this anxious and she had never noticed? She thought back to how he had clung to their bag of rice on their first boat trip to the island. And now, he clung to Aru. She stretched out her stiff shoulder. What would he want from her tonight – more prayers? More holy water? No matter how dutifully she stood and prayed and fasted, he appraised her devotion, and then asked for more.

Maybe she would go up North with Jonson. He could contact Peterson, the District Agent. He had seemed normal enough in Vila. Maybe he could convince Max to take a holiday, away from the island. They could sleep late, eat tunafish sandwiches. She thought of the dingy hotel with the peeling paint they had stayed in when they first arrived on Efate. What a luxury that seemed now.

Bea walked up towards Bambayot. The tops of her thighs were chafing on the damp fabric and she itched to pull her underpants away from the skin, but she daren't risk it within sight of the village. From the slope she could hear a commotion from the village. A woman was wailing. It seemed as if there were a lot of people on the hill, outside their houses. Like a festival. Bea wondered if maybe it was Christmas Day, and she had lost track of what month it was.

Mabo-Mabon appeared from the bush further along the coastal path. She was waving delightedly, then began to run towards her. Bea had never seen Mabo-Mabon running, not ever. Not even the time when Jinnes had set her bushkitchen on fire. She was holding her breasts in place with one elbow as she jogged. With the other hand she was waving. Bea wondered how it could possibly not hurt her to run on the sharp pebbles of the path. The soles of her feet must be so tough. Bea started waving back, perplexed. She felt self-conscious in her wet clothes.

Mabo-Mabon called out, 'Beatriz – come, come!' She almost ran straight into her. Mabo-Mabon's breath was hot in her ear. She rapped Bea on the shoulder and pushed her back towards the ocean. She stopped, looked back at the village, and spat on the ground. 'They're dead. Mr Garolf. He's dead.'

'What? But I just saw him –' Bea felt unsteady. She looked around her for somewhere to sit.

'No!' Mabo-Mabon pulled her up by the arm. 'The white-man. He's dead, too.'

Bea's vision went green. She gripped Mabo-Mabon's fore-arm. 'Max?'

'No, no – the other whiteman.'

'Jonson? What? But –'

'Yes.' Mabo-Mabon raised her bushknife and mimed slitting her own throat. 'Like pigs.'

'Oh my God.' Bea put her hand to her mouth. The other arm gripped on to Mabo-Mabon. 'But how did this happen?'

Mabo-Mabon shook her head, as if Bea's question had entirely missed the point. 'They are looking for you,' she said.

'For me?' Bea's knees began to shake.

'They say –' Mabo-Mabon blinked, then looked her in the eyes '– they say they need to find the devil in the village.'

'Oh, shit.'

28

Bea climbed uphill. The bush was dense, and webs broke across her face. She thrashed in front of her with the bush-knife. The air was close and humid; she couldn't draw enough of it into her lungs. She took strides as wide as she could manage, trampling through wet plants and deep, gummy puddles. Loose rocks rolled in the mud, and the earth was slippery with dew. She needed to get up to the old colonial house. From the top floor she could see downhill, down to the village. She would see them coming.

Bea's right foot caught in a divot in the earth and she careened forward, grasping for a branch but instead catching hold of a barbed vine. She cried out as a stab of pain shot through her right leg into her buttock. She groped at her ankle, convinced a shard of bone would be sticking through the skin. But it wasn't broken. Probing in the mud, she guided her right foot out of the snare of a tree root. As she moved, a wave of nausea rolled into her throat. She let out a sob of frustration. She fell back on to her behind and tentatively rotated her foot in the air, the muscles in her calf quivering. There was blood, she could smell pennies. She dabbed at the wetness on her shins, but the blood was already drying into a thin tidemark. It was coming from her right hand. Holding her palm up in a column of moonlight, Bea saw the vine had stripped a belt of skin from the middle of her palm and lacerated the side of her little finger. She pulled out several sharp barbs from her hand, as her palm lazily oozed blood.

The bushknife had flown somewhere as she tripped, and

Bea crawled forward, trying not to push the open scratch into the mud. As she crawled, her right leg rotated in its socket and the spear of pain jabbed into her lower back. She took a deep breath. She needed that bushknife. She patted blindly in the mud for it, groping at wet leaves, the hollow shell of a snail, then hard wood – her heart lifted in relief. But it was a nodule of tree root. She crawled further, scrabbling around in the earth. A dim glint caught her eye. The blade of the knife reflected a sliver of moonlight. She lunged for it, as if it might disappear if she took her eyes off it for even one second. Relief drummed through her chest. She stood up on her left leg only, dragging the right off the ground, and stabbed the bush-knife into the mud. Propping herself up on the knife, she took a stride forward, and sagged. She was going to have to switch the knife to her bad hand. The handle stung in the palm of her hand against the cut, but no matter.

Slower now, she climbed the hill towards the colonial house. She rested on her left knee, took a step on the right, dug in the knife, hoisted up the right leg. She travelled for a few minutes, but kept catching her island dress. Above the waist, it was so large it was basically a smock, but the seam underneath her knees snared her at each step. She sat back in a squat, and dug the knife between her legs to cut the fabric, and ripped a strip of material away. She rested the knife carefully on the earth, and wound the strip round and round, over her right ankle. It was cushioned now. It was fine. She hoisted herself back up and began her scrabble-climb-knife-scrabble up the hill. She made a game of it. She breathed in on the left leg, out on the right, in on the left, out on the right. She counted ten breaths. Then stopped for three. Then on. Blood from her hand dripped down the handle of the bushknife. On for ten.

The forest was starting to clear now. She must nearly be at the top of the hill. She couldn't see much slope in front of her.

She was close. She tossed the bushknife over the top of the ridge, and used her elbows to pull herself over the edge. Her exposed knees grated on rough bark and a feathery insect skittered over the skin on the back of her legs. She could see the pallid columns of the colonial house looming out of the murk. Her arms were shaking. She crawled the last distance to the door, sliding the bushknife ahead of her on the grass. When she clambered on to the porch, she nudged at the door with her head, and it yielded. She crept over the threshold and into the house, as mildew showered sharp-smelling spores into her hair. She leant her back against the door and it shut with a creak. Yet more spores sprinkled the dust. Bea doubled over and threw up a mouthful of liquid on to the wooden floorboards.

29

It was still dark when she woke. Bea heard the shriek of a crow and sat up in one motion, disorientated. She held her breath, her heart drumming. The bird screeched again, but it wasn't a crow. There were no crows on the island. It probably wasn't even a bird, she thought. She shuffled herself backwards against the wall, straightening her legs out in front of her. The place smelt acidic and dank.

Moonlight streamed through the windows on to the bare floorboards. Bea patted the bandage on her right leg, convinced it would be wet with blood, but it was only damp and crusted with mud. She desperately wanted to undo the wrapping and check on her ankle, but she was counting on the compress to squeeze it back to its normal size. Her right hand was stinging. The handle of the knife had dug deep into the gash, and she could feel the wound thrumming with each pulse. She wiped her other hand on her thighs and, wincing, tentatively probed the cut, rolling out grains of grit stuck into the soft flesh. She was going to have to clean it somehow.

Now her eyes were more adjusted to the gloom, dim shapes appeared in the shadows. There was a wooden chest against the far wall, and a card table on the left-hand side, near the window. The rest of the room was bare. Bea squatted forward on to her right leg and stood up shakily. Her whole body was stiff and aching. She didn't want to leave the house. She listened for the sounds of people approaching, but there was nothing.

She opened the cracked door, leaking more mould, and

limped as fast as she could to the bushes. She didn't even look around her – worried she might see people coming. Bea poked in the undergrowth with her foot until she found a couple of bamboo stalks. She twisted a green stem over and rinsed her hand with the dribble of water within. She tried to drink from the second stalk, but it was barely enough to wet the inside of her mouth. The not-a-crow sounded again. She didn't want to be outside any more.

Bea hobbled back towards the house, and stood still by the open window, convinced she would hear them coming now. She took the bushknife in her left hand and walked through the big open room to the back, where there was a narrow staircase. It was almost totally black there, and Bea moved tentatively on to the first step, worried it would be rotten through and collapse under her weight. The boards creaked, but they were mostly solid. The third step was sodden through in the middle. She put her legs either side of the sagging wood and crept upwards. A thicket of webs coated the staircase; she spun the bushknife in circles to clear a passage, gathering soft white bundles.

At the top of the staircase, she turned into the room on the right. It was bare. A white lizard scuttled heavily across the roof. She crossed to the window, and leant forward to look out over the hill below. In the distance she could see moonlight on the close water of the coast. The tree cover was so dense, she realized she might not even be able to see anyone coming, after all.

Her foot scuffed against something concealed in the dark under the window. It appeared to be a rectangular wooden box. Bea prodded the box with the bushknife and the blade made contact with something loose and spongy. She knelt to look more closely. It looked like a shrine. A chicken bone, half a coconut shell, and what looked like a braid of hair were piled on top of the box. Bea probed the plait with the tip of the knife, and a flurry of tiny white mites poured from the fibres. Suddenly, she didn't want it in the house with her. She kicked it with her good leg. The coconut shell wobbled. She picked up the box and threw it straight out of the window. She heard a soft crack as it hit the grass underneath, but fluffy tufts of the hair flew back from the window and stuck to the fine webs over her arms. She coughed and scraped, and then curled herself into a crescent at the back of the room.

Bea woke on the floor, instantly alert. A noise had woken her. She lay perfectly still, blood singing in her head. The sound again. It was the noise of someone climbing the stairs. She heard a heavy tread, a musical chime from the blade of a bush-knife against wood. Bea's heart stammered. A wave of adrenaline shook her body. She set her teeth together. If she played dead, maybe whoever it was would go away.

She tried to hold her breath, but it came heavily out of her nose like snoring. Her right arm was pinned under her. She tried to move her fingertips but they were stiff and useless. The handle of her knife was cradled in her stomach. She inched her left hand to touch the handle of the blade. It was crusty with dried blood. There was no point. What would she do with it anyway? She held her breath.

'Bea?' It was a woman's voice. A bare foot pressed down beside her. Bea felt her chest rising and her eyelids twitching.

'It's Santra.'

Bea heard the knife being laid on to the floor. Santra put her fingers on either side of Bea's head, and pulled her face roughly into her lap. Bea couldn't understand what was happening. Was Santra sent here by them? Bea stopped struggling. God knows it didn't matter. If she was going to die, better that Santra should do it. She gave up. Let it be over quickly.

Santra shuffled round so she was crouching over Bea's face. Her eyes were large, but the expression was unreadable. 'You are crazy,' she said.

She rubbed Bea's left arm, and probed at the impromptu dressing on her leg. She pushed Bea's head back roughly and opened her eyes with her fingers, inspecting her pupils. 'OK?' she said.

Bea stiffly pulled herself up, and the room swam. She thought for a second she might be sick.

Santra braced her by her shoulders and gave her a few smart pats on the head. 'You're fine,' she said.

Bea nodded dumbly, and then looked up at her. Santra's face was expressionless. 'It's so nice of you to come,' Bea said. Then she spluttered helplessly with laughter.

Santra ignored her hysterical giggling, and instead pulled Bea's right hand towards her. Bea let out a yelp as Santra's hand touched the swollen flesh. Santra forced her fingers apart, even as Bea tried to wriggle away from her. Santra looked into the cut, and pinched hard at each of Bea's swollen fingers.

'This is one bad hand. It's really bad. Can't you smell it?'

Santra held Bea's hand under the wrist and flopped it towards her. Bea could smell something – a dirty, sweet stink. Was that her own hand?

'You're going to lose this hand.' Santra made a chopping motion at Bea's wrist.

Bea prised it out of Santra's grip, and held it protectively against her chest. 'No!' she shouted. 'No, Santra – I cut it, on a bush. That's all. It will be fine. I just need to wash it.'

Santra pulled her impatiently by the left shoulder over to the needles of light coming in from the window. She pulled open the hand and stepped back. Bea peered at it, now afraid to look. The whole palm and fingers were swollen. The sore that extended up into the little finger was pulpy and grey and overlaid with a long oozing cut. Soft patches of peach-coloured pus were seeping through the skin all over her smallest finger and into the palm.

Santra watched Bea's face carefully, then took Bea's smallest finger, and gave it a hard pinch. Bea yelped from the antici-pated pain. But there was none. She couldn't feel anything. It was like an alien thing attached to her.

'I just need penicillin, that's all. It will heal just fine,' Bea said.

Santra looked into her eyes. 'And where are you going to get medicine?' she said.

Bea realized with a creeping horror that Santra was right. Where could she even get the pills from now? Everything was back in the village.

'Maybe on the main island? Or up in the North?' Bea heard the pleading in her own voice, and stopped talking.

She would never last long enough with it in this state. She'd die of blood poisoning before she even got there. The veins would go black and track all the toxic stuff back to her heart. She'd die on the road. They would find her and say Ukunu got her in the end. Well, to hell with that.

'Let's take it now,' she said to Santra. 'I can't bear to wait. You do it. Do you know how? You do it. Can you do it? I can't do it.'

Santra chewed on one side of her lip and pointed at Bea's torso. 'Wait here,' she said. She picked up her bushknife from the floor and walked straight down the stairs without even looking back.

About an hour later, Bea heard Santra coming back through the forest to the house. She knew it was her this time because Santra was singing in her high, girlish voice. Bea was crouch-ing in the corner of the downstairs room. She had tucked her hand under her other armpit. What was she supposed to do? Sit there looking at it, reminiscing about all the wonderful times she and her hand had spent together?

At the doorstep Santra motioned with a smart whistle for Bea to come with her. Bea rose stiffly and limped after her, suddenly reluctant. She didn't want to lose her hand outside – in the jungle. It would drop into the dirt and rot. She had imagined it in the house. But then – her hand. Not attached to her. Lying on the wooden floor. What would they do with it? Would she pick it up and take it with her? Bea had an image of leaving it propped on the shrine she had destroyed.

Santra whistled again more impatiently, and Bea picked up her pace, too tired to think any more. Let what was going to happen, happen. Santra led her out of the house and to the left, under a striped bush. The light was dropping, it must be about 4 p.m., thought Bea aimlessly. Santra walked quickly, following a trail Bea couldn't make out. She ducked under palm fronds, climbed under the exposed root of a strangler fig tree. They walked for less than ten minutes and came out by the edge of a small, muddy stream. Santra stopped and waited for Bea to catch up with her, then motioned further downstream. Bea wanted to say she had changed her mind – but no words came out. Bile swam in her stomach.

There was a fire smoking, nearby the bank of the stream, and littered around, Santra had been cutting something, Bea couldn't see what very clearly. Santra held out her hand for Bea's bushknife, then balanced it over the edge of the wood-pile so the blade rested in the fire. She picked up one of the bits lying on the ground and held it out to Bea. It was a piece of breadfruit, and Bea felt her eyes widen. She stuffed as much as she could fit in her mouth and chewed it roughly before swallowing. She wanted another two hundred breadfruit. She looked at them wildly, waiting for Santra to offer them to her, but instead, Santra guided Bea to the edge of the stream, and pushed her on the shoulders until Bea was on her knees in the grass.

'Put it in there –' Santra pointed to the water '– don't touch the bottom,' she said. Bea held her hand under the stream. Her shoulder was aching. She shuffled round until both her feet dipped into the shallows, and watched the stones glowing under the water. After ten minutes, Santra came over and gently touched her on the shoulder. She inspected the very cold hand, and told Bea to come back to the fire, holding her hand up over her head. Bea felt a little silly walking back towards the fire with her one-armed salute. Icy water dripped down her arm.

Bea sat in the grass out of the direction of the smoke, and Santra offered her another piece of breadfruit. When Bea reached to put it in her mouth, Santra suddenly gripped her arm at the wrist and above the elbow joint, and, putting her whole body on top of her, smashed Bea's elbow down on to a slab of flat rock. The nerve at Bea's elbow rang all the way up her arm. She screamed out, and tried to grab the arm back from Santra, but Santra pushed her to the ground.

This is when she kills me, Bea thought, in panic. She was going to kill me all along. Bea was flat on her back. Santra sat on her outstretched arm, facing away from her. Bea felt sudden pressure as Santra bound tight strips of vine around her wrist. She tied another two around her fingers. Bea's heart was hammering. Pins and needles prickled over her scalp and her back. Santra grunted as she smashed down on Bea's elbow again. Bea tried to spit out the breadfruit, but the huge piece was still in her mouth, it was choking her. She bit down on it and tried to struggle against Santra but she couldn't budge her even a fraction.

Bea gave up flailing and tears ran from her eyes, drips of

snot from her nose mixing with the huge shard of breadfruit in her mouth. She closed her eyes and began to whine.

Santra took her knife, and laying Bea's hand flat against the rock, in one sudden swift chop, sliced off Bea's little finger. The pain pulled at a seam in her body, a runner-bean string that shot through her elbow and spine and rimmed the sockets of her eyes. Bea screamed. She screamed and flailed and moved and pushed. Wet, warm blood dripped down her forearm. Still, Santra didn't budge. Bea could smell the iron. Another chop and the fourth finger came off, too. Bea screamed even louder. She couldn't have imagined more pain could be added to her pain. She felt breadfruit coming into her throat, she was choking on the vomit, she couldn't breathe. Was Santra going to take the whole thing off, one finger at a time? She couldn't take any more. She would kill Santra herself before she took any more. She would push her into the stream. She would stab her in the eye with her own damned bushknife.

But it had stopped. Bea felt herself jerked forward as Santra held her hand under the stream of icy water. The pain was also a throb now – a pulse-pulse throb that Bea could feel inside her eyeballs. Her whole body was shaking. She struggled to sit upright and threw up vomit and spittle down the front of her body, wiping her neck feebly with her good hand. Bubbles popped at the edge of her vision. She felt far away from her own head.

Santra took Bea's bushknife out of the fire, and covered Bea's eyes with her good hand. Bea leant her head back down again. It didn't hurt any more. She felt sleepy and confused. Santra pressed the burning knife on to the wound and Bea smelt cooking. From very far away, she realized that she was the one cooking.

30

That evening, they sat around the fire by the stream. Bea never wanted to see breadfruit again, so Santra had collected a pile of naus for them to eat.

'You were gone for so long,' Bea said.

Santra scrunched up her nose in confusion.

'Before, I mean. I thought maybe we weren't friends any more.' Bea pushed her fingernail into the pith of the naus. She felt her cheeks redden.

'I came,' Santra shrugged. 'But he told me to leave.'

'Who?' Bea sat forward. 'Max?'

Santra nodded. 'He told me not to come to the village any more.'

Bea said nothing. The silence went on for a few minutes. 'How did you know I was here?' Bea asked her.

Santra smiled. She threw a slice of peel into the fire, where it smoked wetly. 'I followed you. It wasn't hard.'

'You followed me? From the village?'

Santra raised her eyebrows in a 'yes'.

Bea imagined Santra watching her scramble up the hill, only a few steps in her wake. It made her feel like a fool. She had been flailing about like a madwoman, when Santra was calmly walking behind her the whole time. But then, Santra hadn't come to the house until today. She must have traced the mess of a trail she had left behind. The scramble didn't seem so foolish or rushed now. The men must know where she went, too. Everyone must know.

'Why did you follow me? Why did you come here?' Bea was

afraid to meet Santra's eye. She felt embarrassed by the debt she owed her. For Santra to come to find her – it meant trouble. When Aru and Max found out, she would probably be locked in the church, marched to the ocean. She would be cleansed and saved and purified for who knows how long. Her husband would be so ashamed.

Santra still hadn't spoken.

Bea couldn't help herself. 'Does Charles know you're here with me?' she said.

'He knows.'

Bea rubbed her right forearm. She massaged it up the arm, towards her heart. Somehow she felt that rubbing it down-wards towards the hand might make the blood come out of her fingers. Like squeezing a tube of toothpaste. It pulsed with pain at every heartbeat. She would never be able to sleep.

Bea leant her head back against the wall. 'Will you tell me a story?'

'What story?' Santra picked her teeth with her fingernail.

'A real one. Just a real story.' Bea wanted to hear about something – with no demons. No magic. Something normal. 'A happy story. A wedding story,' she said. 'Tell me about you and Charles, your wedding. Were you happy?'

Santra rocked back on her heels. 'The other day, there was a woman whose name was Santra. She was married up in Central to Charles. Her wedding was happy, with singing and storyan. The old whitewoman missionary came to the celebra-tion, even though she wasn't invited. But she made gato so it was OK. There were many flowers because it was in July. San-tra's family had a feast, with a roast pig, and simboro and poulet fish. After the wedding, Santra and Charles lived with his par-ents, and they built their own house together. Their new house was small, but it was close by the gardens so it was OK. Some-times a black puppy came to the door and Santra fed it taro.

'After a year past the wedding, the couple still had no babies. A man called Aru came, he talked to Charles. He said they needed prayers over Santra so she could have babies. Charles did not like that. But Aru came anyway. He came to the house and he said prayers over her. Many prayers. Many words and spells. And then Santra, she had one baby die. It came out after pains, it was small – not like a baby – like a bird. She was very sick. But after some time she wasn't sick any more. But then Aru came again and he prayed more. He told Santra she can't have any babies, because of darkness in the forest, darkness in her soul. Aru made a mark on her head with a pen and a needle. But it didn't help to make babies. Santra told him it wouldn't help – only one thing can make babies anyhow, and that's a man's cock.'

'What did you do?' said Bea.

'Me or Santra?'

Bea goggled at her.

Santra smiled, then her face dropped. 'He's stupid but he has all the spells. People listen to him. He wants to get all the girls on the island with his pen and needle.'

Bea watched as Santra gnawed on another green naus. She squeezed her arm again, away from the wound, back towards her heart. 'I wish he were dead,' she said.

Santra spat out a shard of stone, and rubbed the shrapnel from her lips on the back of her hand. 'I know,' she said, 'you and me.'

31

As soon as the sun began to rise, they set to work. With only one good arm, Bea couldn't help much. And whenever she stood upright, the world changed angles, and she felt seasick and confused. Santra pointed her into the bushes around the house to dig up a pile of weeds, prising them out of the earth with her bushknife to keep the roots intact. When Bea had collected a heavy pile, Santra walked her around behind the house. She motioned for Bea to stand with her back against the wall, while she walked tentatively in the open grass, pausing after every step and piercing the ground with her bushknife. The wall of the house was rough against Bea's palm. She could feel bubbles in the plaster, like blisters.

'Are you doing leaf magic?'

'Be quiet.'

Santra stepped and tapped, and stepped and tapped, until she seemed to find what she was looking for. She crouched and dug around in the dirt. She cut into the liana with her bushknife.

'Are you burying something?'

Santra ignored her. Bea came behind her, to see better, but Santra swatted her away and pointed back towards the house.

It seemed to take hours. Santra burrowed and poked. She lay flat on her belly and scratched at the red clay with her nails. She coughed and sweated while Bea stood and watched. Eventually, Santra laid a rough circle of twigs on the ground. Bea wondered if it was a holy circle. Would she have to stand inside it? More spells, more prayers. Santra called her over to stand behind her.

'Slide your knife there,' Santra said, pointing to a place in the grass.

With her shaky left arm, Bea pushed the blade into the turf. It met something hard, then yielded to a hollow pocket of air.

'Oh!' Bea said. 'There's a gap!'

Santra levered her own knife in the earth on the other side of the circle. They jiggled the blades back and forth like a saw, then clumsily lifted out a jagged circle of vegetation and a thin wooden raft. The earth released a wave of putrid air. Bea turned and retched over the grass. Santra covered her mouth with the skirt of her island dress, coughing, her eyes running water. Bea carefully approached the hole in the ground. And there it was – a huge, stone well. Hot-coloured, open-mouthed flowers gawped from the aperture. The smell was sickening. Santra stood over the edge of the well, her elbow over her nose. She picked up a pebble and threw it in. It landed in water with a distinct splash. What the sound told her, Bea had no idea. She crawled closer to the basin of the well. It was almost perfectly circular. She hadn't seen anything like it on the island. It was so big, she and Santra could have swum in it.

Santra disappeared, bringing back with her an armful of the weeds they had collected earlier. She bound a rough thatch of twigs together, while Bea sat with her back against the wall of the house. She kept raising her injured hand in the air and rubbing it towards the elbow. She tried to move the stumps of her fingers until she felt something awful wiggle. I'll only ever count to eight and a half, she suddenly thought.

Santra plaited the weeds through the thatch, and lying on her belly, slid the weave over the well. It looked odd, like a tufty bouquet of half-dead vegetation had sprouted in an orderly allotment. Santra smiled, and Bea gave her a thumbs up. Santra looked perplexed for a moment, then leant forward and pressed her thumb on to Bea's.

'It means we've done well!' Bea giggled. She felt giddy.

Santra stood back up and brushed red dust off her forearms. She nudged the well covering with her foot, and looked down at Bea.

'Wait in the house,' she said.

So Bea waited.

The day grew darker. Santra had been gone for hours. Bea was limp with hunger. She sat against the far wall, her head dropping in brief lapses of something like sleep. When her body relaxed, her arm dropped, grazing her knee or the wall or the floor, and she was startled awake again by peals of rolling pain.

And then she heard Santra coming back again through the bushes. There was the distinct sound of crunching and chopping. Bea half stood, bracing herself against the wall. Her vision lurched. She stumbled closer to the window. The chopping sound was large and clumsy. Light from a hurricane lamp streaked dimly across the grass. Stepping out into the clearing, was Max. He rubbed the muscles at the back of his neck, and set the lamp down. He looked around the clearing, breathing heavily. Bea's heart squeezed; she felt woozy.

His face was coated in sweat, a pink flush high on his cheeks. He called into the dim light, 'Bea?' His voice was hoarse. He coughed into his fist, swallowed, and called again, 'Bea, are you here? It's me.'

Bea's heart was beating so hard she felt it was pressing up against the front of her throat. Pain from her arm curdled into her stomach. She put her left hand on the window frame to steady herself. A dribble of dry plaster dust crumbled as she touched it.

Max walked towards her, towards the back of the house, peering uncertainly through the open window. Bea felt her intestines contracting; her mouth was dry. Where was Santra?

She started to cry. She couldn't help herself. Maxis. If he could just take her home. If he was just normal and he could just take her home.

'Sweetheart.' He stopped walking. 'Don't cry.'

Bea gave up to the sobbing. It started in the hollow of her stomach and travelled to the top of her hand and back again. She crouched on the floor of the building, curled up over the centre of the agony – a hard walnut pit somewhere in her chest. She heard him walk towards the window, and half stood again, the world turning as if on a ship.

'No!' she screamed, white drops of spit falling over her lips. 'No, Maxis! Round, come round, come round.'

He stood for a second. Then he followed her gestures and began walking round to the front door. She stopped crying. She rocked back and forth on the floor until he was there. He was so tall. His hair was greasy.

His stubble scuffed against her forehead. His breath smelt sweet. 'Sweetheart, what are you doing here? Why did you run away?'

'Santra took my fingers.' It was all she could think to say. She held out her hand towards him. She looked up at him.

His eyes widened as he gripped her forearm. 'What have you done?'

Bea felt her eyes rolling in her head. She felt so hot. 'I didn't.'

'What did she do? What have you done?' He was shaking her arm now.

'I haven't – we had to – it was dead, but it's OK.'

Max dropped the arm. He wiped his hand over his face. His freckles were dark. He looked over his shoulder, back towards the front door. The light from the lamp shone over half his face. The pouches under his eyes stood up from his skin in crescent puffs.

'Looking for you has caused us a lot of trouble.' He turned

back towards her, holding her left hand to help her up to her feet. Unsure how to touch her injured fingers, he put his palm under the elbow. Bea grabbed on to his shirt, standing awkwardly. 'Are you well enough to walk?' Max looked into her eyes appraisingly.

'I don't want to go back there.'

'Beatriz,' Max sighed. His eyelids lowered in exhaustion. When he opened them again, his eyes looked red and wet. 'We don't have a choice,' he said softly.

'I can't – I can't bear it –' She shook her head, feeling the quivers go all the way into her shoulders.

'You can't bear it?' His face was full of astonishment. 'You?' He took a jagged inhale of breath. 'How should I bear this? What more can I do for you?'

Bea began to cry again.

'Answer me – what more can I do for you? I've tried so hard to help you. Now it's out of my hands.'

'I don't need help.' She wiped the spittle from her lips with her good arm.

Max held his fingers to the other. 'You don't need help? Look at what you have become!' He shook her good arm. 'Look at what has become of you!'

'This wasn't my fault,' Bea said, feeling her head swim. 'Max,' she said quietly. 'We don't need to stay here. This isn't right. You know it, I know you do. What happened – to Garolf, and to Jonson –' She stuttered over their names. She could see Jonson's face in the light of Mission House. He had asked her to leave. It felt like years ago.

'Not your fault!' Max was shouting now. He stood back from her, pointing down the hill towards the village. His body was twitchy with agitation. 'Don't you understand? Your pride, your stubbornness. You let it in. You let it in – you've brought this upon yourself, upon all of us!'

She felt so tired. Her skeleton was heavy.

'Come along,' he gestured finally with his head, his voice calmer now. 'We should begin at once. Let's not lose any more time. They are waiting for us in the church.' He nodded towards the front door.

Bea looked over to where the bushknife was lying against the far wall.

'Come along, Beatriz,' he said again.

Reflectively, Bea rubbed the naked hollow of her palm where the handle of the knife should fit. Outside the window, the clearing was dark and empty. Santra had gone. Maybe she had never meant to return. Bea shuffled past Max. Floorboards beneath her feet creaked. A sour smell rose from the dust.

Max waited for her to pass, then followed. He walked behind her, and placed his left palm directly on the small of her back.

Bea swallowed. She felt that hand, and something popped at the base of her skull. Something popped and tore open.

That hand on her back. She was already walking. He wasn't hastening her. He wasn't guiding her. She was not stumbling. He was not helping. He was not quickening her steps. He was not touching her with love, with concern. He was not steering her. So, what purpose, then, did it serve? That hand on her back. The something tore, and it bubbled, it bubbled and it soared into her bloodstream.

She stopped abruptly at the door lintel. He almost crashed into her. She felt his breath on the back of her neck.

'Take your hand off me,' she said. The bubbling bubbled. Her teeth bit down on the words.

She felt him stiffen. The hand remained.

'Remove your hand,' she whispered again.

She paused at the door frame. The night smelt cool. Droplets of dew flickered in the grass by the light of the lamp. Soft clouds hung in the sky.

Bea bent down towards the lamp, and picked it up. The handle was warm. She turned on the spot and swung it across her body, upwards towards his face. Glass shattered.

She ran.

Max cried out. He brushed the shards from his hair, spat them out of his mouth. He tossed the guttering candle in the grass, he plucked a piece of hot glass from where it had lodged in his arm and dropped it into the earth.

Bea ran, unsteadily. Her leg twisted underneath her. Max followed, barely hastening. In two short strides he had caught up with her. His face was white, his nostrils opened.

He threw his weight on to her bad arm and she screamed so loudly she heard it echoing in her own eardrums.

And there was a cracking, a soft crunching, a sweet stink rising.

Bea slithered forward in the grass, clutching her arm to her, her body shaking in agony. She rolled forward over the weeds. A low yowl of pain came from the hole. A stirring, splashing sound.

'Beatriz,' he called. 'Beatriz!'

Bea rolled on to her side. The world spun backwards.

'Beatriz. Beatriz? Are you there?'

'Yes,' she said. Her tongue was swollen. She could taste blood in her mouth.

'I can't – the smell, I can't get out –'

'I know,' she said.

'Sweetheart,' he called. He paused to swallow. His voice was high. 'I'm sorry. I promise. I won't hurt you. You don't understand – we won't hurt you. We're trying to help you. You need me. I can help you. Please.'

Bea lay by the edge of the hole. She said nothing.

'Bea!' Max was shouting now. 'Bea! Help me! You don't know what you're doing.'

But Bea was concentrating on the shape on the other side of

the house. Santra was standing by the corner of the wall. She was just standing there. She nodded her head at Bea, and disappeared out of view.

When she reappeared, she was carrying the grassy wooden lid. The well covering. She waddled over to Bea, resting it against her legs above her knees. She sat in the grass and hovered it above the opening.

'OK?'

'OK.'

Santra pushed it slowly across the grass. Slowly, it closed over the hole. Over the drooling flowers and the sickly smell and the sounds, the sounds.

Bea lay on her back in the grass. The stars were starting to come out. White, like speckles on a goose egg.

It's only flesh, Bea thought.

Acknowledgements

Thank you to my parents, Marion and Ahmad, for your inspiration and encouragement, and thank you to Walid, Hussein, Alya and Yasmin.

Thank you to Judith Corrente and Wim Kooyker for your support during my DPhil, and your belief in my writing skills!

I'm very grateful to my first readers: Natasha, Maria, Dave, Patsy and Photeini – thank you all for your insights.

To my agent, Hattie Grunewald, your confidence in this book has changed my life, I can't thank you enough. Everyone in the team at Blake Friedmann has invested so much positivity and enthusiasm into this project, thank you.

To my editor, Juliet Annan, thank you for your humour, tireless energy and sharp eye. Thank you to Anna Steadman, to Shân Morley Jones, and to everyone at Penguin Fig Tree for the time and care that goes into their work.

To Struan, the thank yous are never-ending, for the rounds of editing parties, hours of discussions, your confidence, patience and love – I'm so grateful.

Extra-special acknowledgements are due to my comrades through exorcisms and hedge: Andrew, Chris, Kat, May, Rebecca and Robin: thank you. A particular thank you to Tabisini for your regional expertise.

Finally, I am indebted to my Ni-Vanuatu colleagues, students and friends: *tankyu tumas*.

We love stories.

Fact or fiction, long or short, exploring distant lands, imagined worlds or your own back yard – anything can be a story, and every place has stories waiting to be told. And we want to find them.

Do you have a story to tell? Want help cutting through the jargon, answers to your burning questions or advice from top authors, agents and editors across the industry?

Find out more about how to get published at:
www.penguin.co.uk/publishmybook

He just wanted a decent book to read ...

Not too much to ask, is it? It was in 1935 when Allen Lane, Managing Director of Bodley Head Publishers, stood on a platform at Exeter railway station looking for something good to read on his journey back to London. His choice was limited to popular magazines and poor-quality paperbacks – the same choice faced every day by the vast majority of readers, few of whom could afford hardbacks. Lane's disappointment and subsequent anger at the range of books generally available led him to found a company – and change the world.

'We believed in the existence in this country of a vast reading public for intelligent books at a low price, and staked everything on it'
Sir Allen Lane, 1902–1970, founder of Penguin Books

The quality paperback had arrived – and not just in bookshops. Lane was adamant that his Penguins should appear in chain stores and tobacconists, and should cost no more than a packet of cigarettes.

Reading habits (and cigarette prices) have changed since 1935, but Penguin still believes in publishing the best books for everybody to enjoy. We still believe that good design costs no more than bad design, and we still believe that quality books published passionately and responsibly make the world a better place.

So wherever you see the little bird – whether it's on a piece of prize-winning literary fiction or a celebrity autobiography, political tour de force or historical masterpiece, a serial-killer thriller, reference book, world classic or a piece of pure escapism – you can bet that it represents the very best that the genre has to offer.

Whatever you like to read – trust Penguin.